INCESSANT

D. R. WALKER

Suite 300 - 990 Fort St
Victoria, BC, V8V 3K2
Canada

www.friesenpress.com

First Edition — 2019

ISBN
978-1-5255-3089-0 (Hardcover)
978-1-5255-3090-6 (Paperback)
978-1-5255-3091-3 (eBook)

1. *Fiction, Science Fiction*

Distributed to the trade by The Ingram Book Company

INCESSANT

Prologue

"This is all a big dream, right? I mean ... this can't really be happening!"

Deacon couldn't tell if he was living, dreaming, or living within a dream. His experiences had taken him well beyond the realms of Plato and Aristotle. At this point, he needed some proof, some evidence of his existence ... and his sanity.

After performing the age-old test, pinching himself, the pain brought him rushing back to the temporary conclusion that he was very much alive. Deacon's rational mind tried to debunk any conclusion before making any assumption, no matter how obvious or questionable it was. Dreams could be vivid and real, in some cases causing certain sensations even while asleep. Could this be one of those moments? After surveying his surroundings, he hoped it was.

He didn't recognize anything. It all seemed alien: the colors, the furniture, the room, even the shape of the couch. It was all oddly functional. He couldn't explain it, and he didn't even try. He had higher priorities on his "What the hell?" list as he picked himself up from the ground, such as, *What the hell am I lying on?* and *Where the hell am I?*

Then, just as fast as he had come to himself, a surge of knowledge coursed through his brain, like a thought library streaming from a global Wi-Fi brainwave modem. In an instant, he was theoretically as smart as everyone on the planet. He could access just about any subject he pleased, just by thinking about it. However, when applied to his current situation, he reached a mental roadblock and developed an intense headache. All these occurrences happened in a controlled manner, like the information was there, but he wasn't allowed to probe it. It puzzled him, and after many attempts to access this mental database, the headaches became more intense and longer lasting. Where was this knowledge coming from, and how could he control it? He had to get out of there and find Phoebe. He knew how to talk to her.

Chapter 1

I

Stop and go, stop and go. The traffic was unimaginably slow, the same as every morning for commuter Deacon Russell. He was the incarnation of every middle-class worker trying to make ends meet. Two jobs, three kids, a wife, and two intolerable in-laws equaled a full house with little privacy or cool-off time. The house came fully equipped with a noisy teenager, a spoiled daughter, a confused twelve-year-old, and an obnoxious mother in-law who hated every fiber of his being. However, the constant help and support from his wife and friends gave him the motivation he needed to carry on from day to day without doing anything stupid. At the moment, sitting in bumper-to-bumper traffic, he just wished he had another Red Bull.

Deacon lived in the suburbs but worked in the city as a writer for *Critical Thinkers*, a science magazine located in nearby Hollowsprings. It was only a twenty-mile trip, but it took an hour and a half to get there in the busy morning traffic. He was good at his job but never received the credit or recognition he felt he deserved. He toiled at his laptop for hours, writing magnificent reports and editing his own work, and yet his supervisor couldn't even get his name right. He constantly called him Leroy. Leroy was the smelly security guard who always picked his nose and wiped it on the inside of his pants pockets. He was almost ten years older than Deacon and was also African American. He took offense at his supervisor's unintentional suggestions, but he tolerated the humiliation for the paycheck.

His second job was much more laid back as far as coworker encounters were concerned. He was a night cook at a local smokers' bar called Cuban Stogies that didn't have one Cuban employee in the entire company. Alcohol, cigars, and greasy food were the three parts of a deadly combination that attracted thousands of guests from all over the state on a weekly basis. They were also the only three things in the place that were Cuban, in a sense. Deacon was the well-respected head cook with a taste for fine dining. He didn't have a culinary degree; he was just an avid fan of the Food Network and could create masterpieces with the right ingredients.

Phoebe, his hot soccer-mom wife, supported him one hundred percent on anything he undertook. She used to be the head nurse at the hospital in Hollowsprings but had to quit when her father became sick. Her mother had rheumatoid arthritis and could hardly take care of herself, much less her husband, so Phoebe decided, against Deacon's wishes, to quit her job and invite her parents to live with them.

Her mother, Janice, openly hated Deacon and seized every opportunity to humiliate him publicly. He tolerated her blatant disrespect, and Phoebe understood his position.

Chalmers, Phoebe's father, was bedridden. He was a depressed old man who despised the fact that his son-in-law was the head of the household. Still, Chalmers appreciated Deacon's kindness and hospitality, in addition to his toleration of Janice, a feat Chalmers had achieved for over sixty years now.

Deacon's three kids were his entire world. Even though he loved them all equally, Junior, the oldest of the three, was his favorite by far. Deacon was tougher on Junior, so it may not have seemed like a close relationship from the outside, but he did it because Junior was so smart. He wanted Junior to utilize his full potential.

James, the twelve-year-old, who was trying to find himself, was a curious case. His weirdness wasn't attributed to his age; he had always been different from other kids. Deacon jokingly blamed the unplanned pregnancy. Janice blamed Deacon's genes.

Jessica, his seven-year-old daughter, was the apple of his eye. She was spoiled, but not by choice. She didn't ask for things; things were given to her. She was an attention magnet and cuter than a Big Eyes painting. All three were well mannered, respectful, well behaved, and outstanding students, and Deacon rewarded them constantly for that. They must have realized at an early age that good behavior came with certain benefits.

Just a little over halfway to work, Deacon started to sweat. His car's air conditioner had broken at the end of the previous summer, and the driver's side window hadn't worked for years. As a bead of salty sweat eased into his right eye, he caught a convex glimpse of the chemical plant through the wide-open passenger-side window. "Heptagon Chemicals," the sign read, but nobody really knew what was made inside. Some said it was a factory for WMDs, and some said it was a cover for a secret military project. It was actually a pharmaceutical plant, but Deacon didn't care the least bit. He had never been much of a tree hugger, so until he saw a three-legged baby or a two-headed moose, it was none of his concern.

As he approached his parking spot, nearly half a mile away from work, he gave a deep sigh of relief. Stepping out of what he referred to as "the sauna" was like stepping out of a hot shower when the cold bathroom air hit. As the goose bumps started to protrude, he cracked a smile and enjoyed a moment of relief. Then his smile morphed into a frown when he realized how long of a walk he had and to where he was walking. "Damn. Walking half a mile from the sauna to the hellhole. I need another cold Red Bull!"

II

"Ah, home sweet home." Deacon pulled into his driveway later that afternoon and didn't even bother opening the garage. As soon as he was inside the door, his sweet home instantly turned sour when he was greeted with a menacing grimace from Janice. No words were exchanged, they had decided it was best to communicate only when necessary.

Even so, the way she scowled at him was enough. He proceeded to his bedroom, trying to ignore the encounter. "If I could ever get my hands on her," he whispered to himself. He never finished such sentences, just envisioned different ways to murder her with his bare hands.

After taking a steaming shower and changing into fresh clothes, Deacon felt like a million bucks. He decided to take advantage of being off from his second job that day to spend some quality time with his kids.

Junior, being a teenager, had some female company, so Deacon didn't want to interfere with or embarrass him. He just popped his head in the door to say hey and then left him alone with his company.

James was playing his geeky computer games and eating ice cream with popcorn—weird indeed. Deacon didn't want any part of that, so he said hey and left him alone too.

That left Jessica, his little cupcake. She was helping Phoebe cook dinner in the kitchen, so he snuck up on her and then let out a yell. "RAHHHH!"

Jessica unleashed a bloodcurdling scream before she realized it was just Daddy messing with her. He scooped her into the air and gave her a big kiss. "How's my little princess today?"

Her dimples were like craters accenting her playful smile. She gave him an in-depth, description of her day.

"Just like your mother," he said when she was finished. "You know why I call you my little princess?"

Again, with the smile and the dimples. "No, Daddy, why?" she asked in the cutest way possible.

Deacon threw her up onto his shoulders. "Because I'm the king of this house!"

"More like the jester!" Janice said from the next room.

Deacon grimaced. "If I could ever get my hands on her … "

III

After dinner, it was time for Deacon to take his unwinding process to the next level. He called his pot dealer and lifelong buddy, Chuck. "Come on over and bring some of that good shit you had last time."

He and Chuck had known each other since elementary school and had always been best friends. During childhood, their families lived only a block away from each other, so they hung out every day. Even though they were from similar backgrounds, they had chosen different paths in life but remained close friends. They even introduced themselves as brothers, and Deacon's kids called Chuck "Uncle Charlie."

Chuck had been selling pot since high school and had never been caught (knock on wood), but Deacon didn't buy too often anymore. "My shit ain't done curing," Deacon said. "I'll need about another ounce to hold me over." Deacon had a green thumb when it came to pot and had three hydroponic kits in his basement.

"Gotcha," Chuck replied. "Gimme 'bout twenty minutes."

Twenty minutes later, just like clockwork, Chuck showed up. He greeted Janice with a hug and a kiss on the cheek. For some odd reason, she liked Chuck, and they engaged in conversation every time they were around one another. Deacon said it was because they have a lot in common: they were both rude and obnoxious.

After his rundown of the basketball game with Janice, Chuck made his way through the kitchen, where Phoebe was diligently cleaning up from dinner. He made his presence known with a gentle hug.

"Hi, Chuck," she said, smiling. "Are you hungry? There's plenty of food."

Chuck graciously declined, saying he had already eaten. Truth be told, he just didn't like her cooking.

After saying goodnight to the kids, Chuck finally made it to the basement, where Deacon was waiting for him. "Damn, it only took you twenty minutes to get here, but it took an hour for you to make it to the basement. What happened? You get caught by tha Janiconda?"

Chuck smiled and showed Deacon what he had brought. "Just in from Cali," Chuck said. "and it's all tha way lime and frosty!"

"Well let's get it all tha way rolled up, so I can bust yo ass on this pool table."

After a couple of fat blunts and a four-hour conversation, Deacon finally looked at the clock and realized how late it was. He glanced at Chuck, who was asleep, and realized something else: he had been talking to himself for the better part of an hour. The phrase "time flies when you're having fun" is doubled when you're high. They hadn't even played pool; they just sat there and ran their mouths until Chuck passed out. That's how it had been for years.

Deacon went to the closet, got Chuck a blanket, covered him up, and then went upstairs, whispering to himself. "Lucky dog. No wife or annoying mother-in-law. Stay out late, sleep wherever and with whoever he wants. Lucky dog." They envied one another in opposite ways. Chuck envied the fact that Deacon had an amazing wife and family. The subject had never come up between them though, because it wasn't a big deal. Why bother?

Upon entering his bedroom Deacon was confronted with a pleasant surprise. Strawberry-scented candles and incense dimly lit the room as Barry White resonated softly in the background. Phoebe was sprawled across the bed in her newest Victoria Secret splurge. He couldn't get his clothes off fast enough. What a glorious ending for a day that had started off dreadful at best.

Chapter 2

I

Once again, the traffic on the interstate was bumper-to-bumper chaos. It was six degrees hotter than the day before, but Deacon didn't even notice. He had his extra Red Bull and decided to leave his shirt off until he got to work, so he could take full advantage of the single operating window. He was in an oddly elated mood from the previous night's erotic escapades, nodding his head frivolously and emulating Eminem playing through his car's expensive sound system. He was still hot and sweaty, but the sex, and the extra Red Bull, made the heat easier for him to bear.

Halfway to work, the ride seemed to be going faster for him, although he was ten minutes behind schedule. Just as he reached to replay the song again, he paused, noticing an odd smell. Upon investigation, he observed smoke coming from one of the four large conical structures at Heptagon Chemicals. Deacon was no chemist, but he was smart enough to know that where there was smoke, there was fire, and this was the first time any of the buildings had ever smoked. Not a good sign at a chemical plant.

Unsure of what to do, he slipped into a hypertensive panic mode. *Should I call the cops? I'm sure they know by now. I'll just get a busy signal or be put on hold. Maybe I should call my family. Should I get out and run? Is it too late?*

He grabbed his cell phone in desperation, pressed the emergency call button, and selected Phoebe's cell. It rang until the voicemail played. He hung up and tried the house phone, but as soon as he heard the first word of the answering machine, he hung up. By then his frustration was uncontrollable. "Goddammit, Phoebe! Answer the phone!"

He tried her cell again as he continued his tirade. On the third ring, she finally answered, but the only thing she heard was "Baby I—" followed by a burst of static, and then nothing.

II

Phoebe hung up her cell phone, enraged. She tried to call Deacon back a few times, but it kept going straight to voicemail. "Don't gimme dat shit!" she exclaimed in frustration. "I was just talking to him!" She had missed his first call while she was finishing up in the shower, and she only heard a few words from the second one, so she dried off, got dressed, and then made her way to the kitchen, somewhat confused.

"Deacon tried to call," Janice said, "so I didn't answer it. Figured I'd save my insult for later. I've got a good one for him today."

Phoebe started to walk away in fury when Janice grabbed her attention again. "But wait, there's actually something happening in this boring-ass city. It's on every channel, something about an explosion at a chemical plant."

Phoebe turned up the volume and took a seat as the dashingly handsome anchorman made his announcement. "Breaking news ... no more than ten minutes ago, Heptagon Chemicals experienced an explosive chemical reaction of catastrophic proportions. Due to unknown causes, one of the plant's chemical containers malfunctioned, resulting in an explosion that took out the entire plant. The blast radius was so big, it reached the neighboring interstate and demolished everything in its path. It's total pandemonium, to say the least. Death toll estimates are now well over fifty-six hundred. Our sources say radiation poisoning isn't a factor in the wake of this horrendous tragedy. Stay tuned, and we'll keep you posted."

It didn't take Phoebe long to realize she had just heard what could have been Deacon's last words, and it was too much for her to cope with. She didn't know if she was mad or sad. More importantly, she didn't know how she was going to break the news to the kids or how to help them cope with it. Hundreds of thoughts flooded her head, each question leading to another. She tried to maintain her composure, but it lasted for only a few seconds. She frowned, and then her lips began quivering, and then the full waterworks display and banshee wails broke out. She rushed to the computer room to look up the disaster on the news station's website. *Maybe there's more information online. The media is always the first to know.*

The website already had a memorial for the plant workers posted on their home page. They even had a link to a helicopter that was streaming live footage from ground zero. The wind was blowing so hard into the reporter's microphone that Phoebe couldn't hear what he was saying, but she didn't need to hear him to confirm her nightmare. On her monitor sat a mangled version of the Ford that Deacon had driven to work that morning. The ratifying clues were the Carolina Tar Heels logos that adorned the trunk and the mismatched alloy wheels. That was indisputably his car.

Once again, Phoebe conceded to the hysteria and the waterworks. "I've gotta get out there!" She sped out the door with her keys, her purse, and the general location of Deacon's car in her mind. "He may still be alive!"

The entire time Phoebe had been ranting, Janice was oblivious to what was going on. "Hell, I thought she hated the place; I did. Never shoulda been built. Gimme tha chance, I would've blown it up myself."

III

Ringing, boisterous screams and random moans were all Deacon heard as he slipped in and out of consciousness. As he lay there in desperate need of a tourniquet, he couldn't help but think about his love for his family. Not solely the parental love he had for his kids but also the strong, unconditional, everlasting love he had for his wife. They always knew they were meant for each other. All the times they'd laughed and all the pleasant moments they'd shared flooded his brain. He was tickled by the thoughts, because their relationship seemed to have never left the puppy-dog stage.

He felt his heartrate slowing and his body losing its strength. The longer he lay there, the more inevitable his demise seemed, but he was okay with that. Each time he regained consciousness, the recurrence of moans and screams were fewer and farther between. Death was all around him, encompassing the scene, but he had come to accept it. "Well ... at least ... I don't have to ... go to work today ... I hate those assholes."

It felt like hours had gone by, but it was only about thirty minutes, give or take. Then, like music from heaven playing in his ears, he heard ambulances wailing in the distance. In his case though, it seemed to be too late. Deacon had suffered broken bones, multiple lacerations, and internal hemorrhaging, but his will to live was as strong as a farm mule, and he wasn't about to submit when help was so close.

He tried to reach the horn on his steering wheel, so he could make a few random honks for the medics when they arrived. Since horns were going off everywhere, one erratic horn could be a signal from a survivor to a medic. However, his attempts were futile. He had lost so much strength that he could barely even move or speak. Even if he could move, the steering wheel was so mangled that the horn may not have worked anyway. Desperation set in as he ran through countless ideas in his head with his last bit of strength, to no avail. He felt his consciousness drifting away again, and he prepared to embrace death.

As he faded away into listlessness, he heard what he discerned to be an angel's voice beckoning him. It was soft and beautiful, yet the closer it got to him, the more it sounded like it had a serious sense of urgency to it, not what one would expect to hear when approaching heaven's gates.

It was not until this angel called him by his nickname, "Deak," that he noticed the angel's voice was strikingly similar to Phoebe's. Suddenly, his adrenal glands kicked into overtime and coursed raw epinephrine throughout his system as love reinvigorated his will to live. With just enough power to open his eyes, he saw Phoebe crouched over him and yelling for help. All he could do was cry.

"We're gonna get ya outta here, baby," she said while cradling his head and wiping the blood from his face. "You're gonna be just fine."

IV

"Breaking news ... in addition to the four thousand nine hundred employees at Heptagon Chemicals who met a tragic death in the explosion today, an estimated seven hundred people died on the interstate and another fourteen hundred in surrounding areas of the blast radius as the explosion took out buildings that were thought to be out of harm's way. This is a disaster of mammoth proportions as the death toll now eclipses seven thousand. We at the network would like to formally express our condolences to the families of the departed."

At first Janice was pissed off by the repeated interruptions of her game show for the constant updates on the explosion. She wasn't prepared for the conversation she was about to hold with her daughter.

Phoebe was the calm and collected type, so Janice had never had to deal with her in this condition. She tried to calm Phoebe on the phone, so she could understand her, but in the back of an ambulance with her dying husband on the gurney, calmness wasn't an option.

"What? Get the ... what? Calm down, sweetie. Now you say get tha kids outta school and ... meet you where? Tha hospital? Wha-what?" Janice was suddenly thrust into panic mode as Phoebe's cell phone lost reception. After a brief episode of hyperventilation, she salvaged her wits, smoked a cigarette, and got changed. She didn't want to show up at the kid's schools in her plaid pajamas with rollers in her hair.

V

In the back of the ambulance, Deacon was still slipping in and out of consciousness; however, he felt as if consciousness was being brought back to him instead of it being regained. It was more of a lower level of listlessness, one that he wouldn't have come back from if left to himself. Every time he saw that beautiful white light, he felt a surge before he was pulled back into the pain and agony of his mortal body. All the drugs they were pumping into him and the needles they were prodding him with were useless. Only the defibrillator and Phoebe's persistent encouragement kept him alive. He died five times on the thirty-five-minute drive to the hospital.

"Janice is gonna meet us there with the kids, and we'll all see you through this, baby." Phoebe fought her hysteria and tried to give some optimistic words whenever Deacon was alive and aware. "The kids and I love you, Deacon. Everything's gonna be okay." She really didn't believe he would be okay, but stories were told every day, where someone would befall a bitter becoming, and bounce back. Unfortunately, Deacon seemed a little too mangled to be reconstructed and survive.

As the paramedics wheeled Deacon into the hospital, Phoebe showed him a family picture that she kept inside a locket. It was of their trip to the mountains the previous summer and had been taken using a tripod while they stood on a popular cliff. It was the happiest moment of their lives as a family. "We're here for you, baby; all of us are." As Deacon saw the photo, he displayed how well his tear ducts were still working. Even the nurses were crying as they rushed him to the operating room.

"I'm sorry, but you can't come back here with us, ma'am," a nurse said as they passed through a pair of large double doors. Phoebe fell to the floor in despondency as they departed with Deacon in his dire state of dissolution.

Another nurse stopped to help her up from the germy hospital floor. "Ma'am, these are trying times for us all, and I'm truly sorry for your misfortune, but we need you to have a seat in the waiting area, and please don't block these doors. This is a very busy day, but we'll try to keep everybody informed. Thanks for your cooperation."

As Phoebe tried feverishly to contact Janice from the waiting room, Deacon died two more times on the operating table.

Chapter 3

I

AHHHH!

Deacon unloaded a barrage of bullets in a sweeping motion. Hot shells flung out of the chamber in rhythm and hit the ground beside him. With bullets whizzing pass his face, he blasted his last few rounds straight ahead, discarded the empty clip, and reloaded with the speed of a Navy SEAL. Then he sprinted approximately fifty yards and dove behind another tree. Spotting two more enemies, he swiftly disposed of them both without any hesitation and kept moving. With every advance, he heard the scurrying of what he assumed were his comrades behind him. He presumed this, because if it were his enemies, they could have killed him a long time ago.

He didn't know where he was or how he got there, but he knew he had to survive. He didn't even know who he was killing, but if one of them came within his field of vision, Deacon Russell would be the last thing they saw—if they saw him at all. Right now, he was persevering purely by instinct, like muscle memory.

He operated his automatic weapon with amazing speed and accuracy, even accounting for the slight inaccuracy of the camouflaged Colt AR-15. He darted from tree to tree, slaughtering enemies and creating a path for his fellow rebels. How he got there was the last thing on his mind. Getting out of there alive was the first.

Deacon massacred his way five hundred more yards downhill until he spotted a small cluster of cabins, where the enemies seemed to be convening. Taking cover behind a tree, he wiped the sweat from his eyes and grabbed from his back an object he hadn't even realized he was carrying until he stopped. He loaded the rocket launcher and aimed at a generator on the side of the largest of the four cabins. Holding his breath to steady his aim, he squeezed the trigger.

The blast leveled two of the cabins and created a large mushroom cloud in its wake. The absence of electricity momentarily disoriented his remaining enemies, allowing the rebels a window of opportunity for a swift invasion. None of the enemies survived the attack as the rebels raided the camp, taking no prisoners and sparing no life.

Without even a hint of celebration, one team plundered the camp for all the remaining weapons, medicine, and food while the other team hotwired the few vehicles that hadn't been demolished in the explosion. The rebels' disposition was dead serious. Even though they had just slaughtered everyone in the vicinity, they knew it wasn't over until they got home.

Deacon didn't even have time enough to clear his thoughts before they were all packed up and ready to head out. Everyone, including himself, was on full alert as a ride up an unfamiliar path lay ahead. Deacon had assumed leadership from the beginning. It was *his* dream, right? So, his vessel led the convoy back up the path.

The vehicles they had commandeered from the enemy were of a highly sophisticated military grade but seemed to be somewhat aged, as if their looks didn't match the technology. The geek in Deacon drooled in awe after the driver pressed a few buttons to activate a three-dimensional holographic image of the surrounding one-hundred-yard diameter. The image seemed as if it had come from nowhere, Deacon noticed no projectors or cameras. *Only in my dreams,* he thought. It even highlighted edible or dangerous life forms and vegetation. Other than a few wild animals, the ride uphill seemed like a clearly laid out path.

II

The ride back to base was fast and intense. With the rebels at attention and fingers on triggers, not a sound was made as they crept their pilfered buggies up the hill. The futuristic radar was clear, but they kept their eyes open until they had safely reached the sixty-foot tall, twenty-foot thick gateway to their base.

The base was more of a small city than a headquarters. It sat one hundred feet above sea level on a plateau that spanned some two thousand acres. The eighty-foot tall, fifty-foot thick wall that encircled it sat on top of the hillside and was dotted with watchtowers full of snipers and windows for rocket launchers and machine gunners. As Deacon and the rebels approached the enormous fortress, they heard the massive doors creaking and moaning to life, as if it hurt them to open.

The team was greeted with cheers of victory as they drove the stolen vehicles to the scrapyard for disassembly. Deacon felt like he could finally let his guard down. Then he began to assess his situation. *Shouldn't I have woken up by now? I must be in a coma. But if I am, would I be aware of it?* As he exited his ride, he checked his body for any scars and found nothing. *It has to be a coma, because there are no remnants of the wreck, but this feels so real!*

Deacon decided to take a stroll through the city. Everything seemed foreign to him. The city was mapped out with dusty dirt roads, all of which branched off one main dusty dirt road down the center of the city. It put Deacon in the mind of the Wild West. There were no familiar landmarks, no flashing billboards, no automobiles stuck in traffic, no junkies begging for spare change, and no car alarms sounding off in the distance, none of the things to which Deacon had grown accustomed. Yet, he could tell this was indisputably the city. It was huge!

The main road was riddled with shops, bars, and people. Deacon made his way down the dusty road, and people seemed to make way for him. He was really confused when they started saluting him. Confounded, Deacon picked the most extravagant-looking bar and hurried inside, figuring the money he had just stolen off the enemy corpses would be accepted there.

III

Deacon sat at the bar for hours, pondering his situation and drinking the strongest liquor he had ever had (if Everclear and Bacardi 151 had a baby ... that strong). *Where am I? I've never seen any place like this in my life! This has to be a coma ... it has to be.* It took him all of two hours before he asked himself how he could be drunk if he were in a coma. The question only caused him more concern.

The strip-bar was full of patrons, many of whom had participated in the slaughter that afternoon. All the dancers there were fully naked, well endowed, and promiscuous. They scampered about from person to person—drinking, frolicking, flirting, and smoking, hoping one of the patrons would eventually request some private time with them upstairs. The tantalizing women approached Deacon numerous times over the course of the night, but no matter how tempting each vixen was, each more beautiful than the last, he would look them straight in the eye and decline their company—the Latina almost got him though. Considering the day's events, all he wanted to do was to cuddle up next to Phoebe in *his* bed and go to sleep.

Deacon sat there alone, just a man and his thoughts, ordering drink after drink and sulking in his bewilderment. *I miss my family!* He downed another double shot and ordered another when a slender, well-built gentleman approached him cautiously.

"Permission to speak freely, sir," the young man said as he clicked his heels and saluted.

What would R. Lee Ermey say in this situation?

"At ease solider. Permission granted."

After a deep sigh, the solider studied Deacon in his confounded state and then proceeded. "What's wrong with you? You've been acting funny since we got back from the killing. Don't you see all these titties in here? Aren't you the slightest bit happy about our victory today? Are you paying attention? What are you looking at? Do you even know who I am?"

Deacon gazed slowly at the solider, who had a concerned look on his face, one that was eerily familiar. *Lose the muscles and the scar, grow a mustache and a beer belly, and then he would look just like ... hey, wait a damn minute ...* "Chuck? Is that you?"

IV

Deacon was confused, tired, drunk, and hungry, but at least he wasn't alone anymore. His childhood friend had surfaced, as he always did in times of duress. He had a long, jagged scar across his face, but other than that, he was Chuck. *Now I know this is a dream! How can he have a scar on his face that he never had growing up?*

The young man came to attention and saluted as he addressed Deacon's inquiry. "Colonel Charles Terrence reporting, sir, also known as Chuck by my associates."

Deacon wasn't used to seeing Chuck so sharp. It scared him. "Settle down, homie. You ain't gotta speak dat army lingo wit me," Deacon said as he started to feel somewhat like himself again. "Why is everybody saluting me anyway?"

Chuck seemed rattled. "You really don't know who you are, do you? Do you even know your name?"

The thought had never crossed Deacon's mind. Maybe he wasn't who he thought he was. Maybe he and his band of murdering rebels were the bad guys. "Deacon Russell?" he said, sounding unsure of himself.

Chuck frowned. "General ... you're General Deacon Russell. You're our leader, homie. Get it together! I was right behind you when we invaded that camp, and not one of those bastards laid a finger on you. Your execution was flawless, like always. But ever since we got back, you've been acting like you have amnesia or something. Do I need to get a medic over here?"

Deacon wanted answers, and he knew he could get them from Chuck. "Sit down," he said, motioning for the bartender. "We got a lot to talk about."

Chapter 4

I

Round after round, question after question, Deacon and Chuck exchanged unbelievable stories. To Deacon, this was some sort of dream world. To Chuck, Deacon's story sounded like it had *come* from a dream world. Neither one wanted to believe the other, because both stories seemed too far-fetched. They asked sarcastic questions regarding what the other held to be solid truth. The more information they exchanged, the more confused Deacon became. He felt as if they were being counter-productive.

"Soooo," Deacon said continuing his sarcastic inquiry. "you're saying, the Germans went nuclear before us and throwed a few bombs around the world. If there was a nuclear war, shouldn't there be some three-headed cyclopses running around or somethin'?"

Chuck gave Deacon a disgusted look. "Stop playing with me, man. You seriously don't remember *anything*? So, you just suddenly think you're from somewhere else or something? I don't know what's going on in that head of yours, but something must have happened to you out there in the field. You were perfectly normal when we were talking before deployment."

That's another thing that seemed to befuddle Deacon: Chuck constantly referencing the past, yet he had only just arrived there. *Who am I?* By this time, Deacon's rational mind was straddling the fence over whether it was all a dream or if it was real.

All his senses were on full alert, the smell of stagnant water and overheated pheromones permeating the air. He could hear the conversation he and Chuck were having over the loud music in the background. The liquor looked and tasted watered down, and he certainly felt drunk. "I don't understand either, Chuck. Like I said, I was on my deathbed, and the next thing I knew, I was in the middle of a war zone killin' people for no apparent reason. By the way, who *was* I killin'?"

Again, Chuck brandished a look of utter disgust. "You're serious, aren't you? I'm going to say this the nicest way I can. Deacon, you're the most decorated officer this army has ever had, the most respected person in this camp, and it's a true honor to be your friend. I don't know if you remember this or not, but we've been through a lot together. I've always been there for you and vice versa. Now I'm telling you, friend to friend, you need to get some counseling. Whatever you got going on is obviously out of my league. You got some serious psychological damage or some shit."

"You might be right," Deacon admitted. "Where should I go?"

Chuck smiled. "I'll take you there. Now I think you should see Torres, Phoebe don't—"

"Phoebe?" Deacon interjected. "Phoebe is *here*? What about my kids? They here too?"

Chuck smiled again. "So, it's coming back to ya, huh?"

"No, it's not," Deacon replied. "Phoebe is my *wife*, homie! Where is she?"

Chuck's smile turned to a look of surprise, then confusion. "Wow, I wonder how *that* worked out for ya. I don't know how she was where you claim to be from, but here she's your overly obsessive baby mama. I noticed you said 'kids.' How many do you think you have?"

"Three," Deacon said angrily.

"You have one," Chuck said, sensing Deacon's hostility. "That's all you said you could have with that control freak. You know you've had her detained before? She's crazy, man. I don't think you need to go to her with this."

Being that everything there was different, Deacon understood Chuck's concern. *Chuck seems to be the same person, so how much different can she be?* Phoebe could be some psycho maniac stalker bitch, or maybe that was just how she was made out to be. Either way, Deacon was willing to find out. The bartender brought them another round and disappeared again.

"She's my wife, Chuck, I miss her and my kids. I have to see her, man. Besides, I know how to talk to her."

"Alright, you win. I'll take you to her. Just remember, you've been warned. Now let's toast: good times and good friends."

Deacon clinked glasses with him. "Good friends, good times."

Chuck smiled. "See? It's coming back."

"No, it's not," Deacon said. "That's been our toast forever. This shit is confusing!"

II

On the way to the counseling center, Chuck explained the history of the war being fought. "So, to make a long story short, what used to be the Soviet Union was overthrown by Germany and its allies. Then the Brits double-crossed America and sided with the Germans. So, it was like America versus the world. We didn't stand a chance. The invasion was swift. Our government collapsed overnight, and it was total anarchy. Those of us who weren't killed or imprisoned by the invading Germans formed rebel groups. And ... here we are."

Deacon, who was still unsure if he was dreaming, completely understood Chuck's rundown. He knew his history well, particularly World War II. In the back of his head, he always wondered how it would be if the Germans had taken Moscow. *Well, I guess this situation answers my question!* "Fuckin' Germans," he said, shaking his head in disgust.

Chuck stopped mid-stride and gave Deacon his most surprised look of the night. "You don't know how many times I've heard you say that phrase—in that exact manner. I know you're in there somewhere. Maybe seeing Phoebe is a good idea after all. Her office is in the next building over. You need me to go with you?"

Deacon pondered the question for a few moments. *She's my wife ... right?* "Nah, I got this. Just hang out here for me." He figured he could just feel her out and see how the conversation went before he explained the situation. "Once I explain everything, I'll come get you, and we can all figure this shit out together."

Chuck gave Deacon a concerned look. "I don't want to see her if I ain't got to, but if you somehow pull this off, I'm in. It'll be worth it just to see somebody get along with her."

Deacon felt intimidation set in. *She can't be that bad, can she?* "It's Phoebe, man. What's she gonna do? Kick my ass or something?"

Chuck shrugged and cocked his head with a questioning look on his face. "Probably. Who knows, homie? I'm just saying, stay on your toes in there."

III

As Deacon entered the empty edifice, his heart began to race at what felt to be triple pace. The dark, quiet atrium was an enormous feat of architectural genius. The sound of his combat boots on the wooden floor echoed throughout the gloomy expanse, like he was in the Batcave. As he marched through the void, he couldn't shake the feeling that he was being watched. The entire experience was sobering to Deacon when added to the fact he was about to meet his wife for the first time ... again.

This is nice. All it needs is some light! I can't even see where I'm going!

Once his eyes began to focus, he saw a slim line of light piercing the darkness. Once fully adjusted, he realized the light was coming from the bottom of a door. He also saw that he was about to run into a wall and quickly stopped in his tracks.

Deacon took a deep breath and regained his composure. Standing there, motionless, he noticed it wasn't entirely quiet anymore either. Indistinct laughter, like a child at play, feebly permeated the air. *Is that ... Junior?* Deacon strode toward the door. He knew that sound well and was sure it was his son. *He's got to be about three years old with a floor full of toys and a smile full of teeth! That's m' boy!*

Approaching the door, he slowed down and eased it open just enough to where he could see between the crack on the hinge side, between the door and the frame. He was right. A cute, innocent, three-year-old version of his eldest son sat there happily at play and totally unaware of being watched. Every parent wishes to go back in time to see their child at that innocent stage again. For Deacon, the wish had just come true. The sight brought forth the sincerest tears Deacon had ever cried. *That's him! But wait a minute, how old am I?*

He stood there sobbing quietly yet trying to recuperate, so he could enter and interrogate his son. Still, the undeniable sensation that someone was watching him demanded a look behind him. Conceding to the urge, he turned around slowly, and as his field of vision crested his shoulder, he saw the loveliest, most magnificent specimen of womanhood: Phoebe Marr. The vixen was aiming some contraption, which looked to be quite deadly, directly at his head.

"Deacon, you scared the godforsaken *shit* out of me! Why didn't you call? You just about got yourself decapitated! And are you crying?"

For a moment, Deacon stood there, speechless. The elation of being reunited with his love and their firstborn was overwhelming. He needed a few seconds to clear his mind and formulate a response, reminding himself that Phoebe didn't know his current situation and that they weren't married in that reality.

"Uh ... nah, I just got some dust in my eyes. I lost my phone killin' people. That's why I didn't call."

She cocked her head in disbelief. "That's what you said the *last* time you wanted some ass, and one of your hoes called you while you were sleeping. I told you, if you want some, just call me, baby."

Deacon's initial thought was to take her up on her offer, but he needed answers. Besides, Chuck was waiting outside. Sex could wait. "That's not what I come here for this time," Deacon said as he gradually brought his emotions under control. "I have some serious issues that I need to discuss with you on a more professional level."

She again cocked her head, this time with a look of wonder. "Deacon, as long as I've known you, you have sounded like this only once: when you found out I was pregnant. If I'm not mistaken, that's the sound of fear. Let's go to my office. You look like you need some counseling."

IV

Phoebe's office was warm and inviting, the type of atmosphere one would expect from a counselor trying to make patients feel comfortable opening up to them. The soft earth tones were pleasing to the eyes, the smell of lavender engulfed the air, and the ergonomic couch was the most comfortable thing Deacon had ever had the honor of being situated upon. However, opening up to Phoebe was the least of Deacon's problems. Finding out a way to explain his situation proved to be a daunting task. If he just told her he was having a problem deciphering dreams from reality, she would think he was joking. If he explained everything in detail, she would think he was crazy and have him committed. *I've got to handle this one delicately.*

"Do you ever remember your dreams?" Deacon already knew the answer. They talked about their dreams frequently, and Phoebe seemed to remember them more often and more vividly.

"Yes, all the time. You know that," she replied. "Why?"

Deacon took a deep breath before he continued. "Well, you ever have one that seemed so real that you woke up in total shock and awe? I'm talkin' 'bout one that made you question its authenticity, even though you *knew* it was a dream."

She rolled her eyes around, as if she was pondering the question, then nodded. She seemed intrigued, and then her expression transitioned smoothly from wonder to concern. "Yeah, I have those all the time. Where are you going with this?"

Deacon sat up from the ergonomic couch, which put him in a terribly uncomfortable position, but he wanted to emphasize his point. "What if you couldn't wake up from that dream, like a coma or something, would it be considered your reality?"

Phoebe gave Deacon a look of utter confusion. She understood the question perfectly fine; she just didn't know how to answer it. "Um, I guess so. I've always believed reality was based upon one's perception of their environment. So, if your dream is all you can perceive, I suppose it would be, in a sense, your reality."

Deacon was astonished by her amazingly intellectual answer. *Still got the brains of the Phoebe I know. I just hope she's retained the open-mindedness.* "Okay," he said hesitantly. "I don't quite know how to say this, but ... I'm living in that dream right now."

V

Outside the counseling center, Chuck was antsy, his nerves a network of confusion. "This is some serious shit! I hope he still smokes pot, because I can't take this anymore." Chuck rolled one of the largest joints he had ever held in the hope of enticing Deacon with a buzz. It looked like he was holding a miniature baseball bat. "It's a long shot but well worth it if he'll smoke with me. On second thought, fuck it. I'm smoking this one and rolling another. Knowing Phoebe, I might be out here for a while."

Chapter 5

I

Flabbergasted, Phoebe found her way through the darkness to the wet bar on the other side of the facility after checking in on Junior. *He's serious, and he isn't crazy. I don't know what to think about this one.* After Deacon explained his situation to her, she was stunned. For the first time in her career, she was speechless. They sat there in silence for a moment—Phoebe in astonishment, Deacon waiting for a response. Finally, Phoebe broke the silence, proclaiming her need for a drink, and left the room, shaking her head in bewilderment.

Deacon was still slightly drunk from the bar that he and Chuck had attended after the raid. When Phoebe left the room, she offered him a drink, but he politely declined. *I just need a joint and a cigarette, and then I'll be straight.* He had all but forgotten about Chuck waiting outside. When the thought crossed his mind, he rose from the ergonomic couch and headed outside to get him. *Maybe he's come up with something, sitting out there with his thoughts.*

"Man, if Deacon don't hurry his ass out here, I'm smoking this one too!" Chuck wasn't even thinking about the situation at hand. His mind had been everywhere but where it needed to be. He stood up to stretch his legs, took a deep breath, and just as he was sitting back down, the door to the counseling center swung open. "Phoebe! What a pleasant surprise! How's everything goin' in there?"

"Cut the sarcasm, and put some fire to that joint," she said angrily. "I don't know what to think about your buddy in there." She didn't know how to handle this matter, and it irked her, because she always knew what to do. This, however, had her on the ropes. "He's not displaying any signs of dementia or blunt-force trauma to the head or anything like that. He sat there and told me that insanely outlandish story totally straight-faced. Not even a smirk. But the oddest thing about the entire ordeal, the story that he told was *my* dream last night!"

"Okay," Chuck said with a perplexed look, "just when I thought things couldn't get any more confusing, here you go complicating things even further! We come here looking for solutions, not more problems! Now pass that joint!"

"Did someone say somethin' 'bout a joint?" Deacon asked as he rounded the corner, rubbing his hands together like a housefly. "You seriously need to turn some light on in there. I just got lost and somehow ended up in the back of the building."

Phoebe and Chuck erupted in laughter. "Pass it to him, Phoebe," Chuck said. "he needs it more than we do."

II

After smoking, they decided to go inside for a few rounds to complement the joint. Phoebe, who was toasted by then, managed to slur a complete sentence to Deacon. "I'm going to check on our son and then go to bed. I've had enough excitement for one night—unless you wanna come join me."

Deacon and Chuck had much higher tolerances for pot and alcohol, so they weren't even close to being done. Chuck already had another joint rolled and ready as Deacon poured two shots for them. "Okay, I'll be in there after this one," he said, knowing she'd be asleep by then.

After she left, Chuck gave Deacon a wide-eyed look of approval. "I've never seen her like this. She's glowing with delight! You are too. Maybe there's something to this entire marriage story. The more time we spent together, the more I believed you. You guys *never* get along this well! I mean, joking and laughing, not arguing and fussing. It's not the weed either; it's *you*! You really know her, like you two have spent your entire lives together. Before tonight, you couldn't even spend twenty minutes together without having sex or an argument."

Deacon smiled. "I told you, homie, she's my wife. I know how to talk to her."

Another two hours passed as Deacon ranted about his life prior to the wreck. Then he realized Chuck was sound asleep. *Typical Chuck.* He left the wet bar and went to check on Junior. The sun had surfaced slightly, so he could find his way to the room, where he had previously seen his son at play.

Deacon cracked the door open and peeked through the hinge side, like before, but saw nothing. He cracked it a little farther, so he could poke his head through to survey the entire room. He saw Phoebe lying on the couch with Junior lying on the floor in front of her. *How cute!* He couldn't see their faces, so he thought they were asleep, until he noticed how awkwardly they were lying. Both had their hands behind their backs. *That's weird.*

He reached in to turn off the light when Phoebe raised her head to where Deacon could see her face. She looked at him with the most horrified look in her eyes and the corner of a cloth hanging from her mouth. Deacon realized instantly that she was bound and gagged. Then the familiar sound of a gun cocking resonated behind his ear, followed by words in an unfamiliar language, though he knew full well what the assailant was saying. "Move and you're dead."

III

Deacon, who was also bound and gagged, watched as the German intruders dragged Chuck into the room, bound and gagged. Then he heard gunshots and explosions in the distance and deduced their base was being raided. *Payback is a bitch!*

A few minutes passed, long enough to secure the perimeter of the counseling center, when a tall, slender guy entered the room with a smug look on his clean-shaven face. Deacon knew he wasn't German, judging from all the words on his outfit being in English and the way he walked with a slump, unlike the upright-walking Germans. It wasn't long before Deacon recognized who the slouching guy was either. Deacon worked the gag out of his mouth, so he could give the traitor a piece of his mind. "Ken? If you don't release me and my family, I'll fuckin' *kill* you with my bare hands!"

His former supervisor from *Critical Thinkers*, Kennedy Wallace, gave him a questioning look that matched the looks Chuck and Phoebe had displayed. "How the hell do you know my name?"

Rather than reply, Deacon just glared at him with enough fire in his eyes to burn a hole in him.

"It doesn't matter. All of you are about to die anyway," Ken said. "I understand you're the general of this outfit who's killed countless numbers of my colleagues. So, you will have the pleasure of watching your family die, then dying a slow, painful death yourself. Sounds like fun! Let's get that gag back in your mouth, so we can get started."

Ken yelled a few words in German to two of his soldiers. One grabbed the gag Deacon had spit out, spit on it himself, and then shoved it back into Deacon's mouth. The other soldier cocked his sidearm and walked over to the four helpless Americans after the first soldier made sure the gag wasn't coming back out. The second soldier aimed his gun at Chuck and pulled the trigger. Chuck's head exploded. Blood and brains spattered all over the other three captives as they burst into muffled screams and tears.

The soldiers returned to Ken's side with looks of satisfaction. "See?" Ken said arrogantly. "You aren't killing shit! There's nothing you can do! What are you going to do, cry me to death?" He laughed as he brandished his sidearm and walked toward them. The intent to kill emanated from his evil grin as he waved the gun barrel slowly from side to side in front of their faces with his finger on the trigger, adding to the fear factor that was already established. Deacon tried to talk, but the cloth was shoved so far in his mouth, his gag reflex took over, and he had to stop, so he could breathe.

Ken stopped waving the gun and grabbed Phoebe by her hair, jamming the gun into her chin while looking Deacon square in the eyes. Deacon expelled a muffled yell, and even though he was gagged, his words were clear. "I'll do anything (muffled gag). Let her go!"

Ken laughed even harder at Deacon's futile plea for mercy. While still holding Phoebe by the hair, he aimed his gun at Junior and fired, spattering his brains everywhere.

Phoebe fainted, her head going limp in Ken's hand. Deacon's entire countenance changed. He didn't know what he wanted to do the most: kill Ken or die. Either would have sufficed at that point. *This is by far the worst dream I've ever had! I know one thing: when I wake up, Ken is a dead man!*

His former supervisor gave Phoebe a few gentle slaps on the face to awaken her. "I'd hate to murder you while you're unconscious. Wake up and get what's coming to you, so the general can suffer all the agony I've had to endure throughout the years."

He looked Deacon in the eye while continuing to speak to Phoebe in an angry tone. "He killed my parents right in front of me, no questions asked. Why? Because we chose to side with the Germans instead of being executed or imprisoned. I happen to *value* my life and the lives of my loved ones. What he saw as treachery we saw as a chance for survival." He put his sidearm in its holster and pulled out his field knife. "Now *he* will experience *my* pain!"

Deacon wasn't even listening. He and Phoebe shared a moment of sorrow while looking at each other for the last time. Then Ken slid the razor-sharp knife across Phoebe's neck, cutting all the way down to her spinal cord with one slice. When he let her go, her eyes were still open and looking at Deacon as her head flopped backwards, exposing her esophagus. Blood squirted out from her neck onto Deacon's face in rhythm with her heartbeat. Deacon was thunderstruck with emotion, speechless.

IV

The German language is drastically different from English, phonetically speaking. So, Deacon knew the conversation Ken was having with his minions wasn't about cruising or falling. "*Kreuzigen oder pfahlend*," they repeated while glancing at Deacon like he was a ten-ounce filet.

After lengthy deliberation, the trio seemed to reach an agreement. *Pfahlend* it was. The two henchmen scurried off, leaving Ken to explain the slow and painful death Deacon was about to endure.

A few moments passed, allowing Deacon to fully grasp the situation. Then, with his back still turned to Deacon, Ken finally spoke. "This one is Lukas's idea. I suggested crucifixion, but Lukas ... Lukas is twisted."

Ken turned to face Deacon with the most sinister yet satisfied smile on his face. "Bram Stoker's Dracula was based upon a real prince in Hungary from around the fourteen hundreds. He earned the nickname, 'Vlad the Impaler,' from what he would do to his enemies."

Ken, who was still smiling, walked slowly toward Deacon as he continued his monologue. "He would take a long stake, shove it up their ass, and then bury the stake outside his walls, so everybody who considered entering saw what had happened to his adversaries. As gravity pulled the body down, the stake slowly drove its way up through the intestines and ribcage. No telling where it would eventually pierce the skin. Maybe through your chest, maybe your mouth, maybe your throat. Who knows? Entire armies would just turn around at the sight and smell of thousands of rotting corpses."

He stopped right in front of Deacon and knelt, so they were face to face. "And that's what we're going to do with you, General. We're going to impale you and bury the stake in front of your city walls, so all your fleeing citizens can see their fearless leader dying in agony."

As Ken stood up, the two soldiers who had left earlier scurried back into the room, accompanied by two more soldiers who were considerably more broad chested than they. The larger of the two burly Germans grabbed Deacon by the ropes around his ankles and dragged him outside. Ken lit a cigar and strolled out behind them, still smiling.

V

I don't care how, I don't care why, just do it, so we can get this over with, and I can wake my ass up.

After the horrific events that Deacon had witnessed, he concluded that he was, in fact, dreaming. He wasn't even paying attention to Ken during his villainous speech. Knowing he was dreaming helped him calm down a little, and he even decided not to kill Ken when he woke up from his nightmare. He just wanted to get this impalement thing over with, if that was what it would take to wake him up.

The large German tossed Deacon into the back of a jeep, and then they headed to the front gates. All Deacon saw was the bottom of the truck bed, but he heard the chaos surrounding the truck on the way to his final resting place. Explosions and gunfire were the prominent sounds, along with women and children crying and Germans yelling. "*Zerstören*!" The attack on the city was totally unexpected, and everybody was caught off-guard as the unrelenting Germans laid waste to the entire place.

The sounds of anarchy started to fade away, then the truck finally came to a sliding stop. Deacon realized they were there. *Good, let's get this thing over with!* He was fully aware that the impalement just might hurt him for real, but he was ready to deal with it the best way he could. A stake up the ass wasn't exactly something for which a person could prepare. *If I can get through this without screaming, I won't wake up everybody in the hospital.*

The Germans dragged him off the truck bed and tossed him onto the ground like he was an inanimate object. He hit the ground with a thud that knocked the air out of his lungs. As he struggled to breathe, he saw Ken's boots step out of the driver's seat and then walk around the truck toward him. Upon arrival, he kicked Deacon in his stomach, then reached down and grabbed the gag from his mouth. "I want to be able to hear your screams," he said, "and I want all the remaining citizens of this city to hear them too."

The two husky Germans stood to Deacon's sides, grabbed him by his wrists and ankles, and started walking. Once off the ground, Deacon ducked his head, so he could see what was going on in the direction they were headed. Everything was upside down, but he could clearly decipher the scene. Two guys were holding shovels, and two other guys had a fifteen-foot pole that was sharpened at one end and flat on the other. *Jesus! That thing has got to be at least five inches thick!*

The two guys with the pole took aim and started swinging it back and forth. Then Deacon felt his own body swaying back and forth in rhythm with the pole. The farther back he swung, the closer the pole got. He gradually saw Ken materialize from foot to head with each swing, and he was wearing the largest smile of the night, a cigar hanging out of it.

"*Man*!" the Germans yelled in rhythm with the sway. "*Zwei*!" they yelled again right when Deacon felt the pointy end of the pole poke him between his thighs. At that point, he realized they were in a countdown, and most such countdowns only lasted until ... "*Drei*!"

In the split second he was airborne, he saw his life flash before his eyes. The odd thing about it was the fact that it wasn't the life he had lived. This life was full of violence and mercilessness. Death was prominent. He saw friends and family murdered, people dead in the streets, and Germans marching in unison as he watched from a window. He saw himself murdering other people: men, women, even innocent bystanders and children felt his wrath. He saw his parents lying on the floor in a pool of blood. This was not the life he knew.

Then the scene changed. He saw his family—the family that he knew: his beautiful wife and kids, his best friend, Chuck. The unconditional love he felt for them engulfed his entire being, and he became excited about the possibility of seeing them once he awakened. *I can't wait to wake up from this nightmare!* That split second felt like an eternity. Then the oddest thing happened: he saw a brilliant flash of bright white light, and then he went numb. He felt weightless.

Is this death?

Chapter 6

I

"The dedicated detectives who investigate these vicious felonies are members of an elite squad known as the Special Victims Unit. These are their stories."

As Deacon heard the famous intro to Phoebe's favorite TV show, *Law and Order SVU*, he laid there without opening his eyes and cracked a slight smile. *I knew it was just a bad dream.* He felt as if it was no coincidence that the show was on, and he could almost sense his beloved wife nearby. He took a deep whiff, trying to smell her distinct perfume, but only procured the strong scent of bleach and hospital disinfectant. Besides the episode of *Law and Order,* and the heart-rate monitor beeping in the background, the room was silent. No nurses or doctors scuttling about or patients writhing in pain. No telephones ringing off the hook or impatient family members trying to locate their loved ones in the operating room; none of the mayhem from before. *How long was I out?*

He squinted his eyes open to survey the room and quickly spotted his wife, who was sleeping soundly in the recliner next to his bed. Ignoring his pulsating headache, he conducted an analysis on his body, which seemed to be in pretty good shape, as opposed to when he was brought in. He was expecting whatever limbs that were still attached to be in casts. All his limbs were there, although one leg and one arm were in casts and his head was bandaged. He quickly used his operable arm to check the "important limb" and was overwhelmingly pleased to find it still there and seemingly unscathed. *I survived in one piece.*

II

He laid there and watched half of the episode of *Law and Order*, unable to sleep from fear of another nightmare. *I've slept long enough.* Just as a commercial ended, a beautiful Latina nurse entered the room cradling a clipboard and whisking a pencil across it. "Oh! I didn't know you were awake," she said, erasing what she had just written. "How are you feeling?"

"Better than I thought I would feel, considering the situation," he said. "I thought I was gonna be an invalid!"

The sexy nurse giggled and walked over to his bed. "Well, you're far from that, Mr. Russell, but I'll take good care of you. First, I just need to take a few tests. Phoebe wanted me to wake her up, but since you're awake now, I have to do my job first."

The nurse buzzed the front desk to notify the doctor in charge of Deacon that he was awake and coherent and could have an examination. Then she scoured an upper cabinet for a bottle of pain medication as she asked him what he preferred.

"Hydro please," he replied as he turned his head to check on Phoebe, who was wide awake.

"Hi baby," she said. "How are you?"

"Much better than before," Deacon replied, feeling like everything was finally back to normal. "They thought they could take me out, but you gotta wake up pretty early in the morning to get me!"

She laughed. "Whatever, baby."

The nurse administered his medication, and then the doctor arrived and examined Deacon. Once the doctor was finished, he spoke with the nurse, gave Deacon and Phoebe a vague smile, then took his leave. "He's going to sign your release papers," the nurse explained. "and you're good to go."

"Wait a second," Deacon exclaimed, "what about all the casts and bandages?"

The nurse gave him a confused look. "You're healing quite nicely, Mr. Russell. A few weeks or so, and we'll be removing those casts. Until then, try to be more careful."

As the nurse left the room shaking her head, Deacon sat up in his bed, bewildered. *How long was I out? It can take two or three months for a broken bone to heal. Have I been out that long?* He turned to Phoebe. "What's happening to me?"

Chapter 7

I

The SUV was full of pot smoke, and Archie was still half-naked when he got the text saying they were on their way down. *Damn, how long was I sleeping? It should've taken her hours! Wait a minute, she said "we." Is he with her?*

He hustled to clothe himself and get the vehicle clean of condom wrappers and pot. The fact that he was stoned didn't slow him down one bit. He wasn't as worried about the roaches and pot as he was about the condom wrappers and sex smell. Deacon knew his wife smoked, but if he found out she was sleeping with Archie, he would divorce her, take everything, and Archie's entire plan would be washed up. *I've worked too hard to get caught slipping. Why won't he just die already?*

After getting dressed, Archie rolled down the windows to air out the vehicle. Then he sprayed musky cologne to mask the sex smell. On his way to the trash can, he saw them exiting the elevator backwards. The leg cast Deacon was sporting stuck straight out, and they couldn't turn him around in the elevator with other passengers aboard.

Glad we parked so far away. The fourth floor of the parking deck was crowded near the elevator, but nearly vacant on the outer edge where they were parked. He quickly got back in the car and gave it a once over before Phoebe arrived with Deacon. He only had one chance to get this right.

As they approached the car, he saw the confused look on their faces through the rear-view mirror. *Did she tell him? Goddammit!*

Phoebe wheeled Deacon slowly, to give Archie enough time to make sure everything was in order, and so she could gather herself from the conversation she had just had with Deacon.

Archie started the car and gave the vents a nice coat of cologne before blasting the heat. Then he held his breath and rolled the windows up with crossed fingers.

It works with the police.

11

Phoebe was taken back. *First the wreck, and now this? I don't know how much of this I can take!* For her, the past six months had been an emotional rollercoaster, with the death of her parents and children being the apex and the ensuing weeks being a downward spiral.

Her husband, the sole survivor of a brutal accident that killed every other passenger, was losing his memory. She had just explained the past few months to him in painful detail, and he didn't remember one bit of it. He also didn't believe it and rebutted her with some absurd story of his own. *For Christ's sake, he thinks he's in a dream!*

She didn't know how to take it. Either he was delusional and really believed those things happened to him, or this was some sort of sick joke. *I'm mad, but I'm sad ... but I'm mad!*

Phoebe used to be supportive of her husband, but it was hard for her to support the person who had killed her parents and children, regardless of whether they were his children too. *Accident shmacksident!* She blamed him for their deaths. He blamed himself too, but the state had ruled it as a random automobile accident.

However, her most recent hardships came when Deacon started getting sick. Since then, they'd been in and out of the hospital every other week. He would get sick, see the doctor for a few days, then get well again. He had gotten so sick this time, he had passed out and fallen down the stairs. Nobody could figure out what was wrong with him. She thought it was depression. Archie said it was guilt.

She still loved Deacon, being that he was her husband, and she had married him for that reason, but she still hated him, being that he was the person who had destroyed everything else that she loved. Archie, her friend from med school, had been a big "shoulder to cry on" and "really supportive" for her, which further confused her situation. Her marriage was on the line, and her husband seemed to be losing his mind.

This is going to be one long ride home!

III

Deacon didn't know what was going on. *A dream within a dream? Maybe ... .* The idea had been explored before in movies, like *Inception*, but Deacon's instincts were telling him that it was more to it.

This feels too damn real to be just in my head! His bones were aching, his stomach was queasy, and Phoebe was serious when she said he had "killed the family."

He was overwhelmingly confused. To add to it, Phoebe was wheeling him toward a mid-sized SUV that reeked of pot, sex, and cheap cologne. The wiggler who stepped out of the driver's side and greeted them with a large smile rang a distant bell in the far reaches of Deacon's memory.

"Who the fuck are you, homie?" Those were the first words that come to Deacon's mind. He didn't even have to think about it. Just the way Archie approached them set Deacon off. Maybe it was the way Archie was dressed or his devilish grin formed out of pearly white teeth. There was something about Archie that Deacon didn't like, and this was before introductions (but really, he already knew him). "Who the fuck are you, and what are you doin' with my wife?"

IV

Upon seeing the immediate hostility, Archie threw his hands up by his shoulders in submission, then glanced at Phoebe for an explanation, or at least some support. *He doesn't remember me? That shit is stronger than I thought! A few more doses, and he's a goner for sure!*

His diabolical plan seemed to be getting back on track. Soon Deacon would be dead, and Archie would have Phoebe all to himself. The insurance money she got from her parents, her kids, and her soon-to-be dead husband would be enough to set them straight for the rest of their lives.

The plan went off track when Deacon survived the wreck. Archie hired a muscle to cut the brake line, they all were supposed to die in what looked to be like a freak automobile accident. Deacon's survival called forth alterations to the plan. Now, Archie had to figure out how to kill Deacon without drawing suspicion toward him or Phoebe.

Luckily, he was in medicine and had a minor in chemistry. The poison he concocted would go undetected by doctors and was lethal over time, when given in small amounts. Archie had been slipping it to Deacon in his pain medication and anti-depressants ever since he came home from the wreck. One small pill amongst a handful of others that were taken daily was hardly noticeable. The effects were though, and Deacon didn't have many more trips to the doctor left.

However, the memory loss seemed to be a slight hindrance. The doped-up, depressed Deacon was much less curious about Archie and Phoebe's relationship, and yet it was the first issue Deacon addressed as soon as he saw Archie.

This might be a problem. If he doesn't remember what happened, he won't remember to be depressed, and he'll start caring again. This might be a big problem!

V

"Didn't she tell you I was driving?" Archie asked as he tried to keep a straight face while Deacon arose from his wheelchair, ready for some action. Archie found it entertaining, watching Deacon work himself to his feet with the leg cast. What Archie had no chance of knowing was the training that Deacon had received in his previous lifetime was retained, and Deacon had every intention of killing Archie right there in that parking deck with his bare hands, then shoving his leg cast up his ass.

"Deacon, stop," Phoebe interjected, stepping between the two men. "I didn't tell you about him, because I wanted to know if you really didn't remember. Judging by your reaction, I can see you're telling the truth. Now calm down, so we can talk."

Deacon looked Phoebe square in the eyes. Then he paused to consider his options and take in all this information. Looking around, he saw condom wrappers in the trash can that the jerk had been walking away from as he emerged from the elevator. Deacon cocked his head in curiosity when he saw them, then looked back at Phoebe, who realized what he had seen. Then he remembered the slight aroma of sex and weed when they approached the vehicle. He tilted his head the other way and glanced at Archie, who had the smuggest look he could muster. That was the last straw.

VI

Archibald Stockholm met Phoebe Marr in med school years earlier. The British intern eventually moved to America to finish his education and try to win the hand of the loveliest woman he had ever laid his eyes on. The cheerleader was the sexiest on the squad, the smartest in her class, and hot in the pants. She had been on and off with an inadequate English major who would never be able to provide for her like Archie would.

During one of the off periods, Phoebe granted Archie the pleasure of being his French maid date for a Halloween party. Things went a little too far, and it was a life-changing experience for the British virgin. Advancements in social media made it possible for him to find her years later and rekindle the lost flame. That flame turned into a raging inferno of lust and jealousy, which spawned his murderous plot. He never liked or respected Deacon anyway. He regarded Deacon as inferior, a pheasant with a queen. Archie would enjoy killing him and his offspring to start over with Phoebe.

VII

There's no way this guy is serious. Half his body is in a cast. What's he gonna do? Archie was so tickled that he could barely stand it anymore, and the look on his face displayed that fact in full glory. His genetic smugness took over, and he didn't care anymore. *So what if he knows? What's he gonna do? What can he do?* Archie stood tall and puffed up his chest, indicating he wanted to squabble. As he made the mistake of his life, Phoebe saw fire in Deacon's eyes and dove for cover.

The arm cast seemed to materialize out of thin air and place itself firmly across the top of Archie's eyebrow with atomic force and a deafening thud. Archie didn't even see it coming. Deacon continued the onslaught with a flurry of cast blows to the head and face as he pinned Archie to the SUV by his throat with his good arm. He was going to kill him.

VIII

Everything happened so fast that Phoebe could barely tell what was going on. She knew Deacon was a jealous man, but he had never taken it so far. *He's fuckin' psycho! If I don't do something fast, poor ol' Archie doesn't stand a chance!*

She didn't really think Deacon was going to jump on Archie; hell, he was crippled. She had never seen this side of Deacon before. Save for the past few depressed months, Deacon was usually quite the jester, always joking around and laughing. She rarely saw him angry at anything other than work and had never seen him engage in combat. Then again, she had never cheated on him before either. Realizing that Deacon was about to kill a man over her, she fought off the flattery and brought herself to her feet to save Archie's life.

The volume of crushing blows that Deacon was delivering to Archie's head was totally unexpected. The beating made consciousness a luxury for Archie as his body went limp and afforded Deacon a wealth of uncontested brutality. Just as Deacon was getting into a rhythm, Phoebe thrust herself on him, knocking him off balance and sending him to the ground with her on top. Archie slid down the side of the SUV with a slight hint of breath being the only sign of life in his otherwise lifeless body.

The look in Deacon's eyes was one that Phoebe had never seen before, and hoped never to see again. It terrified her. With all that had been going on, she had forgotten the true love that she and Deacon had shared before the wreck. It was a love that she didn't have to cheat on, because she already had all that she had ever wanted out of life. The fact that he got that jealous over her incited blandishment, yet the length at which he had just gone incited fear. He didn't seem mad at her, just jealous of Archie. "Oh my god, Deacon, I think you killed him," she said, her voice quavering.

Deacon took a deep breath to calm down. "Ain't nothing wrong with him," he said. "He's still breathing. He'll make it. Let's go."

Phoebe was stunned at the harshness of his tone. "Well, we gotta call the cops or an ambulance or something, right?"

Deacon looked at her with surprise. "We're *at* the hospital, baby! He'll be fine right here. Fuck him. Let's go."

Phoebe was mortified. She couldn't blame him though. After all, she *had* just fucked Archie, and she had been doing so for the past few months. That didn't justify murder, but a temporary insanity plea would definitely hold up in court.

She knew the right thing to do would be to contact the hospital and let them know a man was dying on the fourth floor of the parking deck, but the way Deacon had just pummeled Archie scared the socks off her. "Okay, let's go. Fuck him," she said with a slight sigh and a nod, as if to apologize to Archie's soul.

Chapter 8

I

"They're getting in the vehicle now, sir. Yes, sir, looks like they're headed right toward you ... No, sir, they're going the speed limit, and it looks like there's a few people in front of them too." Leroy Jenkins had just given the head of security a rundown of the brutal beating he had witnessed only seconds earlier on one of the fourth-floor parking deck's security cameras. *I'm pretty sure that guy is dead.* He radioed for a team of medics to be sent there with a gurney.

Leroy leaned back in his chair with a sense of satisfaction on a job well done. *I love camera duty.* Some of the things that went on in hospitals, particularly the parking decks, was surprising. He had just seen a couple smoking weed and getting it on in an SUV. He was going to report them then, but the female was hot, and he thought he recognized her, like maybe she had worked there before. Either way, he decided against reporting it.

When she returned with another guy in a wheelchair, he felt bad for the crippled guy, who also looked familiar. All his sympathy faded away when the crippled guy rose from his wheelchair and mangled the other "pretty" guy. It was no ordinary fight; the cripple was going to kill the other guy. That's when Leroy decided to radio the head of security to apprehend the assailant. *I mean, it looked like he tried to shove his cast up the dude's ass before he left him there to die. Twisted shit right there, buddy, really twisted.*

He scanned his array of monitors to find the first floor of the parking deck. Once he found it, he dedicated all four of the available cameras in the area to watching the security officers lining up at the exit. *I'm not going to miss one second of this!*

Once the cameras were at the proper angle, zoomed in, and recording, he dug in his nose, wiped it in his pocket, then reclined in his cushiony leather spin chair to enjoy the show. *That guy takes his job waaay too seriously!*

II

On the first floor of the parking deck, the head of security was busy barking orders and getting everyone set for action. The camera guy said they weren't speeding away, so he had a minute or so to ensure everything was in place to apprehend the suspect. The five-man crew hated him to the core. He didn't care who liked him, as long as they followed his orders and did their jobs. *This isn't a popularity contest.*

"Guns off safety, everybody. This is not a drill! The suspect is considered armed and dangerous and has a female accomplice driving the car for him. She is also armed and dangerous. Three cars are in front of him, and he seems to be unaware of the situation down here. Once he rounds the bend, I want the vehicle surrounded. One in the back, two on each side, and me up front. I'll attempt to get him out of the car. If I succeed, you know what to do. If not, you know what to do in that situation too. Take 'em down, but do not kill. I repeat, do *not* kill! The goal is for everyone to come out of this alive, people, *alive*! Here they come. Places, everyone, places!"

The head of security wasn't being totally honest with his crew; he knew the two weren't armed. However, he hadn't shot his pistol since he had gone to the range the previous month and had never fired it at work. *About time we had some real action!* He was ready to fire some shots at a murderer with intent to kill.

His men were hidden so well between parked cars that the first three cars that passed didn't notice them. His men waited for the suspect's car to get far enough past them before they popped out of the shadows, guns drawn. "Freeze! This is security! Lay your weapons down and step out of the vehicle with your hands up!"

III

No way! Really? This asshole again? Deacon couldn't believe it. Ken was aiming a pistol at his head with the intention to kill him, yet again. "What weapons? We don't have any weapons. What are you talking about, Ken?"

"Keep your hands where I can see them, asshole!" Ken was ready to shoot this guy and get it over with. He knew all he had to say was, "It looked like he was reaching for a weapon." This was a black man who had just beat a white man to death *on tape.* The case wouldn't even make it to court. However, the pressing issue in Ken's head was, *How does this cocksucker know my name?*

"Step out of the vehicle with your hands up!"

"I can't, smartass," Deacon said. "I have an arm and a leg cast on!"

Ken was aware of this fact; he was just being an asshole. As soon as the crippled man tried to adjust to get out of the car, he was going to be a dead man. Yet the fact that he had called Ken by name still sparked his curiosity. *Maybe he heard someone call me in the hospital hallway or something. If I kill him now, I'll never know.*

IV

Phoebe was in such deep thought that everything seemed to be going in slow motion. Everything in her brain was working double time, so everything else around her seemed to be going at half speed. If those cars hadn't cut them off, they would've made it out of the parking deck before those cop wannabes were able to pull themselves away from their coffee and donuts. *He knew he wasn't gonna fit that cast up Archie's ass! That was just a waste of time. Furthermore, how did he not know who Archie was, but now he's calling out random security guards by their first name?* The entire situation was too complex and confusing.

The two security officers to her left motioned her to get out of the car, but she wasn't moving anywhere while those guns were pointed at her; she knew better. The head of security looked to be legally crazy, and there was no telling what he had told his crew. *They might really think we have weapons for real!* She looked at them, horrified, and then she looked back at Deacon, who was popping attitude at the head of security. She didn't know who she was more afraid of: the puppets with the pistols or the maniac who had just mangled a man with his bare hands.

Phoebe knew she had to do something. She was usually the decisive one, but she was on the fence about this. *Well, at least the maniac beside me loves me.* That seemed to be enough for her as the guards backed away and allowed Ken to take control the situation. As Ken got closer to the car's passenger side, Phoebe got closer to making her play. Just as Ken reached for the door handle, Deacon looked at Phoebe with desperation, and she made her move.

V

Leroy was awestruck in the camera room. *I can't wait to upload this one! My Facespace followers are gonna love this. It may even go viral!* He couldn't believe what was taking place in the parking decks that afternoon. He was so engulfed that he totally missed a nurse stealing pain pills in pharmaceutical and two surgeons making love in recovery—and the patient that was jerking off to it. He had been watching this story develop since he noticed the SUV pull up and then start bouncing, and he wasn't about to miss a glimmer of the action. He had seen a lot take place on those cameras, but nothing like what was going on in the parking deck at that moment. He was transfixed by the screen, glued to it like a child with his favorite Saturday morning cartoon. *This is blockbuster shit, even without the audio!*

He watched as Ken eased his way over to the passenger side, and just as he reached for the door, the SUV made a mad dash for the security gate. The suspects escaped in a barrage of bullets. All the officers unloaded on the SUV as it smashed through the gate and drifted flawlessly into traffic. *She's one helluva driver!*

VI

Deacon knew he was hit, multiple times, but he didn't mention it to Phoebe. She was preoccupied with weaving through traffic and dodging the police. He held his nerve throughout the ordeal as part of his training from the previous reality, but the thing that had him in awe was how readily Phoebe sacrificed for him. He looked at her, and at that moment, he was reminded of the love he felt for her in his original lifetime and rued the fact that he had brought her into this mess, even though Archie had it coming. *You can't go killing people in public.*

Deacon turned back to the road to regain his orientation. It looked like she was headed toward the highway. When he looked back at Phoebe, she was looking at him in total devastation. "Deacon," she said, "you're hit!"

He looked down and noticed one of the bullets had gone all the way through. If she had seen the other wounds riddling his back, she probably would've fainted. "Don't worry about me. Just get yourself to safety," he said as he found himself fighting death yet again.

Phoebe cut off three lanes of traffic, jumped a curb, and skidded onto the southbound ramp, effectively eluding the police. The plan was to double back at the next exit and head north, because she had family in Canada that she hadn't seen in years, and they were the type of family who wouldn't mind harboring fugitives. A bullet hole in Deacon's chest really dampened the escape plan though. Deacon wouldn't make it out of the state, much less across the border.

"We've gotta get you to a hospital! You're bleeding out," she said as Deacon grimaced in pain.

"We just left the hospital, honey. I don't think they'll be very welcoming to our return either," Deacon responded in his usual comical form.

"Well, they can't turn you down," she replied. "Hippocratic oath."

Deacon knew he was going to die, but he didn't want Phoebe to throw her life away in the process. This was a woman who had buried her entire family and who would now have to bury her beloved husband. "Don't worry about me, baby. I'll be fine. You need to get somewhere safe, call the police, and turn yourself in."

Phoebe was flabbergasted. "Excuse me? I took a vow till death do us part, and you're not about to die, not on my watch!" She didn't care what Deacon had to say at that point. She was not going to let him die too.

They had gotten much farther up the highway, to the point where the next hospital was closer than the one they had just left. It would be much faster to keep straight than double back. "We're almost in Springfield. They aren't aware of us there. We can get you stitched up and head north from there."

Deacon felt himself fading again, the same feeling he had when he was dying after the explosion that had started this entire mess. He had to fight death to make sure Phoebe heard his last words. "I'm so sorry I got you into this shit, baby."

Phoebe grasped Deacon's hand. "Don't you die on me, Deacon!"

He was already on his way out. "I love you, Phoebe. See you in my dreams."

VII

As a life much like his original one flashed before his eyes, Deacon couldn't help but feel at peace. Then that peace was shattered by horrific images of the wreck that took his family. Flipping and tumbling, bodies flying about, blood splattering all over the van's interior. Apparently, they had gone off a cliff. The event flashed before his eyes like a high-speed slideshow, image after image, until only one image remained ... Phoebe's angelic face.

It seemed like he could do no wrong in her eyes. He had killed the entire family, and judging by her reaction to the current situation, he concluded that she still loved him with the same intensity she had when they got married. Her level of devotion warmed Deacon's heart to its core. Even now, as he was knocking on death's door, he was sure she wasn't listening to him. She was on her way to the hospital to make some poor nurse attempt to revive his dead body. She wasn't worried about going to jail; she was trying to keep him alive.

Then images from his original reality came to the forefront of his mind. None of them were negative either. These two lovebirds had the perfect relationship. They had lots in common, they never argued, and the sex was epic. They never had to worry about giving each other space, because they always wanted to be around each other. At that point, the love was so thick in the air that Deacon felt like he could reach out and grab it. Even though he didn't know where he was going, he knew where he had come from. The memories of her brought him back to a peaceful feeling.

He was ready for death this time, but for some reason, he knew that wasn't what was going to happen. *Am I immortal?*

Then everything went bright white, and for a moment, he felt as if he were floating in a vast nothingness. All his senses were heightened, like a body buzz, yet he couldn't feel his body. He was just a single point of energy in an empty whiteness. There were no walls, no floors or ceilings, and no boundaries, just whiteness. There was no physical presence to be observed.

Then, just as fast as he was there, he was gone. Everything went black, and he could feel his body again. This time he felt no pain at all. No casts or bandages; however, he did feel one prominent difference. And it was awesome.

Chapter 9

I

As Deacon opened his eyes to a familiar sensation, the most apparent thing was the blowjob he was receiving. Lying in his California king-sized, memory foam, heated, canopy bed, he realized he was stark naked and drooling with ecstasy. After ejaculation, Deacon was in bliss. *Phoebe has changed her style a little bit, but still, that was perfect and very much needed!*

"Thanks, baby, I needed that!" he said as he watched her crawl out from under the covers.

When a voluptuous brunette Latina emerged from under the spread, Deacon was surprised yet slightly intrigued. "My pleasure, Mr. Russell," she said as she trotted to the edge of the bed to retrieve his breakfast and newspaper.

Damn, she looks familiar!

She placed the silver tray on his lap as he lay there, still recovering from the morning top off.

"Let me know when you're ready for your bath," she said while strutting away.

Talk about room service!

Deacon sat up to eat, and for the first time took in his surroundings. Two flat screens and a surround-sound system were integrated into the oak and cashmere canopy.

Shit! This is the nicest hotel bed I've ever seen, much less got head in! Upon further investigation, he saw satin curtains, bearskin rugs, golden doorknobs, custom crown moldings with words carved into them, and all the luxurious stops.

It was when he looked up at the headboard that he was sent reeling. It was a colossal mirror with elegant negative-spaced wording. He had to twist around to see what it said: "Russell." He twisted back around in astonishment, looked closer, and saw his last name engraved on just about everything. Mink slippers with a big R stitched into them, his pajamas were lying across a nearby similarly marked chair, and so were the bedsheets and covers. Even the custom crown moldings read "Russell." That was when he realized he must be rich and, in fact, in his own house rather than a hotel, but it didn't fully sink in till later. Until then, he just played along. He still thought he was dreaming anyway. *Yep, this is precisely how I would do it ... precisely.*

He ate his breakfast and smoked the blunt that he found while hunting for his silverware. Then, just as he was sitting up from his immaculate bed, the Latina returned. "You ready for bath, Mr. Russell?" she asked as she started removing her maid's attire to reveal her perfect body.

Was she just reading my mind?

"I most certainly am," he replied with a devilish grin.

Wow! A man could get used to this!

11

After his extended bath, Deacon made his way downstairs. He had fully enjoyed his morning, but it was time to get down to business.

The beautiful Latina didn't seem to understand much English, and he didn't understand a lot of Spanish, but through their combined efforts, he was able to discern a wealth of information while they were in the bath. He was surprised at how much she knew about him. Apparently, she was his shrink too. He would talk to her every morning in the tub and every night when she "put him to bed."

"You marry *bruja*," she said as she rinsed the soap off his shoulders. "You love secretary, but you enjoy my company best. We talk. You teach me English. We make good sex. But why you ask this today?"

Deacon didn't know how to answer in Spanish—or in English, for that matter. So, he mustered the best bullshit excuse he could think of. "I just wanted to hear the truth from somebody."

She smiled, then told him about a lucky lottery ticket and a big investment. She also mentioned how poorly his wife was treating him and how he hardly saw her or his four kids. He replayed the conversations in his head on the way down to the kitchen.

By the time he made it down the long spiral staircase, he was exhausted. *Damn that's a workout! I may need another bath!* He rounded the elegant newel post and saw the Latina in the kitchen rolling another blunt. *Does she have a twin or something? How did she get down here so fast?* "So, I see the teleporter is working well," he said with confidence. *There's no telling what's going on in this dream.*

She looked at him in bewilderment. "Or you can take elevator, like me."

Smartass, Deacon thought as he glanced over at a stainless-steel elevator door beside him. "Uh, yeah," he said trying to throw her off. "Elevator, that's what I meant."

"It's first time you not use it in years," she said. "You okay? You act strange today."

Man, if I play my cards right, I could live in luxury for the rest of my life—well, at least till I jump into another dream.

He and the beautiful Latina sat at the kitchen bar to have a few cups of coffee. Both were wearing thick, plush bathrobes with names embroidered on them. He looked down at his to admire the stitching. *Hey, that's my first name!* He stole a glance at the Latina's perfectly perky breast and saw "Gloria" stitched into it. *That must be her name ... unless she's wearing my wife's bathrobe. I'm pretty sure Phoebe is the secretary, if I truly love her. But she could be my wife, and Gloria is the maid's name. If Gloria is the maid's name, then Phoebe could be either one. Guess I just have to take a chance.*

"Listen, Gloria," he said as he lit the blunt that she had rolled for him, "it seems like we talk a lot, and I feel like I can trust you."

Intrigued by his statement, Gloria cocked her head slightly and lifted an eyebrow. Partly because he hadn't used her full first name in years, but also because the tone in his voice was so sincere, it almost sounded like he was afraid.

"I've been having these dreams," he continued, "and I can't explain it, but they seem so real. I can't tell if this is real or what. I mean, imagine being face to face with death and then waking up in a mansion to a beautiful woman like you, and all the wealth and power you could ever want. Sounds like the stuff of dreams, right?"

III

Gloria De Rosario grew up in Veracruz, Mexico, in an open-minded atmosphere. Anything to do with the paranormal was a daily topic of conversation in their household. She wanted to move to America to get an education and a career, so she could help her family back in Mexico. Even though Spanish was her native language, she knew enough English to survive in America, so she enrolled in school and found a job online. Three months later, she was living in an apartment in America with a job as telemarketer and going to medical school. She wanted to be a nurse.

One day after class, she was standing in line at the corner store, and the guy in front of her bought a fifty-dollar scratch-off lottery ticket and winked at her. "Good luck," she said (which was a phrase she had happened to pick up the day before from a clerk when she purchased her own ticket), and then she winked back at him in a mildly flirtatious manner.

The guy smiled. "Thanks, I might need it," he said and then left the store. She didn't understand what he said, so, thinking nothing of it, she bought a pack of cigarettes, ten dollars of gas, and walked outside to her pump.

As she started to pump her gas, the stranger ran up to her and planted the most exotic kiss on her that she had ever experienced. "I won!" he exclaimed. "All the numbers matched. I'm a multi-millionaire! You're my lucky charm, baby!"

Gloria didn't understand what he was saying, but she knew what was happening. "You want a job?" he asked. "I'm going to build a mansion. Come live with me as my maid, and I'll pay you a preposterous wage. Sound good?"

She understood that.

IV

"The stuff of dreams you say?" Gloria sipped her coffee as she pondered the issue. "You know, Mr. Russell, I thought something was wrong as soon as you woke. You always pull the covers back to watch when you wake. You never eat all of breakfast, and you always have TV on, looking at stock market. When you didn't take elevator, I knew then, something is wrong."

She then lit a cigarette and took another sip of coffee. "And you ask a lot of questions, like you don't remember your life. You even stroke differently when we make sex. I believe what you say, Mr. Russell, and I want to help. I have always been here for you and will always be here, no matter what nightmare you have. I'm your lucky charm! What can I help you with?"

V

Deacon was a smart guy, no matter what reality he was in. He took his winnings in increments but invested it in a few start-up companies and franchises. Then he began to think outside the box and invented a few of the era's most innovative technologies. He held twenty-eight patents and had money streaming in from all directions. His main base of operations, Woven Dreams Enterprises, was just a few blocks from where he built his mansion in Hollowsprings. There, his secretary ran the show; she was the boss when he wasn't there. Partially because she was the only person he trusted, but mostly because he loved her, and it justified her healthy salary.

Once Deacon wrestled his way through the revolving door, he felt like nothing could stop him from seeing Phoebe. Running through the lobby at full sprint in nothing but his bathrobe and mink slippers, Deacon searched frantically for his office, spilling coffee everywhere. *I bet it's on the top floor ... stairs or elevator?* DING! *Elevator it is.*

The top floor was virtually empty, much like Nakatomi Plaza in the first *Die Hard* movie, only with more technology and security installed. They were the only business with spaces rented out on the floor, so it made finding their offices a cinch. As Deacon neared the secretary's office, his heart raced. He couldn't tell whether it was the anticipation of seeing the love of his life, or the sheer excitement he got from the pot smell steeping into the hallway. *Now that's some good shit!*

When he reached her office, the door was open. The room was full of smoke, and he saw someone in the corner typing so fast that there was a higher chance that the smoke was coming from the keyboard. Her back was turned to him as she pounded at the keys like she was mad at them. As she turned to ash her roach, she caught Deacon's eye, and he stood there, speechless.

VI

Word had it Phoebe Wallace was sleeping with the boss. She didn't pay any attention to the rumors though. As long as her checks were signed, she could care less what everyone thought of her. She had a family to take care of. She and her husband were still living together, but were separated enough to where they slept in different rooms and never spoke to one another. The only reason they stayed together was the kids—that and he was out of work and had nowhere else to go. She would've hated to be the one to split the family apart, since he had practically begged to stay, so, she put up with him and paid all the bills while he got to stay home with the kids and do absolutely nothing.

Her boss was a savvy businessman who had everything to offer in life. He was extremely wealthy and quite handsome, with a boyish charm. He radiated confidence and energy with the swagger of a young Kevin Bacon as he entered the building, greeting people and shaking hands with his ape-like grip. His perfectly straight, bleach-white teeth were displayed in a huge, welcoming smile that made the ladies sink in their office chairs, trying to hold their hearts in their chests and gasping for air.

The fact that the entire office thought she was having an affair with him was flattering to Phoebe. *I'm not in his league. Hell, we're not even playing the same sport!*

Her boss wasn't the shallow type though. To him, money wasn't a factor when considering who to love. He also wasn't the type to sleep with just anyone. He had a reputation to keep and was constantly in the public eye, given his celebrity status. The business mogul also had a wife whom he was in the midst of divorcing. An affair would devastate his divorce; it would make a difference of millions of dollars. A fling with his personal secretary wasn't worth it. *I'd fuck him though, just based off principle. Never pass up a chance with a millionaire, and I bet he's hung like a sperm whale!*

Phoebe was one of the hardest workers on staff. Sure, she had days where she just sat there in her comfy office chair and relaxed, but most of the time it was balls to the wall—and she didn't have any balls to put to the wall.

It happened to be one of those days: working nonstop from the moment she entered her office. She received calls, set up appointments, reviewed reports, conducted interviews, and fixed computer problems all day, to the point where she had to neglect her daily duties. *Working overtime again. Oh well, I'll see it in my overtime pay.*

She was sitting there, just before five o'clock, clacking away at her keyboard, when she heard footsteps approaching her isolated office on the top floor. *Got to be the boss. Everyone else is getting ready to leave.* She continued to pound at the keys when her prediction was confirmed mere seconds later. Boss man was standing at the door, dressed for the occasion, and looking quite confused. She stopped typing for a moment. "Is there anything I can help you with, sir?"

Chapter 10

I

Deacon stood in the doorway of his secretary's office like a deer caught in the headlights, slightly embarrassed but more disappointed than anything. The nameplate on her desk read "Cassandra Camden," and she was stunning. The brunette bombshell had the naughty librarian look with her hair tied back, black framed glasses over her big brown eyes, a chiseled facial structure, pouty soft lips, and a swimmer's body. "Mr. Russell, I didn't expect to see you *this* early," she said as she tipped her glasses down to peer at him over the frames, "but I can always ... fit you in."

Okay, so she's hot. And I think I know this chick from somewhere too. I could probably fall for her. Still, she's not Phoebe. Deacon regained his composure and realized he was entirely naked under his bathrobe. *I own this place; they'll get over it.* "Yeah, uh, I just needed to see you. I'm having a rough day."

Cassandra shut her laptop and walked over to the window. "Come on in, baby," she said as she pulled the blinds shut. "And you can tell me all about it"

II

Phoebe locked up her office and rushed out of the building, checking the time and fumbling though a massive set of keys to find the one that matched her Mini Cooper. *I can't believe this is happening to me!* Just moments earlier, her boss had asked her if she would accompany him to a red-carpet event going on in downtown Hollowsprings that night. At first, he wasn't sure how to approach her, being that they both were still married but somewhat separated. After weeks of being shy, he finally mustered up the confidence to ask her out mere hours before the event. *The limo will be there at eight. Limo! I've got to hurry!* She weaved through traffic to make it home as fast as possible to prepare for the night of her life.

III

Deacon trudged home, deflated. After the amazing sexual escapade, he had the most unintellectual conversation with Cassandra he had ever had with another human in any reality. He quickly pegged her as the self-centered, materialistic type. *How could I ever be in love with someone like that? I mean, I've had more stimulating conversation with pets. The sex was incredible, but it doesn't compensate for the lack of brains. How could I love someone like that ... unless I was like that too? Shit, is that what I've been reduced to?*

During the slow walk home, Deacon couldn't stop memories of Phoebe from flooding his thoughts: the first time they met, their honeymoon in Jamaica, Junior's birth. All were life-altering events, and now they seemed to be all for nothing. His entire life was leading up to a future that no longer existed. This was the first time he had been forced to ponder the option of a life without his family—his original family. There was still a chance that his family in this reality was a distorted version of themselves, but to him, the odds of that were slim. The thought of not being with them again was enough to send Deacon into tears.

He moped up the driveway and took a few laps around the giant Poseidon fountain in his front yard as he contemplated suicide. *So, let me get this straight: lead a luxurious lifestyle where I travel the world, sleep with dazzling women, and live the proverbial dream without Phoebe, or end it all right now and start over. Quick and painless.*

He was serious about it too. He didn't understand what was happening to him, and nobody had explained the rules, but he had noticed a certain pattern developing, and a life without Phoebe just might be enough to test his theory. *If it works, I'll run the chance of being reunited with Phoebe. If it doesn't, I'm dead, and I'm not so thrilled about leaving this lifestyle either.*

He stopped to take in his surroundings. The first thing that gathered his attention was the twelve-foot-tall fountain portraying Poseidon wielding his trident in attack stance. He was riding a wave and was intimidating yet majestic. Water spouted from the three forks of the trident and Poseidon's mouth. Truly majestic.

Then he gazed upon his estate, which featured his massive three-story mansion with a huge two-story guest home to one side and a six-bay garage to the other. He thought about all the stuff in the back that he hadn't seen yet. The indoor/outdoor infinity pool and hot tub, the marina by the dock, and the helicopter. The grass was thick and green, and all the trees and vines bore fruit and berries. *I've also slept with two of the most beautiful women I have ever seen in my life, in one day. I mean, I miss Phoebe and all, but ... .*

IV

Phoebe ran inside her house to greet her family and then rushed into the shower to prepare for the event. Her boss hadn't given her any details concerning attire either. "Just come as you are," he said. *I can't do that, unless he wants me to embarrass him in front of hundreds of other millionaires.* She hadn't been so nervous about her appearance since senior prom. The event weighed heavier on her scale than her wedding, but a lot weighed heavier than the wedding.

She rummaged through her closet and came across an old dress that she hadn't donned since she was her aunt's bridesmaid fifteen years earlier. *This will do.* She kept digging and found the perfect pair of heels and an elegant sash that she had forgotten about. *Get ready social elite, here I come!*

V

Deacon sat on his Poseidon fountain contemplating his situation when he had an epiphany. *Hey, wait a minute, I'm rich! I'm filthy fuckin' rich!* After all the confusion and false Phoebe chasing, his brain finally registered all the information he had gathered, and for the first time that day, he realized he had the world at his fingertips. He vaguely recalled Gloria mentioning something during his bath about him being the youngest multibillionaire ever. At the time, he paid it no attention, because he was so concerned with finding Phoebe. *I'm filthy fucking rich, and I have everything I've ever wanted! What more could I ask for?*

He had a slight wave of guilt associated with selfishness, but the exhilaration of sudden wealth was enough to send adrenaline coursing throughout his body and brought him to his feet. *I want to go see what all I have in there!*

Since Gloria was sympathetic to his cause, he felt comfortable asking her for a tour of his estate. She took him through every room, showing him all the attention to detail they had made with the construction of his mansion (she helped with the design). Each of the fourteen bedrooms had some unique feature and had a full bathroom and a large walk-in closet. Any of them could have been the master bedroom. The mansion was decked out with twenty-one bathrooms, seven living rooms, three full kitchens, two elevators, a library, and a basement the size of most people's homes. The open floor plan allowed Deacon to see a lot of the house from the front door. Walking into it, he could see all the way up to the third floor at the top of the cone-shaped spiral staircase. Original paintings and sculptures were on display throughout the mansion, along with velvet furniture and thick carpeting.

After showing Deacon the guest house, which was more like a quarter-million-dollar dream home, Gloria led him across the front yard to the six-bay garage. Deacon took time to appreciate how perfectly spaced the apple trees were down the long, curved driveway. Then he noticed headlights at the end of it. "Are we expecting somebody?" he asked as Gloria turned to look.

"*Ayee! ¡Dios Mio! El charrito!*" she exclaimed. "*¿que hora es*?"

Deacon scratched his head. "Uh, six ... six fifteen maybe? But what charity are you talking about?"

Just then, the long, white stretch SUV pulled up beside them with one of the back tinted windows slightly cracked. "It's six thirty," a voice said, "and you're still in your bathrobe!"

Chapter 11

I

Chuck seemed to be having the luckiest day of his life. His company had made a marginal profit that month, his wife had granted the divorce, and he had won the hand of the most beautiful woman he had ever known for a date. His goal for the night was to allow her to see him for who he truly was. Considering that, everything had to be perfect. He had spent well beyond expected expenses to ensure that everything was flawless. Brand-new tailor-made tuxedo, expensive champagne, extra-strong pot, even a last-minute upgrade on the limo. Everything was top shelf.

All the extras were in hopes of showing that he was a different guy outside the office. Nobody there knew that he smoked or drank or even had a sense of humor. It was all work while he was at the office, but once he got home, it was all play. He tried not to let his personal life interfere with his business, because it was a gift that he refused to let fail.

As a child, Chuck grew up with the uncanny ability to get along with anybody, no matter their race, gender, or color. This led to him having a lot of associates, but throughout life he considered himself to have had only one true friend, only one person with whom he shared a mutual respect. That person was Deacon Russell. They had fun hanging out and had shared countless laughs. They were there for each other through the good and the bad. Loyal. So, when Deacon hit the jackpot, it was like Chuck also hit the jackpot.

Deacon bought Chuck a mansion, a car, and a yacht. Then he asked him what kind of company he would like to own and invested seven million into it for a thirty-percent profit share. Chuck was now the owner of a multi-billion-dollar armament company and had contracts with governments worldwide.

He had hired Phoebe the previous year, because she was the perfect blend of beauty and brains. His secretary would be frequently handling calls and meeting with important people from all over the world. She had to be able to keep things in order, give clients a pleasant encounter, and, in some cases, promote the merchandise with a little womanly persuasion. The British minister of defense called every month to check on his order—and to hear her voice.

Since Chuck had hired her, they had doubled the number of contracts, which, in turn, nearly quadrupled their revenue. Her marketing abilities, coupled with her powers of persuasion and a top-notch product, had made his company the highest grossing armament dealer in the world. She was in line for a big raise and a gigantic bonus to cap off a night of hoity-toity entertainment.

II

It was almost seven-thirty at the Wallace residence, and Phoebe had just got her twelve-year-old daughter, Gwen, to straighten her hair. Gwen was almost as excited as Phoebe and planned to put a butterfly clip in Phoebe's hair to pin her bangs back. "Mom, you're about to be the main attraction," she said. "You're absolutely beautiful!"

Phoebe blushed. "Stop it. You're gonna make me cry and bleed my mascara." She was thankful that Chuck had called to tell her that he was running a little late, but she still wouldn't have time to re-apply her makeup.

"So, who's the lucky man?" Gwen asked.

"It's not like that," Phoebe said. "Chuck is a good guy. It's ... complicated."

Gwen paused to finish a section. "Well, what's he like then? Is he gay or married? Jabber says those are two of the main issues as to why good guys are hard to find."

Phoebe grimaced. "You know what? If you read your schoolbooks as avidly as you do those damn magazines, you'd be a genius."

Gwen giggled. "We don't have books in class anymore. Besides, you didn't answer my question."

Phoebe squinted once she realized she had been figured out so quickly. *She's still a genius.* "I told you, it's not like that. I mean, yes, he's married—separated—but that's not the issue. He's my boss, a multi-billionaire who's known worldwide, and we're headed to an event that's being hosted by another multi-billionaire—and billions of billionaires will be there! I just hope I don't embarrass him—or me!"

Gwen smiled and gave her mom some much-needed advice. One thing she knew well was relationships. "Calm down, Mom. Just be yourself. He asked you to go with him for a reason. He likes *you*, so just be you. I guarantee you'll be the most beautiful woman there, so be confident and smile. Go have a good time with the guy. By the way, I kind of figured he was married."

III

Deacon's tuxedos were tailor made and customized for different occasions. He had one for formal events, one for dress-casual events, one for weddings, one for dances, one for operas, and he even had a long-tailed tux for masquerades and similar events. He had a wardrobe devoted to tuxedos, and Gloria was having a tough time scouring them for the perfect style for that night. *Maybe the penguin tux? Yeah, perfecto.*

She was so upset with herself for forgetting about Deacon's charity ball that when Chuck said he was picking someone else up, she jumped at the opportunity to make it up to Deacon by being his date for the night. She had learned her grace and elegance from being around so many wealthy people through the years, and her mother was a magnificent Spanish ballroom dancer, who had taught Gloria how to rumba and mambo at an early age. However, she had received her beauty directly from God. She possessed all the necessary skills to frolic with the upper class and enough beauty to turn every head, no matter what she wore. Her main objectives were to ensure that Deacon had the time of his life and to help make the ball a success. With her sultry dancing and godly body, they would be the center of attention amongst the wealthy, which would draw in more donations for his charity, a cause that also touched her personally.

The dress she chose was a thigh-length, sleeveless, low-cut, black-and-white masterpiece that was tight enough to show all her curves yet stretchy enough to allow nimbleness on the dance floor. The pattern also matched Deacon's handkerchief and the vest on his tuxedo. *Perfecto.*

IV

The stretch SUV Chuck had picked out was exquisite and one of a kind. Heated leather seats to accommodate eight comfortably, double-tinted windows for maximum privacy, soft LED lighting inside and out, surround-sound audio system with a nineteen-inch projector display that reflected off the driver's partition, and a bar that was stocked with the most expensive champagnes and wines that Chuck could think of at a moment's notice.

When Deacon saw it pull up the driveway, it was stunning, but nothing could prepare him for all the amenities that came with it. Once he sat down and realized the chair reclined, he was astonished. "Chuck, you've really outdone yourself this time, homie," Deacon said. "I mean, it even has foldout tables and shit!"

Chuck lifted an eyebrow in curiosity. "You don't recognize it? It's the one you had *custom made* last year for the opening of the studio."

Deacon winced. "Oh yeah, I forgot about that," he said, trying to throw Chuck off.

"Dude," Chuck replied, "it's *your* limousine company! You sure you're up for this tonight? You've been acting suspect ever since I got here."

Deacon smiled. "I'm good; I've got this. We're gonna have an awesome time, homie! I mean, we're about to go listen to some wiggler speak for a few minutes, then get fucked up and dance all night! I'm ready!"

Chuck's countenance changed to concern. "This is *your* event. *You* are hosting it! *You* are gonna be the wiggler delivering the opening and closing addresses. Please, tell me you're ready. Do you even know what charity this event is benefitting?"

Deacon didn't know he was going to be delivering speeches, so all he could do was respond with a blank stare.

"Don't worry," Gloria interjected. "I'll have him ready before we get there."

"I sure hope so," Chuck replied. "A lot of innocent lives are riding on it."

V

"They're on their way. We've got about twenty minutes before they get here, so any last-minute touches need to get finished." Phoebe and Gwen had a unique mother-daughter relationship. After her husband lost his job seven years earlier, Phoebe had to work two jobs and still find time to be a mom. She had worked one or both jobs every day for five years.

One year she took a three-day maternity leave, and the bills backed up so far that she had her tubes tied. With all the hours her mom was working, and a father who would rather lie around all day drinking moonshine and smoking pot, Gwen had a significantly condensed childhood. By the time she was eight, she was raising her siblings and cooking and cleaning up as much as she could, so her mom could come home and get a bit of rest. That led to a firm bond between them and a level of trust that rivaled marriage.

"Aaaannd done!" Gwen clipped her mom's bangs back and gave her sides a flick. "See? you can still dance your ass off, and your hair will bounce right back."

Phoebe smiled and then got serious. "Gwen, you're not mad at me for going out tonight, are you?"

Gwen took a step back in shock. "Of course not! Listen, it's obvious dad is a lowlife. He doesn't deserve us. I'm so excited for you! You need this, Mom. Go and enjoy your date tonight."

Phoebe smiled. *Such a smart girl.* "Thanks for always being there for me, kid. You're absolutely irreplaceable."

Gwen blushed. "No problem, Mom. Better go say your goodbyes to everyone else before they get here in that fancy limo. I've got to go run bath water. Bedtime is still ten, whether you're here or not. Goodnight! Go have some fun with Romeo, and I want to know everything tomorrow—all the juicy little details!"

Phoebe giggled. "Okay, I'll make sure I take pictures too."

VI

Thousands of miles away, a small family in Honduras packed a few small bags and left their inadequate, one-room shack in search of a new start in America. The cartel had taken over the government and infiltrated the police in much of Mexico, Central America, and parts of South America. Crime, poverty, and murder were all on a steady increase. The best chance of raising a family was either to join the mob or flee the country.

However, most of those who chose to flee were being turned around at the border. Even if they did make it past the border, it was only a matter of days before they were caught and deported back to a life of dodging bullets, only this time with all hope of survival demolished.

The statistics were staggering, and it seemed like no one could solve the situation. To sponsor a relief effort of that magnitude could easily run into the billions. That's why Deacon and a few of his billionaire colleagues had decided to host a charity event on the refugees' behalf. They could charge admission, accept donations, eat, drink, and be merry. All the music, food, and drinks would be from Latin America, and they could hold a draw for an all-expenses paid trip to Cancun.

Explaining all this to Deacon was the easy part for Gloria. Getting him to stop playing with the accessories and pay attention was the problem. All this wealthy lifestyle business was new to Deacon. He didn't know how to be rich. Where he was from, he had to work two jobs just to classify as lower-middle class. "Are you getting all this?" Chuck asked in frustration. "Because if not, I can stand in your place and say a few words."

"Naaa, I got it," Deacon replied. "Homeless refugees getting denied entry to America by insensitive politicians. It's a classic rich and poor political battle that's been going on for ages. I could speak for hours on that shit."

Chuck looked relieved. "Well, we only need a few minutes from you tonight."

Just then, the movie they had been watching paused to allow the partition to roll down slightly. The chauffeur tilted his rearview mirror down, so he could peer into the back. "We're almost there, boss," he said with a thick Jersey accent.

Deacon looked up at Chuck as he poured another drink, and Chuck glared back at him. "He was talking to you, Deacon."

Oh yeah, I own this shit. "Okay, I'll notify the ... uh ... client."

As the partition rolled back up, they heard the chauffeur mumble something.

"What did he just say? What's his name, what did he say?" Deacon asked, slightly angered.

Chuck and Gloria giggled. "His name is Phil, and he said he's glad you're not driving," Chuck said. "You sure you're okay, homie? We can call this entire thing off and go enjoy a night on the town in a badass ride."

Deacon laughed. "I'm good, bro. Relax. I mean, I should be the nervous one here. We're gonna go do this and still have a load of fun. I'm stoked!"

They pulled into the driveway. As Chuck got out of the car to get his date, he looked back and pointed at Deacon. "No more weird shit."

Deacon threw his hands up in capitulation. "I can't make any promises."

Chuck scowled and closed the door. Gloria smiled and took Deacon's hand. "You'll be fine."

Deacon took a deep breath and looked into Gloria's eyes. "Thanks for believing me. I don't know what I would do without you. I can tell Chuck about the situation, but not tonight. With some people, it's all about timing." Gloria batted her big brown eyes at Deacon, and they begin to kiss passionately.

Chuck's door opened, he and his date got in, and Phil pulled away. Deacon and Gloria didn't even notice.

"Ahem!" Chuck acted as if he was clearing his throat to get their attention. "Uh ... ahem! You guys gonna come up for air, so I can introduce my date?" They finally heard Chuck and turned their heads synchronously. Chuck looked at his date. "This is Deacon and Gloria. Deacon and Gloria, this is—"

"Phoebe!" Deacon said, finishing Chuck's introduction.

Gloria and Chuck exchanged a confused look. "So, you guys already know each other," Chuck said, but then he looked at Deacon and thought for a second. "Wait a minute, I don't wanna know."

Phoebe, who was just as surprised as they were, felt the need to defend herself. "I mean, he looks familiar, but I'm pretty sure we've never met."

Chuck looked at her in disbelief. "Well, how does he know your name then? You say he looks familiar."

She looked back at him with all the seriousness she could muster. "I don't know. That's a good question for him though."

Chuck eased back into his seat and laughed. "You know what? We started out on the wrong foot. I'm sorry, Phoebe. I have no right to question your integrity. Let's start over."

Phoebe smiled. "Okay, that's fine, but I still want to know how he knew my name."

"I may have mentioned it earlier," Chuck said. "and he may look familiar from TV. Whatever. Let's forget about it. How about a toast?" They all held up their drinks. "Good times, good friends—"

Deacon finished the toast, as always. "Good friends, good times."

Their glasses all clinked together and signified an agreement to put this foolishness behind them and move forward with the night's events. Chuck and Phoebe were still curious as to how Deacon knew her, but they were willing to drop the subject, so they could fully enjoy themselves. Deacon was silently marveling over how the universe worked. What were the odds of Phoebe being Chuck's date? Gloria fully understood what was going on when Deacon called out to Phoebe. She was just anxious to get out on the dance floor and cut a rug.

Chapter 12

I

Deacon owned dozens of successful companies. He was also part owner of dozens more. After he won his millions, he invested a lot into ideas he had for businesses and inventions. He also reluctantly invested a lot into ideas his friends and family came up with for a portion of their profits. Chuck's companies prospered, but most of the others didn't. That left Deacon with lots of buildings and warehouses that weren't being used, like the opera house that his wife proposed he buy and fix up for her.

He went above and beyond the call of duty to ensure success. He replaced the dilapidated roof with a Plexiglass dome and a retractable steel cover to protect it. Now the audience could see the night sky during the show. He also installed removable seating, so he could utilize the facility for other purposes. The theater also had dimmable lights that lined the walkways and walls, like in the movie theaters, so people could see where they were going and still have it dark enough for the show. The stage and backstage area were renovated to accommodate modern technology, such as cameras, prop lighting, and tethers, and the entire place had been re-painted from head to toe, inside and out.

He even added a botanical garden in the back, so his wife had somewhere to go relax.

Everything about the opera house was perfect, and when Deacon's wife saw it, she was amazed. She had loved opera and stage acting since she was a little girl, so she couldn't wait for opening night. However, when she found out that she had to actually work to run it, she abandoned the idea.

Deacon had used the theater, dubbed Russell Crossings, on several occasions for odd events, but never had it been used for its original purpose. That night, it was being utilized to hold a charity event benefitting immigration reform. It was decorated with plants, shrubs, and small trees from Latin America. Banners were hung, flags were flying, and people were gathering.

The press was up front, as usual, with boom mics, voice recorders, and cameras rolling when all the fat cats began to arrive in a procession of limousines and stretch vehicles. The turnout was inconceivable: actors, athletes, politicians, and other public figures came out to support the cause. Even tycoons and moguls showed up at the thought of cheap labor entering the country legally. Deacon was about to deliver his address in front of hundreds of the nation's most influential people. *No sweat.*

II

The back of the customized Escalade was so full of pot smoke that Deacon could barely see his hand in front of his face. They all stepped out onto the red carpet, giggling, as clouds of smoke billowed out of their ride like it was on fire. Chuck wrapped one arm around Phoebe and strutted inside, waving at everyone with his free hand. Deacon, with one arm around Gloria, was significantly more press friendly. He shied away from questions about his companies and focused more on the issue, along with giving them big smiles and good pictures.

As they made their way through the lobby, Gloria was surprised at how knowledgeable Deacon was about the subject matter and how well he handled the press. "You're better at this than we give credit for. You used to be mean to reporters when drunk."

Deacon laughed. "Well, maybe I'm not drunk enough yet. You know where the bar is?"

She giggled and then pointed toward it. "Chuck is there now," she said.

"Sweet. Have a seat with Phoebe over there. I'll get us some drinks."

Hispanic music was playing softly through the myriad of speakers that were scattered throughout the grand hall. Deacon eased up beside Chuck and poured a glass out of a bottle. "Thanks for doing this with me, homie."

Chuck stared at the stage, not even looking at Deacon. "We do everything together. You know I got you."

Deacon drank his glass quickly and poured another as he prepared to tell Chuck the truth about his awkward situation. Figuring out what to say was the issue. This wasn't the same reality, and it could even be a different Chuck.

How do I go about doing this? He isn't as receptive as Phoebe, but Phoebe doesn't even know me here. Yeah, if I never went to college, I never would've met Phoebe at all. Even if she did know me, I'm not the same person in this place. She would never have married a douche bag like this version of me. Damn, I need a cigarette! So, I guess I should just ease into it like the last time. Sit him down, have a few drinks, and hit him with it. Either way, I can't have this conversation with him in front of Phoebe. Phoebe, that's it … .

"Chuck, are you still wondering how I knew her name?"

Chuck finally looked at him. "The band is setting up. That's your cue. You need to get backstage and prepare for your opening address. Excuse me, did you just say something?"

Deacon shook his head I disbelief. "Never mind. We'll talk after the address. I've got to take this drink to Gloria. I'll get back with you."

III

"They are so cute together. You know, they've been best friends since elementary school. They share everything and know everything about each other. They should've been brothers. Charles looks nice tonight, no? He seems to like you a lot." Gloria tried to spark some small talk with Phoebe. She still seemed a bit shy, and Gloria wanted her to relax and be herself. She thought maybe if she initiated a conversation, Phoebe would be a little more comfortable.

In fact, Phoebe felt like she was in an unbelievably awkward situation. She really liked Chuck and wanted to see how things went with him, but she couldn't shake the feeling that she knew Deacon intimately. *He's so intriguing. I just don't remember where I know him from.* She looked back at Gloria with a giggle. "Yeah, he's cute in that tux, and you can tell there's a strong bond between them. So, what does Deacon do? Is he in the armament business too? I mean, where would he know a regular ol' gal like me from?"

Gloria closed her eyes and bowed her head in disappointment. *Not the response I was looking for.*

Just then, Deacon approached with a glass of champagne and a big smile. "Wish me luck," he said as he leaned in and gave Gloria a passionate kiss ... while looking at Phoebe.

Phoebe watched him as he did this ... so did Gloria. She wasn't jealous or anything; it just went against what was expected. *For this to work I'll have to consume his attention and divert hers.* "Make me proud," she whispered in his ear and then smacked him on his ass as he walked away.

He looked back at her with surprise, then gave her a lustful look, as if he liked it, and then continued his journey backstage. *He's making this harder than it has to be.* Gloria understood what was going on, but she had ulterior motives that didn't coincide with Deacon's. *Yeah, he's committed. Looks like I'll have to work this out through Phoebe.*

IV

Backstage still smelled like brand-new paint. The building was rarely used, the backstage even less. Deacon's dressing room had big couches, bright lights, and pre-rolled blunts. The vanity mirror spanned the entire wall and was lined with globe lights across the top. As Deacon stood there looking at himself in the mirror, he could barely contain his emotions. Love, lust, confusion, excitement, even a hint of betrayal—everything flooded him at once, like his id, ego, and superego were having a fistfight within.

First things first. I've got to nail this speech. Then I can talk to Chuck and go from there. He tugged on his long-tailed jacket to straighten it, tilted his top hat, then put out his blunt. *Even the weed is from Latin America. It's the little things, man.* He pocketed the other two blunts and headed for the stage. Once the band finished their opening number, he took the podium under a roar of cheers and applause.

"Welcome to Russell Crossings, my fellow humans!" he began. "Yes, I said, 'humans.' We are all one species. That's the way we should think. We are all one race of beings. Racism in all forms is senseless. You don't see such acts in nature; only in humanity. You'll never see a Siberian tiger suppressing a Bengal tiger just because of where he's from or the color of his fur. Only humans do that sort of thing. Even dogs and cats get along nowadays! We should all be working together toward one common goal, but until the world is on the same page, we will never evolve past fighting amongst ourselves.

"Some people understand this, mainly scientists, but they are able to cross those language and religious barriers and work together to achieve incomprehensible things. The people at CERN are some of the world's smartest people, geniuses, all gathered at one place performing god-like experiments. Particle accelerators, mass-communication systems—hell, they created the internet! Imagine if the entire world was working together! Just think of what we could achieve if we were to cooperate with one another. The possibilities are limitless. But it all starts here, at home. If we continue such sub-human acts of heartlessness, nobody will ever see the big picture. Earth isn't something that we can section off, and it's downright inhumane to prevent fleeing refugees from finding a place of solace. In all honesty, it's borderline racist. Let's be the example. Let's set the bar. Let's pave the way for other countries to follow. This isn't what America was built on. This isn't us. This isn't humane. *We* have the power to change this. Now let's put our minds, our resources, and our wallets together and show the world what being an American is about—what being *human* is about. Thank you."

The crowd erupted in cheers. Deacon exited the stage to a standing ovation. *Nailed it.* He glanced at his table as he walked off and was elated by their reaction. Phoebe was clapping ferociously. Gloria was too, yet she was also crying. Chuck was crying too, but his were tears of relief. He was also shaking his head, but in a good way, like what Deacon had said was totally unexpected. And his claps were slower than the others, about half the pace. Chuck was genuinely proud of him, and Deacon was happy to make him proud. It was one the greatest moments in his life—of any of his lives.

Back in his dressing room, Deacon noticed that the three blunts he had taken had been replaced, the ashtrays had been cleaned, the floor vacuumed, and the air freshened. After he took off his jacket, he couldn't resist the oversized suede leather sofa and took a well-deserved seat.

Once settled in, he took a deep breath, lit a blunt, and reveled in a job well done. *I told him I could speak on that shit for hours.* A few minutes passed, and then a knock at the door nearly startled Deacon sober.

"It's Gloria. Can I come in?"

"Uh ... yeah, sure," Deacon said as he tried to regain his composure. She came in and sat next to him on the large couch. He immediately passed her the blunt. "So, by now you've gathered that she's the Phoebe I've been ranting about all day, right?"

Gloria took a moment to exhale. "Yes, I did. The universe is so mysterious with how it works, no? When you and Charles were at the bar, she asked a lot of questions about you. Said she feels like she knows you from somewhere."

Gloria paused to hit the blunt and then passed it to Deacon. "At first, I thought maybe he slipped her a roofie one night. But then she said the strangest thing: 'Maybe it was in a past lifetime or something.' Then I *knew* she was your Phoebe. Two problems though: she doesn't know who you are, and right now she and Charles seem to be having the time of their lives together. So, what do you do?"

Deacon thought about it for a second as he smoked, and the hint of betrayal resurfaced. *That's my wife!* Deacon knew she wasn't really his wife in this life, and it hurt, because she hadn't experienced any walks through the park or vacations to the beach with him. All those memories were his alone, and the opportunity to make new ones with her were gone the second Chuck asked her out. *The bro code.*

Phoebe was pretty much a lost cause, but Chuck was not. He was still Deacon's best friend, no matter what. Deacon hit the blunt a few times and then passed it to Gloria before exhaling. "Think you can keep her occupied for a few minutes, so I can talk to Chuck? I know he can't do anything to get me back home, but at least he'll understand my situation. I mean, we share everything."

She nodded while holding in smoke and then exhaled. "I'll see ... what I ... can do." She finished exhaling as she extinguished the roach in the ashtray.

V

"Wow, that was amazing! He never really was a good public speaker—or anything PR related, for that matter." Chuck was blown away by Deacon's welcoming address. Once Deacon exited the stage, Gloria darted backstage to congratulate him, which gave Chuck a chance to get more acquainted with Phoebe. He was still worried about Deacon, but after the epic address Deacon had just eloquently delivered, Chuck felt like he could relax a little. *Deacon has been acting weird all night. None of the egotistical, snobby, rich-bitch bullshit that he's used to shoveling out. He's even press friendly! I was worried at first, but I kind of like the new Deacon. Seriously, he just stood up there and come up with that incredible opening address right off the top of his head? I know he's a smart guy, but damn, that was genius!*

Phoebe was equally impressed. Never once had he come off as smug or bullish. Quite the opposite. He had displayed a childlike innocence and hyperactivity, unlike most of America's snobby social elite. They had a few conversations in the car and connected somewhat. They shared so much in common that she felt like she had known him all her life. *I feel ... drawn to him. But I'm here with his best friend, who just so happens to be my boss. I think I need to focus more on having a good time with Chuck. Besides, how can I compete with Gloria, the most beautiful woman I've ever encountered?*

"Yeah, he did well considering he didn't have any practice," Phoebe said. She sipped her champagne and continued the conversation down a different path. "I've never seen you outside the office. You look nice tonight."

Chuck cocked an eyebrow. *Is she flirting with me?* "And you are absolutely stunning yourself. But thanks; it's Armani. So, what's your situation at home? I heard you guys are separated."

Phoebe smiled, seeing that her plan to divert the conversation had worked. "He's an asshole, to put it simply. I let him stay because I don't want to be the one who breaks up the family, but I'm so ready to move on it's obvious. Even our children know. The youngest calls him by his first name."

They shared a laugh and a drink, and then Chuck proceeded with his interrogation. "Have you dated since you two split?"

"Hell no," Phoebe replied in all honesty. "This is the first time I've been outside the house in years. We don't travel or take vacations; nothing. I lead a normal, boring life."

They shared another laugh and a drink, and then Phoebe decided to ask a few questions. "So, what's your story? I heard your wife just signed the divorce papers. What would make a woman agree to leave a billionaire?"

Chuck grimaced. "Okay, so you know how Deacon and I do everything together, right? Normally, what happens in Vegas stays in Vegas, but this situation left Vegas with us, so I can speak about it. We were young, rich, and fucked up when we came across a set of twins with the best bodies in the nation. So, we took them back to our room, and they swapped us out all night. That's all we remember. Then we came to, and discovered the beautiful twins were actually strippers slash con artists who had drugged us. They didn't even look alike ... they weren't even related! By the time the drugs were leveling off, we had already gotten married in the hotel chapel and were having the best sex we'd ever experienced in the twenty-two years we had been on this planet. When we woke up and they filled us in, we were devastated. Only thing we could do was make the best of a bad situation. So, we brought them back with us. At least they were hot."

Phoebe laughed. "So, why has it taken so long to get divorced? She held out that long?"

"Yeah, because without children, I could give her some money and send her on her way, but with kids, she could have residual income. I don't even sleep in the same room with her anymore, because she tries to get pregnant every time. Like, I'll wake up, and she's riding me. I don't know if a man can cum while he's asleep, but I'm not trying to find out the hard way."

Phoebe giggled. "Isn't that rape?"

"She's my wife. How would that sound in court? 'My wife rapes me, your honor.' The judge would look at me and suck his teeth, 'Case dismissed.'" He slammed his empty glass on the table, mimicking a gavel, and Phoebe burst into laughter.

"Deacon tried to make things work out with Bianca," he continued. "She was ready to leave after the first child, but he insisted she stay, and she kept getting pregnant. It took four kids for him to realize she didn't care about him or their family. That's probably why he's such an asshole, but he's trying to get divorced too."

"Well, it looks like the divorce is paying off already; he seems to be having a great time." *Damn, they are best friends. Let's try this again.*

She finished her champagne and took another stab at diverting the conversation from Deacon. "So, do you travel often?"

Chuck leaned in and answered with conviction. "Yes. A lot of it is business, as you know, but I take frequent vacations to leave the country for the weekend and can be just about anywhere at any time. That's one thing I love about my lifestyle. I was thinking about going somewhere this weekend. You're more than welcome to join me. Hell, you've got, like, two months of vacation time stacked up!"

Finally.

"I would love to join you, no matter where we go. So, where do you have in mind?"

Chuck smiled. "I don't know. Where do you want to go?"

Just then, Deacon and Gloria emerged, seemingly from thin air—air that smelled like pot.

"You two having a good time?" Deacon asked with a smile so big the others could see his molars.

Phoebe and Chuck smiled at each other, and then Phoebe responded with a slight giggle. “Yeah, we seem to be getting along quite decently. By the way, good job on the address. I almost shed a tear.”

“Yeah, good job, dude,” Chuck chimed in. “You had me worried for a second there though.”

“So, what’s next?” Phoebe asked. “All these billionaires here, you do another speech, and then we go home?”

Gloria saw Deacon was in a jam and interjected with the proper answer. “Well, first off, if someone is here, it means they have already spent a large amount, and all the proceeds are going toward the south-of-the-border effort. We’ve received donations from people who couldn’t make the event as well. It was a success before it even started.”

“Not to mention there are enough business transactions going on here to feed a small country for a few weeks,” Chuck added.

Phoebe furrowed her brow. “Business? I thought this was a charity event.”

Chuck looked at her with a grin. “Yeah, everything is about money, even charity. You think all these owners of ‘non-profit’ organizations aren’t making any money? The organization isn’t making money, but the people are. Look around you. There’s a major representative from every facet of the American infrastructure in this room. I’m talking about media moguls, oil tycoons, construction, transportation, energy, even celebrities. It’s a pretty long list. And all of them are talking turkey right now.”

Phoebe looked around and started to recognize a few faces from the news. *Hell, isn’t that Leroy Jenkins? He owns half the city. Three of my monthly bills go to that man.* "So, the event and its benefactors are just a façade for a big business deal?"

Chuck winked at her. "Precisely. Think about it. What would America say if all its tycoons decided to get together and hold a big business meeting? 'Oh, our government is a sham. These are the people who *really* run our country.' They would be right, but we have to maintain a certain level of transparency."

Once Deacon understood where the conversation was going, he decided to participate. "Yeah, if average Americans really knew how this country was run, there would be an upheaval. You also have to consider what an enemy country would do if they found out all our country's leaders were going to be at one place discussing the future. It's easy to bomb that. But bombing a charity event is like bombing a church; you become the *world's* enemy then. This is just a safer way for us to get together without conspiracies being conjured up or terrorist attacks—or media attacks, for that matter."

Phoebe understood. To her it was a win-win situation. Refugees get help, and big business is conducted. "Alright, guys, interesting conversation. Hey, Gloria, would you mind pointing me toward the lady's room?"

Gloria and Deacon looked at each other in surprise. That was the plan, to lure Phoebe away long enough for Deacon to converse with Chuck. Now it seemed like Phoebe had set the plan into motion. "Sure! I can show you a little more of the grounds too. I'm ready for a smoke anyway."

The ladies grabbed their things and walked away, talking and giggling. Deacon took an entire tray of drinks from the server standing near their table, slipped him a fifty, and told him to disappear. Once he put the drinks on the table and sat down beside Chuck, they shared a synchronous laugh and downed a glass together.

"We did it—again," Chuck said with exhilaration. "You have one of the greatest business minds in the game right now, and there are a good handful of people here that you need to be talking to."

Deacon pounded another glass before responding. "You're the only person I need to be talking to right now."

VI

"Ahhh, the smell of a garden on a cool summer night is enough to change your entire perception of plants." Phoebe was astounded at the floral arrangements the botanical garden had to offer. Each section had a dominant flower with accenting flowers that made for a unique scent every time they rounded a corner. There were benches, cobblestone walkways, water features like ponds and fountains, shrub art depicting indigenous animals; everything was breathtaking.

Gloria knew a girl could get proverbially lost in the garden. All the geometric floral patterns and awe-inspiring fragrances were enough to keep a cultured individual occupied for hours, especially if he or she sat down.

The moon was full and bright enough to illuminate the entire garden with a soft, soothing glow. There wasn't a cloud in the sky, and the stars were so big and bright they appeared to be millions of lightyears closer. As Gloria looked up at the night sky, she giggled at Phoebe's comment. "Yeah, Eden tends to have that effect on people, particularly at night."

They continued to stroll through Eden's winding path until Phoebe fell in love with an arrangement, picked a flower, and sat down to enjoy the scenery. Gloria took a moment and then sat beside her. *I wonder if the seed I planted in her earlier has sprouted.*

"So, how are you and Charles getting along?"

Phoebe took a long whiff of the chrysanthemum that she had just picked and then smiled. "You know, at first I thought this was a bad idea. And the incident when I got in the car had me a little confused. I'm just glad Chuck asked me out tonight. I'm having a wonderful time with you guys, and he's shaping up to be a guy that I could be interested in."

Gloria smiled in victory. *That's exactly what I wanted to hear.* "Well, I'm glad you're enjoying yourself with the yuppies tonight."

Phoebe laughed, took another whiff of the flower, and then pinned it in the butterfly clip in her hair. "You guys aren't snobs like the ones I see on TV. You're real, down-to-earth people who just happen to have money. I never would have guessed any of you smoked pot, just because of the social stigma it carries, but I've smoked more in the past few hours than I have all year."

They shared a laugh, and then Gloria was reminded of the blunt Deacon had given her while exiting the dressing room. "Speaking of pot ... ." She seized the blunt from her bra and lit it up. "Trust me, we have time."

VII

So, I'm in a totally different reality, I'm not the same person, and I'm in a completely different situation each time. Deacon felt like he had, for the most part, pieced the basics of this thing together. But then he thought deeper. *But I don't know how it started or how to control it. I think death is the trigger, but I don't know how to go to a specific reality. So, even if I did master the shift, it would be a shot in the dark trying to get home. I could spend eternity wandering aimlessly through reality. How do I explain all this to Chuck without sounding like I've lost my mind?*

Deacon knew explaining it would be hard, but proving it would be the true test. There was nothing he could say that couldn't be taken as a lie, and he had no tangible evidence of his shifts. All he had was memories of a life that he feared he would never see again. *Memories ... I wonder how much of this life parallels with my own.*

Deacon cleared his throat in preparation to speak, but Chuck beat him to it. "Thanks for yesterday. Convincing me to ask Phoebe out was a great idea. I wouldn't have had the balls to do it if you hadn't have said anything. We would be here talking business instead. Man, I haven't had this much fun since ... we went to Vegas—besides the entire marriage thing, which sucked. Other than that we had a blast. Remember that shit?"

So, I've betrayed myself, Deacon thought. *I betray me!* Deacon didn't even answer his question, choosing instead to respond with a question of his own. "Uh, what's your earliest memory of me?"

Chuck took a swig of his drink. "That's easy: elementary school when you beat up Stevie Blake, because he was bullying me. I didn't even know who you were, and you stood up for me."

Deacon sipped his drink and mulled that over for a moment. *I remember that shit. That's how we met.* "You remember when I fell out of the tree and broke my leg—"

"And I carried you all the way home on my back?" Chuck finished. "Yeah, I remember. How could I forget? I just got my spinal column straight again." Deacon laughed along with Chuck as he continued to contemplate his situation.

There must be some variance other than the scratch ticket. I did something different to put me in that store at that time. "Do you remember the day I bought the scratch-off? What was I doing?"

Chuck looked at Deacon as he tried to remember. "Uh, you stopped at the store for some odd reason."

"But why was I over there?" Deacon asked.

"I think you were leaving some chick's house or something. Yeah, you were dating Cassandra at the time. She used to live in that area, and you dumped her once you got rich."

They shared another laugh as Deacon considered the scenario. *Okay, so I remember dating Cassandra during high school; that's where I remember her from. She's extremely hot now, but if I was in my twenties when I bought the ticket, and Gloria was in college, I must have chosen Cassandra over school instead of breaking up with her, like I did in my original reality. That would put me there at that time. It also makes it funnier that I dumped her after I got rich and then made her my secretary.* Deacon laughed again.

"So, what do you think about Phoebe?" Chuck asked, changing the subject.

Deacon's brain scoured his millions of memories of her, all the laughs they had shared over the years and all the movie-like scenarios they had experienced, all the long conversations and all the pillow talk. Then he looked at Chuck and was reminded of all the memories they had shared together as well, the hint of betrayal was then replaced with heartbreaking contentment. *Hell, we share everything else.* "Perfect," he replied. "She's perfect. I'm sure you two will make a lot of new memories together."

Moments later, the women returned from their stroll in the garden, smelling like pot. They had the intentions of showing the dance floor how it was done, and Gloria had a passionate look in her eyes. Chuck hopped out of his seat and met Phoebe front and center with a mashed potato. Gloria dragged Deacon, who felt heartbroken, out on the floor and shook it on him so fast he was twirling and doing splits almost instantly. The two couples danced the night away.

Deacon went straight from the floor to the podium for his closing address—no backstage, no grooming, tie undone, lipstick-stained collar unbuttoned, sweat rolling, glass of champagne in one hand and a lit cigar in the other. The closing comments were short and sweet, with a Russell Simmons feel to them, and Deacon exited the stage, right back onto the dance floor.

On his way through the crowd, Deacon must have shaken thirty hands before making it back to Gloria, who was standing alone. "Where'd they go?"

Gloria bowed her head and closed her eyes, so she wouldn't have to see the heartbreak resurface. "They took a cab. Charles said for us to take the limo."

By the time she looked up, Deacon had his back turned, but he was obviously crying. She placed a hand gently on his shoulder, and he turned to embrace her.

"You know I'll take care of you," she whispered. "I always have, and I always will."

VIII

The ride home from the event, even though it was in an ultra-exquisite SUV, was uneventful. The entire way, Gloria tried unsuccessfully to uplift Deacon. Phil pulled up to the garage and parked the vehicle as they finished smoking and drinking in the back.

"You know, I'm perfectly fine with them being together and all." Deacon paused to blow his nose. "But I can't get that image out of my head. Like ... I know how she is in bed and how she looks naked and all that, and he's probably enjoying all that right now. That which was *mine*! I feel cheated."

He wiped his tears and pounded another glass as he grabbed the blunt from Gloria. Then he continued his rant. "Whatever is happening to me is totally against me! This is the third place I've been to now, and none of them is similar to the one I was in when this entire thing started. I really just want my wife and family back."

Gloria had been listening to Deacon crying and raving all the way home, and this time Phil didn't take the scenic route; he went straight there in a hurry. She figured Deacon needed to vent, so she just kept his glass and his lungs full, and her mouth shut.

Even though Deacon was throwing a fit, she listened to him. He was distraught, and she felt genuine sympathy for him. *I know a good way to take his mind off the pain.* "I understand you've got a lot going on, trying to wrap your mind around this entire reality riddle you've gotten into, missing your family, and now your best friend just ran off with your wife. It's a complicated situation, and I can only imagine how you feel. Why don't we go inside? I'll see if I can make you feel better. They say only time can heal wounds, but tonight, I can at least give you a bandage."

Chapter 13

I

BUZZ! BUZZ! BUZZ! The alarm clock triggered Deacon's PTSD from the war, and he jumped on Gloria and commenced to strangle the life out of her. She tried to scream, but Deacon tightened his grip and twisted, trying to wring her neck. Then, just as suddenly as it had started, he realized what he was doing, jumped off the bed, and fell to his knees with his face in his hands, crying.

Gloria was terrified, and at that point, so was Deacon. It was the first time he had slept through the night in days, and he didn't know being a badass killing machine had such side effects. It was also the first time he had woken up in the same situation as the day before since the fiasco had started.

"I'm so sorry, Gloria! I don't know what happened, I just … ."

She sat up on the edge of the bed and rubbed his back. "You're usually in your own room. I usually wake you up." Deacon continued to sob, and she continued to comfort him. "It's okay. I understand. I know you won't hurt me."

Deacon pulled himself together and picked himself up from the floor. "I think I need to fill you in on the rest of the story. I've done unimaginable things that you need to know about, just so you know who I am and where I'm from."

Gloria got up and grabbed a robe. "Meet me in the kitchen. I'll roll us one, and we can discuss it over our morning coffee."

After getting his robe and taking the elevator down, he met Gloria in the kitchen, where she had already made the coffee and was rolling a blunt. He took his spot at the bar, poured them both a cup, and tried to think of where to start. As Gloria put the finishing touches on the blunt and scoured the kitchen for a lighter, Deacon initiated the conversation.

"Okay, so you know I'm not from *here*, right? The thing is, I think I'm from an alternate reality or something like that. So far, this is the third reality I've visited. They say that life is all about the choices you make—any random choice can send you down a different path—and I'm pretty sure that rule includes decisions made by other people. Take, for example, in the first alternate reality I visited: Hitler won World War II, and I was a general in a rebel army. I just woke up and was killing people. I couldn't help it. It was like second nature, muscle-memory type shit, and I enjoyed it. I think that's what caused this morning's incident."

Gloria was paying full attention, captivated by Deacon's story. She tapped the ash off the blunt, passed it to him, and took a sip of her coffee. "So, are Phoebe and Charles in your alternate realities?"

Deacon looked at her in surprise, and then his face took on a curious expression. "Yes, they are, but that begs the question: are you in them too, since you're such a pivotal person in this reality? At first, I thought you were somebody new, but then I thought about it again, and you do look vaguely familiar. I want to say I've seen you before, but I don't remember where. Maybe it's like what Phoebe was experiencing when she met me, like I know you well from a different reality. Or maybe it's the fact that this version of me knew you so well before I got here. I don't know, but I'm beginning to think we're all connected in some way."

Deacon took a couple of hits as they mulled things over and then passed it to her. He took a swig of coffee before continuing. "The second reality I visited was equally weird. Phoebe was my wife, but I had killed the rest of my family in a car accident. I ended up killing someone there in an explosion of rage that I feel like was imprinted on me from the previous reality. But one thing they all have in common, including my original reality: I die right before the reality shift. Well, I guess I don't die, but I'm right there on the brink of death, in limbo or something. I think that may have something to do with triggering the reality shift."

Gloria passed the blunt back as she looked for her cigarettes. She was astounded. *Wow! He's piecing this thing together!* "So, how is it you remember how to kill without thinking about it but don't remember anything else about that particular version of you?"

Deacon raised his eyebrows. "Good question. I think it has something to do with what the body has learned. It was more of a muscle-memory type deal. Or maybe it's a subconscious thing, because it's more connected with the body than the conscious. It regulates things like breathing and heart rate, shit we don't necessarily think about doing, including muscle-memory type situations."

Gloria tapped the ashes from her cigarette. "How did this all start? What triggered the first shift?"

Deacon put out the blunt and lit a cigarette of his own. "I was on my way to work, and a chemical plant blew up beside the highway. A lot of people died, and I'm pretty sure it set off an EMP shortly before the explosion, because my phone went out while I was talking to *my* Phoebe. I must have died six or seven times. Then, just like that," he snapped his fingers, "I was killing people."

They took a moment to contemplate the situation, finish their cigarettes and coffee, and then Deacon continued as Gloria refilled their cups. "The last time I shifted, I went to this empty white place—"

BRING! BRING!

Deacon was interrupted by the house phone. Gloria left to retrieve the closest one in the next room. Deacon relit the blunt, took a few hits, then put it back in the ashtray and lit another cigarette. When Gloria returned, she looked concerned. "Your wife and kids are coming over in a few hours. She said she needs money. We should get cleaned up."

Deacon sighed. "Gloria, I can wash myself. You don't have to do that anymore."

Gloria frowned. "But we *always* bathe together. It's my favorite part of the day."

Deacon smiled. "Well, in that case ... ."

II

A few hours later, Deacon and Gloria were all freshened up, the mansion was clean, and they were ready for their company. Gloria was lighting incense to mask the marijuana smell when they heard the doorbell ring. She finished lighting the last one and then gave Deacon a final rundown on the way to answer the door. "Your wife is Bianca. Your children are Randy, Baylor, Delia, and Dawn. Delia and Dawn are the twins, and Randy is the oldest. You usually give them all a hundred dollars when they come in. I've got that at the door for you—with interest, because they haven't seen you in so long. They just might leave you alone."

Deacon gave her a puzzled look. "Leave me alone? They can't be *that* bad."

Gloria stopped to give him a horrified look, shuddered, and then continued. "You normally ask Bianca what she wants, do a little negotiating, and then you go and get the agreed amount out of the safe."

Deacon showed concern when she mentioned a safe, because he had no clue what the combination could be. Gloria sensed this and responded immediately. "It's biometric. You don't need a code; it's your handprint." Deacon's concern seemed to lighten, turning to curiosity. Once again, Gloria read his mind. "That should be the same. It's the same body you're in, and *that's* the same size too."

Gloria opened the door and welcomed Deacon's family. "Good afternoon, come on in," she said gleefully as the kids walked right past her, staring her down. Their glares were accompanied by rolling eyes and teeth sucking.

Gloria and Bianca had exchanged negative words before, but they tried not to let anyone know of their bad blood. They simply greeted one another and left it at that.

"Bianca," Gloria said with a slight nod. "Gloria," Bianca replied as she strode in gracefully.

The kids formed a line, oldest to youngest, and stood in front of Deacon with their hands out. Deacon was appalled. He looked at Gloria in shock, and she shrugged with an "I told you so" look. None of the kids even spoke to him; they just stood there with blank stares and outstretched hands. After a few moments, the tension came to a head. The children's facial expressions conveyed shock and disbelief, as if to say, "Is this really how you want this encounter to play out?"

Gloria sensed the situation spiraling south and decided to issue the money herself. Deacon stood there in shock as Gloria distributed the money, and the kids walked away silently, still staring Deacon down. The stone-cold silence was interrupted by Bianca's cell phone. She threw one hand up, as if to put her current situation on pause, rolled her eyes, then walked away as she answered her phone.

Deacon stood there, still stunned, and Gloria approached him with a ferocious gaze. "Why didn't you pay them? You didn't see the look? They were about to detonate! If I didn't step in, they would be doing thousands of dollars' worth of damage to your house. They scream, hit things, throw things, run around, bust windows, attack each other, steal, put holes in walls, break furniture, and they do it all very loudly. Trust me, it's cheaper to pay them."

Deacon still looked shocked. “Hell, I didn’t understand what was going on. I mean, the little bastards didn’t even speak! I was smiling when they walked in, and was going to hug them, but Randy pushed me away like he thought I was attacking him or something. I don’t understand it. Haven’t they been hugged before? Then they all lined up like that, and I didn’t know what to do. I froze.”

Gloria crossed her arms and looked down, as if ashamed. “I’m sorry for yelling. You didn’t know. Just ... next time just pay them and let them go. They’ve had it hard. Bianca doesn’t care about them, and she hardly lets you see them, so they’ve grown up thinking you don’t care about them. Who knows what she tells them about you.”

“Well, why haven’t I taken her to court for custody? I’m sure I can afford the guy who wrote the book on custody law.”

Gloria shook her head. “You can, and you did. But you lost. The court always rules in favor of the mother unless she’s physically or mentally incapable. If she has a job or is well off, she gets the children. Once you get a divorce, everything will be okay, as long as no alimony is involved.”

Deacon was saddened. “But I want to be a part of my kid’s lives. I mean, they need a male figure in their lives.”

Gloria turned to look at Bianca. “She has plenty of those; she’s on the phone with one right now.”

Bianca heard the comment, looked over at them, and flicked her hair as she turned back around to imply she was ignoring them. Just then, they heard glass shattering upstairs. The twins materialized on the front porch. They each peered through a glass pane on either side of the door, then commenced ringing the doorbell vigorously. Randy had put on the knight's armor from the library around the corner and was gallivanting about the house, swinging the sword and destroying everything in his way.

Then Baylor came down the steps behind them and tried to bribe Deacon. "I'm not being bad. Give me more money."

Deacon stared the kid down. "Then who broke the shit upstairs?"

Baylor huffed. "Give me more money, or I'll join my fellow siblings in the mayhem. Understand?"

Deacon looked over at Gloria, and she pointed frantically at his pockets. *Fucking pay the kid!*

Deacon dug in his pockets. "Yeah I got ya. Here, now go be good." He slipped her a twenty and patted her on the head.

Baylor looked at him with the most surprised look a seven-year-old could muster. "Seriously? This is an insult. I'm not a waiter; I'm your kid! Fuck this shit!" She screamed so loudly, it brought Deacon to his knees while plugging his ears with his fingers, hoping they wouldn't bleed. She ran off screaming, and, moments later, they heard glass shattering in the kitchen.

Deacon made it to his feet just in time to receive a good smack across his back with the sword. He dropped to his knees once again as Randy laughed villainously and ran off. The twins still hadn't stopped ringing the doorbell; they were taking turns.

"I think I'm having an aneurism." Deacon rolled onto his back and lay there as the debacle continued.

Gloria giggled. *Bet he'll pay 'em next time.*

II

Chuck leaned back in the custom-made leather chair he had installed in his basement and lit a cigar. He had woken up late and decided to take the day off. *They'll be alright for one day.* His basement was the size of a large apartment with two bedrooms, two full bathrooms, a living room, an office, and a kitchenette with a full bar. The living room was large enough to house a pool table, a poker table, a foosball table, a wrap-around leather couch, and televisions lining the walls. The office had an authentic bearskin rug on display with a small library and surround-sound speaker technology. He liked to listen to classical music while in deep thought.

Chuck sat there, relishing the night's escapades, but he couldn't help but think about the strange way Deacon had been acting the night before. *He really thought he knew Phoebe, and he was so convicted, yet fun. I mean, he started to remind me of the Deacon from fifteen years ago, before the money.* Chuck took a large pull from his expensive Cuban cigar and thought about the rest of the night. Everything was better after that. *Man, she is soooo sexy!*

His moment of euphoria was interrupted by his cell phone, which was set to vibrate, so it wasn't as disturbing. At first, he was going to ignore the call, but then he noticed it was Phoebe. *Oh shit!*

"Hey, how's it ... ." The ensuing conversation led to Chuck rapidly exiting the leisure of his office and running out of his house in a fret, his cigar still in his mouth and his cell phone in hand.

III

When Phoebe got home, the house was church-mouse quiet and seemingly empty. *Where is he?* On her way to her bedroom, she went through the kitchen to grab a drink and noticed a knife missing from the holder beside the bar. *That's odd.* The closer to the bedrooms she got, the stronger the smell of blood and rancidity permeated the air.

She stopped in the hallway bathroom to retrieve a can of air freshener from the back of the toilet, which was adjacent to the door. As she did, she noticed a bloody handprint on the toilet seat. *What the fuck?*

As Phoebe continued down the hallway, she dialed 911 on her cell phone but waited to press send. She poked her head into the master bedroom, expecting to see Ken drunk and passed out on the bed with a nasty cut on his hand. *I've told him about trying to cook while he's drunk.* Nothing. The master bedroom was deserted, the bed still made from the day before, so she assumed he must have passed out on in one of the kids' rooms.

She continued down the hallway, cell phone in hand, and poked her head into the bedroom her two youngest kids shared. It looked like a murder scene. All that was missing was the yellow tape and chalk outlines. The bunkbeds had collapsed in a pool of blood. The comforters and sheets were in shreds and soaked with blood. Feathers and cotton covered the floor from the tattered pillows and shredded mattresses. Blood spatter was all over the walls and created a pattern, like someone's morbid attempt at art. Phoebe decided to make the call before she ventured any farther down the hall.

As she looked down at her cell phone, she was blinded by something shimmering in her peripheral vision. She looked up in fear and saw Ken coming at her full speed from Gwen's room. The blinding shimmer was the knife, raised to attack.

She threw up one arm in self-defense, and her husband took a huge swipe at it, bringing the knife downwards with the blade facing her. The force sliced her arm to the bone. His alcohol took over, and he stumbled to the floor, keeping control of the knife but nearly taking Phoebe's arm off in the process. Once he hit the floor, Phoebe dove into the murder scene room, kicked the door closed, locked it, and leaned up against it.

All the tendons and muscles in her right forearm had been sliced through, so she had to use her left hand to make the call. She grabbed her phone with her left hand, trembling in fear, and hit the send button. Sometime during the attack, however, the "recent calls" button had been pushed, and Chuck had been the last person to talk to her.

Chuck answered gleefully, but she ignored his greeting and started wailing into the phone. "Oh my god, send the police! He's trying to kill me, and I think he's killed my children. Oh, god!"

Ken started kicking and slamming into the door, trying to break it down, causing her to drop the phone and struggle to keep the door closed. Phoebe's body mass wasn't enough to keep him out, and she could see the doorframe separating farther from the wall with each blow. After a few more attempts, the frame and the clasp fell to the floor, and the locked doorknob was no longer a factor. Phoebe braced her back against the door as hard as she could, expecting the next blow to knock her down. A moment later, the knife penetrated the door and stabbed Phoebe in her lungs.

She screamed and fell to the floor as the door swung open. There he stood, the blood of his children on his face to accompany his devilish grin. He wiped his face with his hand and used the blood to slick his hair back. Then he dislodged the knife from the door and glanced at her, giggling.

Phoebe laid there, wincing in pain and mortified as he slowly walked toward her, laughing and brandishing the knife like a tool of death. "I've wanted to do this for soooo long now. Guess I just needed the proper motivation." He waved the knife around as if to animate his twisted speech. "So, some rich asshole comes to pick you up in a limo, and you stay gone all night, and I'm supposed to be cool with that?"

Phoebe inched back as he moved closer. She thought about making a play for the window, but it seemed too far away. All she could do was keep inching back. Soon she would be cornered.

"I gave up a lucrative career that I loved to stay home with these fucking kids, who don't even respect me as their father, and this is the thanks I get? I don't deserve this shit! I'm under-appreciated here, and this shit stops today! You motherfuckers are going to learn to respect me!" He paused, as if he remembered he had already killed the kids and was about to kill her. He shrugged and continued his drunken rant. "Well, someone is going to respect me goddammit!"

Just then, Phoebe's cell phone rang. Ken turned back toward the door, where Phoebe dropped the phone, and the distraction was just enough for her to make a mad dash. She kicked Ken in his knee, hyperextending it, and then scrambled for the window as he fell to the floor.

Ken gripped his knee in agony, then looked at Phoebe's phone, which was right beside his face and ringing vigorously. The name on the screen said, "Charles Terrence," but the contact image was that of Phoebe holding a large, clean-shaven, veiny, black penis in her mouth sideways.

When he looked back at Phoebe, who was hanging halfway out the window, all he saw was red. His knee was numbed with fury as he sprang to his feet like a martial artist. "So, his dick pic is his contact image?" He punched her in the stab wound and then grabbed her by her belt loops and dragged her out of the room, grabbing the knife and her cell phone on the way out. "Why don't you come on in here and join the children, honey? Then I'll take some nice family pics to share with his ass."

IV

"How much do you want?" After hours of chasing kids around the house, defending himself from Randy, playing hide-and-seek Baylor's way (which involved the sound of broken items), and chasing the twins from door to door, Deacon realized he hadn't had so much fun with children in decades. Sure, the kids were ill behaved, but with the proper guidance, they could be managed, maybe even tamed.

They were adventurous and smart beyond their years. Randy was quite the swordsman; with proper discipline and training, he could really do some damage. Baylor was so sneaky, she was virtually impossible to catch, and the twins were a prime example of two heads being better than one. They had fun all day. Once Deacon had Bianca's undivided attention, he asked her a question. "How much do you want to leave us alone? I know you have a price. If I've got it and can maintain my lifestyle, it's yours. What's the number?"

Bianca was stunned. It was the first time that offer had been made where it didn't involve her taking at least two of the kids. She didn't know how to react. After years of abuse, the kids had taken a serious toll on her. For him to take the kids would be priceless. She almost felt like she would owe him some money.

"Look, if you take all the kids and give me enough money to start over, I'll leave, and you will never have to worry about me again."

V

"Get the hell out of the way!" Chuck's road rage kicked in as he raced down the highway to Phoebe's house. He had never driven there, and he hadn't been paying attention when the chauffeur picked her up, so he had to GPS her address. Luckily, he had to pull it up on his computer for the police when he called them, so he just copied and pasted it to the GPS in his phone, mounted it in the holder on his dash, and squealed tires.

At the first red light, he decided to call her back to see if her situation had changed and to let her know the police were on their way. When she didn't answer, panic set in. From that point on, he ignored every light and sign and only braked if it was necessary to keep the car on the road. Weaving through traffic and across the yellow lines, Chuck was determined to reach Phoebe.

And when I get there ... oooohhhh he better pray the police get there before me!

Once he hit the highway, he was home free. It was after normal commuting hours, so it was virtually empty, and Chuck stomped it. Adrenaline coursed through his body, giving him the jitters. Just the thought that she might be dying because he had taken her out was sickening. It was also an indicator of the type of guy he was dealing with.

She's so sweet and smart and beautiful. How could someone hurt her?

The closer he got to the exit, the antsier he got. His leg was jumping so much it almost made his foot dance off the gas pedal. His "sex-cretary" was being attacked, and he was trying his damnedest to stop it. "Hold on, Phoebe, I'm coming!"

Exiting the highway didn't slow him down one RPM. He drifted into his lane, checked his phone's GPS, and eyeballed his next turn. Once he was oriented, his phone went off, letting him know a message was coming through. Since his phone was already open, it automatically showed him the message and the attached image. It was Phoebe, spread-eagled, each limb tied to a bedpost, and a knife shoved into her vagina all the way up to the handle. He saw the children's limbs and torsos piled up in the background with the phrase, "I'm daddy!" written on the wall in blood above them. The message that accompanied the image said, *And this knife is waaay bigger than your dick!*

VI

Phoebe lay there in excruciating agony, bound and gagged and bleeding out. Her husband had tied her up and then stabbed and sliced at her until he was tired. Once he was done, he thrust the knife into her vagina with one swift, fluid motion.

He took a picture and sent it to Chuck and in response got a picture that had been taken the night before. It was of Phoebe, naked and bent over, looking back at the camera. The message that accompanied it said, *This is how I'll remember her. How could you kill your own family? You're fucking sick!*

Ken propped the phone on a dresser in the corner. Then he left the room for a moment and returned with the Glock 9mm that Phoebe had told him to get rid of years earlier. His countenance had changed. Like Dr. Jekyll and Mr. Hyde, Ken had gone from hysterically violent to hysterically crying in a matter of seconds. "I loved you! We were happy! You ruined everything! You turned the kids against me, made them think I was worthless. Even my own parents took your side. I hate you!" He sobbed and snorted as he crept toward her with the sidearm. "God, I love you!"

VII

How could someone be so cold? Gloria and the children stood outside Deacon's bedroom eavesdropping on the conversation, and they were stunned at Bianca's cruelty. The children were heartbroken and devastated, and Gloria was just plain mad. She spied on them all the time, so she knew Bianca didn't care about the kids. That's why when Deacon had called Bianca to the bedroom, she knew what was going down, and had formed an elaborate plot to get rid of her. When the kids first crept up behind her, she thought that them being there to hear their mother's bullshit would be beneficial, so she told them to be quiet and listen. She had no way of knowing Deacon was going to be so straightforward and offer to take the kids. Bianca's response was much less anticipated, and in hindsight, having the kids there was an awful idea.

It's okay though. I've got something for her ass this time.

Deacon stood there in disbelief. "So, pretty much what you're saying is, you don't want the children?"

Bianca lowered her brow. "Since when did you become interested in those brats? You can have them. I just want what's mine. Hell, you only want custody, so you won't have to pay me child support anymore. So, give me enough to leave, and I'll leave. Simple as that."

Deacon was saddened. *How did I end up with this bitch?* "Alright, what about a divorce? Does this agreement include papers?"

Bianca crossed her eyes in frustration. "Listen, take those kids, give me my money, and I'll sign any paper you want. I don't fuckin' love you! I married you for the money, and you know that. Fuck this marriage and those damn kids!"

Deacon turned his back on her, shedding a tear as his wife sold him their children. He didn't want her to see him cry, so he just turned his back to her and controlled his whimpers as he spoke. "I want my kids, because I love them, unlike you. I'm disgusted with you, and after I give you this money, don't *ever* come back around here. Do you understand me?" He turned around and pointed his finger at her. "Don't even call. I mean, unfriended on social media and forgotten about. So, how much is enough?"

Unashamed, Bianca turned her head and looked upwards, batting her eyes in deep thought. Then she shrugged. "Well, Forbes said your worth was almost incalculable, so let me think about this for a second."

VIII

"Your destination is on the right." Chuck's GPS was right on time as Chuck remembered the driveway and drifted the car into their front yard. He didn't even put the car in park when he jumped out and bolted to the door. "You have arrived at your destination."

As Chuck approached the porch, he noticed a broken window with blood running down the wall beneath it. He bounded up the steps, but as he reached for the door ... POP! He paused, *that's gunfire.* He decided to take a more cautious approach when entering the house now that he knew a firearm was involved. He opened his pocketknife while opening the door. *I know, I know, never bring a knife to a gunfight, but it's better than nothing.*

The door was unlocked, and Chuck slipped inside, scouring the scene. He took a few slow steps and spotted blood smeared down the hallway floor, like someone had been dragged back there bleeding. He followed the trail, checking the other rooms on the way. Once his field of vision could crest the half-closed door at the end of the hall, he saw the pile of body parts from the picture. *Well, at least I know I'm in the right place, but where are the heads?* He took a few more slow, calculated steps and then eased the door open with the knife. The door creaked, and he poked his head inside. Nothing could prepare him for what he saw.

As he scanned the room, he was glad he hadn't eaten anything, because he would have lost it then. The children's bodies were dissected to the point where he couldn't tell which limb was where. Arms were cut off at the shoulder, elbow, and wrist, legs cut off at the hip, knee and ankle. But the pile only consisted of arms, legs, and torsos. Phoebe's husband had got a little creative with the hands, feet, and heads. At the foot of the bed, where Phoebe's garbled body lay, were the children's heads, looking back at her, resting on their feet with their hands pegged into the ears. *That was what she was looking at when she died.*

Then he saw Ken in the corner beside him, the obvious victim of a self-inflicted gunshot through his head. He was on his knees, facing the room, yet slumped back into the corner with brains and blood still running down the walls.

Chuck looked over at Phoebe again and felt simultaneously heartbroken and angry. He started to cry, and then he noticed her face wasn't covered with just blood. *Is that ... semen? He jerked off to this sick shit?* That was too much, Chuck blew chunks all over the murder scene.

He knelt to catch his breath and then noticed a cord running from an outlet. He followed the cord to a cell phone that was propped up in the corner and still recording. Chuck grabbed the phone, pressed stop, and went back to the gallery. Apparently, Ken had taken multiple pictures and one long video. The pictures were a load of selfies as he was stabbing and slicing Phoebe. The video was much more involved. She was still alive during the filming, and Ken had taken twisted to an entirely new level.

IX

Gloria had heard enough of Bianca and decided to let her presence be known. She told Randy to wait outside the door until the right moment. "You'll know when," she said. Then she stomped into the room with a massive attitude. "Bianca, you're not getting a dime. Now we would appreciate it if you just leave."

Bianca was stunned. "Well, I'll just go get the children and go. They don't like you anyway."

Deacon let Gloria handle the situation; it seemed like she had something up her sleeve. That is, she was holding something, but he couldn't tell what it was.

Gloria, who had everything under control, was just setting up for the kill. "The kids will be staying, and you will be leaving alone."

Bianca stood up, about to get physical, and then the kids walked into the room and everybody stopped—everybody except Gloria, who held her arm up and pressed the stop button on a digital voice recorder.

Bianca's jaw dropped, and then she regained her composure and cut her eyes at Gloria as she spoke to the children. "Kids; get your shit. We're leaving."

Randy stepped forward. "No. You get your shit. *We're* staying! We heard the entire thing. Fuck you, *Bianca*! We didn't like you anyway."

Deacon was as surprised as Bianca, yet his surprise was a joyful one. His jaw dropped with a slight smile. *I knew Gloria had something going on!* He was elated when Randy walked over to him and gave him a big hug. Soon he was joined by the others. Bianca grabbed her purse and headed sadly to the door. She frowned at Gloria on the way out, but Gloria had no sympathy. "You just lost your entire family ... and got nothing to show for it. You are a cruel, heartless person, so don't try me with that sad shit. You just tried to sell your children. You *should* be ashamed! Now go. You know the way out."

Bianca tucked her tail and trudged away. Gloria watched her all the way to the front door in case she tried to steal something. Then she noticed the condition of the rest of the mansion and grimaced. She poked her head back into the room. Deacon was already playing with the kids. She turned back to survey the damage. *Well, I'd better get started if I want any sleep tonight.*

X

Chuck watched the video in its gruesome entirety. It started with Phoebe lying there, tied up and seemingly dead. Then she started to twist her left arm and almost got it free from the rope. She stopped moving, and he heard Ken in the background, ranting about how the kids never respected him. He sounded cracked. Then he entered the picture, walking toward Phoebe and still ranting. He waved his gun around as he talked. Though he was getting louder, his words were almost incomprehensible. He was telling her how much he loved her and that she had ruined their relationship. Then he mumbled something as he unzipped his pants, pulled his penis out, and inserted it into a stab wound. Phoebe wailed a bloodcurdling scream as he proceeded to stroke, holding her down with one hand and inserting the gun barrel into another stab wound.

Chuck hurled again, but this time, on the way up, he saw a police officer who had his gun drawn and aimed at his head.

Hands up, don't shoot ...

Chuck dropped the phone and stepped back with his hands up. "I didn't do this! I'm the one who called."

The officer lowered his gun. "Well you've contaminated the entire crime scene. Get out of here, now. Give your story to the deputy outside." Then he started to gag and covered his mouth, trying to contain his own lunch.

"See?" Chuck said. "Wait till you see the video."

XI

Later that night, Deacon and Gloria were putting the finishing touches on the mansion after the kids demolished it throughout the day. Each child had chosen a room. They had never slept in the mansion before, mainly because Bianca had told them it was haunted. The twins chose to share the room above the library; they could see the entire backyard from it, and it was the largest one on the second floor. Baylor got the first room on the first floor, because it was the closest to the door. Randy got the room farthest away from everybody, in the basement. It didn't take them long to settle down after eating, and then they all went to their rooms to get acclimated. Once they were in their rooms, Deacon and Gloria double-teamed the cleanup ... it still took hours.

The kids were asleep before they knew it. Then Gloria lit more incense as Deacon lit the blunt that he found in his coat pocket from the night before.

When Gloria finally joined him in the games room, she sat down and sighed, then looked up at him with the most exhausted expression on her face. "It'll take some time and energy, but I think we can manage this."

Deacon looked back with an equally exhausted countenance. "Yeah, I'm going to have to start taking vitamins and supplements to keep up with them." They shared a laugh, and he passed the blunt to her. "You think Bianca will be okay?" Gloria's face turned red. "*Fuck* her. You don't know her like I do. Not even the Deacon from here knew her as well as me. She didn't deserve that. She needs to be in jail.

Trust me, she'll find another sucker soon enough ... not to say that you're a sucker or anything."

"Well, I was, at least once."

They shared another laugh as she hit the blunt and passed it back. Deacon took a massive hit and was choked up. Then his cell phone rang and vibrated in his pocket, scaring the life out of him. "Oh, shit, it's Chuck. I've got to tell him the good news." He hit the answer button. "What's up, man? I've got some shit to tell you—say what? You bullshittin' ... ." Deacon looked as if he just had a heart attack. He dropped the phone and fell to his knees in distress.

Gloria picked up the phone. "What's going on? Okay, yeah, come on over. Bye." She hung up and tried to help Deacon to his feet, but he was dead weight. He was crying so hard, he couldn't even breathe, much less stand. He rolled over and lay there in a pool of tears. Gloria looked on in sympathy as her eyes welled up. *Guess I need to start rolling a few. This is going to be a long night.*

XII

Deacon and Gloria sat in the kitchen waiting for Chuck to arrive. He had cleaned himself up and was discussing with Gloria whether he should tell Chuck what was really going on or not. "Deacon, *you* are not the same person, not even close," Gloria said. "I don't think telling him would be a good idea."

Deacon pondered her postulation. *Perplexing.* "So, you're saying, in this reality, I'm such an asshole, that if I was to approach my lifelong friend with an absurd story, he wouldn't even consider it? He would immediately deem me insane? I don't know ... I mean, I may *have* been that bad."

Gloria extinguished a blunt and spoke as she exhaled (she was good at that). "I'm not saying to not tell him. I'm saying I think it's a bad idea. You have a better idea as to how Chuck will react than I do. I just know you. This is something the previous you would pull as a PR stunt. Just realize, if you don't plan on telling him, you'll have to control your emotions while he's here. And from this day forward, you'll have to choose your words carefully."

Deacon's cell phone buzzed. It was a text from Chuck saying he was outside. Deacon jumped up to answer the door as Gloria emptied the ashtrays, grabbed a few cups, and brewed a pot of coffee.

She lit two blunts, and when the guys came around the corner she handed them each one, then returned to the counter and poured them some coffee as they sat down. Then, she lit a blunt of her own and joined them at the table. They all sat there in silence and smoked.

Once Chuck had regained his composure and figured out where to start, he sighed and broke the silence. "So, yeah, she's dead. Her entire family is dead, and it's my fault." Chuck gave them all the gory details: from the pictures, to the video, to the ride downtown for questioning. Deacon sat there the entire time, perfectly straight-faced. But when he found out her husband was Ken, he got sick to his stomach. Once Chuck was done, Gloria excused herself for a bathroom break, which allowed Deacon and Chuck some time to converse privately.

Chuck lit a cigarette and eyeballed Deacon. "So, you gonna tell me what's going on? I've been your partner all our lives. You think I don't notice shit? You've been acting totally strange the past two days, more like the Deacon I grew up with than the Deacon I have grown accustomed to these past fifteen years. First it was the forgetfulness; you've got the memory of a squirrel. I *know* you didn't forget about an event that *you* planned. Then the entire Phoebe incident. You knew her; I know you did. Funny thing is, you told me to ask her out and didn't even know her two days ago. But at the party, you were all strange around her, like how you were with Cassandra back in high school. I know you knew her well, but she sincerely didn't know you. That's what really got me suspicious. Then the speech. That was no welcoming address; that was a speech, homie. A heartfelt, warm, honest speech that you would never had come up with or had the balls to say two days ago. Furthermore, it seemed like you were trying to tell me something last night too, but you didn't know how to say it. I thought it might have had something to do with Phoebe, but you never said anything. I figured you would tell me eventually, but considering recent events, I know something is up. Don't keep me in the dark. We share everything."

Deacon took a moment to think things over. *I hope he doesn't think I have anything to do with her murder. I loved her! I might have to tell him. He knows. I mean, the jig is up. Apparently, he knows me well in all realities. Yeah, I'm going to tell him, but how do I explain? Where do I start?*

Deacon lit a blunt. Just then, Gloria returned and refilled their coffee cups. She sat down, and Deacon passed her the blunt. "What did I miss?" she asked before taking a large hit.

Deacon stared her down and rubbed his temple in thought. "I'm going to tell him, but I need your help explaining."

XIII

Hours later, after explaining Deacon's situation to Chuck in its entirety, Deacon and Gloria were amazed at how receptive Chuck was. When they told him about the kids, he was sold. Of course, he had questions, but they weren't sarcastic; they were thought provoking and intellectual. Many of his questions led to other questions, and Chuck seemed to be helping them to figure out the situation.

"Well, that explains it all," Chuck said, "as far as the weird behavior is concerned. We can continue to work on the entire 'trans-reality shift' explanation tomorrow. I'm sleepy. Hey Gloria, could you point me toward a room that neither of the kids picked out?"

She smiled. "The entire third floor is free except for our rooms on the end."

He took his leave, and Gloria slid over beside Deacon. She grabbed his hand and bowed her head. "I'm sorry for your loss."

Deacon looked up at her and nodded. Until then, he didn't know she understood how he felt. As far as he knew, she was familiar with the Deacon who didn't even know Phoebe, yet she empathized enough to acknowledge

Phoebe's death as *his* loss. For that, he fell in love with her. It had nothing to do with the amount of time he had been away from Phoebe. It had more to do with the amount of time he had spent *with* Gloria. He couldn't suppress the feelings.

Over the past two days, he had noticed a bond between him and Gloria. Not like the typical boss and housemaid relationship, not even an atypical one, where the boss was sleeping with the maid. It was more of a secret lover type relationship, like maybe they were together behind closed doors. *Or in a different reality! That might be why I feel like I know her!*

"Why don't you come stay in my room tonight?" he asked. "I'd really enjoy the company."

She looked up and smiled. "Of course. Just try to control your PTSD in the morning." They laughed, and Deacon swept her off her feet and cradled her in his arms as she hugged his neck. They kissed as he headed to the bedroom. He took the stairs on purpose.

With a seemingly unlimited supply of wealth and resources, a porn-star hot sex goddess for a mistress, a best friend who was more like a brother, and a rambunctious group of adventurous kids, Deacon felt like he had lost one family but had gained another.

Chapter 14

I

There is no bucket list for a person who has done everything. Skiing, surfing, skydiving, spelunking, scuba diving, even space travel; name it, and Deacon had done it. There was no limit to his insanity. He lived on the edge, like an adrenaline junkie. He was in the best physical shape he had been in since college (well, in his original reality) and could achieve anything to which he set his mind. His research and development department was decades ahead of the curve in terms of technology and engineering, and there was no stopping his success.

He loved his life and his family, yet a big part of him longed for Phoebe and his original family. He missed the smell of her hair after a shower and how she would put her cold feet on him under the covers at night. He also missed wrestling with Junior, playing video games with James, and playing in the doll house with Jessica. Even an insensitive insult from Janice would have soothed his soul. So, even though it may have seemed like adrenaline was the motivation for his madness, it was not.

After fourteen fun-filled years in that reality, Deacon found himself in a catch twenty-two. He loved his current family and didn't want to leave them, but he didn't want to leave his original family to begin with.

His first idea was to get his R&D department on the case, but the closest they came was a teleportation device for inorganic matter. It only worked if the door for the other side was at the destination, and lifeforms that entered weren't reassembled properly on the other side, not even plants or single-celled organisms. Life was just too complicated to reconstruct. But the device was helpful with sending supplies from one person to another, no matter where they were. It was a nifty device and came in handy when they were sending college supplies to the kids or when his space agency was sending supplies to colonies on Mars, but not when trying to return to his original reality.

His second idea was a revisit to the suicide attempt, but he never could carry through with it. He didn't want to die trying to return to his original family and lose both families in the process. He also didn't want to leave his current family without the option of return. He had raised the kids and loved Gloria, who was now his wife, with all his heart. He would hate for her to find his body, even though she would know what happened. She made him happy, and he didn't want her to think otherwise.

He had lived happily with his third idea, which was to ride this life out and see where it took him. For fourteen years it had kept him content, but now he was questioning his decision. He understood that he could shift again and not be home. He also knew there was a slim chance that he could return to his original reality, or a variant of it. There was also a chance that he didn't possess that power anymore.

He had lived there for fourteen years, on the wire, with no shifting. He was content with the life he had, but he lived it to the extreme ... just in case.

II

"So, he looked at me and he said, 'Cats don't like water. I don't care how big they are.' Then, just as the panther leapt out of the bushes, Deacon grabbed me and plunged off the edge of the waterfall. It had to be about a three-thousand-foot drop."

The entire family was sitting at the kitchen table having breakfast with Deacon and Gloria before they left for their trip. It was their fourteenth anniversary, and the kids had bought them a trip to Cancun to celebrate. The kids were in town for spring break but were leaving in the morning. Chuck was there to house sit, feed the sharks and octopi, tend the pot farm, and so on. At the moment, however, he was still drunk from the previous night and sharing one of many daring tales of the adventure that he and Deacon had shared.

"So, either this panther was extremely near-sighted or was pissed off to the point where he didn't give a shit, because on the way down, I was falling backwards, and as I looked up I saw this huge panther dive off the cliff with its claws fully extended and roaring at the top of its cat lungs."

Gloria and the kids were fascinated. Deacon was humbly relaxing in his chair (he had witnessed the event firsthand) and checking the time, so they wouldn't be late for their departure.

"It all happened so fast. He reached into one of his cargo pants pockets and pulled out a little handle with a small box on it. When I saw it, I thought, how the hell is that going to help the situation? He whipped this thing out, grabbed me, and told me to hold on tightly. I was already doing that anyway; I was scared as hell! So, he flicked this little switch on the side of the handle, and the fucking thing popped out into a mini parachute ... blew my mind! We watched that big-ass panther hit the water on his side, and we floated down to the bank on the other side. We didn't even get wet. Man, he's like fucking Batman with the gadgets!"

They all laughed. Deacon stood up to stretch and then started grabbing his bags. "Well, it's about that time. Kids, thanks for coming to visit us on our anniversary, and thanks for the trip; we absolutely love Cancun. Chuck, thanks for that riveting story. It really brought back memories. And thanks for watching the house for me. I'm sure you know it's appreciated."

Gloria signaled Phil to crank up as she and Deacon grabbed the rest of their bags. "We'll call you when we get there," she said. "Bye everybody!" They headed out the door with armfuls of luggage, grinning broadly.

III

Aero-lux Airlines specialized in luxurious flights without all the paparazzi and hassles that celebrities encountered dealing with commercial air lines. The entire jet was first class with food, an open bar, movies, music, and Wi-Fi, and it was all-inclusive. Celebrities used the airline when they wanted to maintain a certain level of discretion, so there was no telling who one might encounter during a flight. Entertainers, politicians, tycoons, even royalty, there are no "average Joes" in those seats. They followed most of the same security protocols as commercial airliners, but the lines were much shorter and the personal searches a lot more discreet. With all the luxurious leather seats and touchscreen TVs, Deacon still felt like they had drawn the short straw, because they were the farthest from the door. *Cheap-ass kids. I could've flown my own shit ... but I guess that would've defeated the purpose of a vacation.*

While cruising at forty-two thousand feet, Deacon was finally able to take a bathroom break. One of the bathrooms was right in front of him, only two rows up, but it was occupied by an aging American actor with some serious IBS issues. The other bathroom was all the way in the back, so Deacon was able to see who else was enjoying the plane ride with him on his way to use it. Apart from the few faces he didn't recognize, the plane was full of American politicians and diplomats, with an entertainer here and there

One that stood out was a Cuban ambassador who had recently been brought up on drug trafficking charges and then mysteriously acquitted. Days after his acquittal, one of the largest drug rings in Cuba was taken out by *los federales*. The implications were obvious; he was a snitch, and there had been a price on his head ever since.

The bathroom wasn't occupied, so Deacon got to waltz right in and do his business. *Better grab this newspaper too.* Once he sat down and began to release his fury, he heard a rumble, and the entire plane began to shake. *She told me not to fool with that clam chowder.*

The rumble was followed by more rumbles, then the entire bathroom started to sway and rotate, and the oxygen mask fell from the top. Deacon hopped up and wiped himself with the newspaper. *Let me get out of here before I get a shit shower!* He dove out of the bathroom with the mask on; the bathroom by that time was sideways and began spilling bile out of the hatch. That's when he realized what was going on.

IV

Gloria was sitting across from Deacon doing Sudoku puzzles on her phone when she noticed him get up and head for the bathroom. *I told him not to fool with that clam chowder.* Moments later, a beeping sound came from the door of the plane. It seemed to be coming from outside the door, but it was loud enough to alert they passengers. They all exchanged confused looks and then ... BOOM!

The explosion ripped a massive hole in the upper half of the fuselage, right above the door, and the door flew off. The plane automatically deployed flotation devices and oxygen masks, but the majority of the passengers wouldn't even get to use them. Those near the door who weren't killed by the explosion were sucked out of the plane due to the difference in air pressure. As the plane continued to split, a series of smaller explosions went off.

The front end of the plane was doing a spinning nose dive, and the tail end was falling straight down, backwards. Most of its passengers had been sucked out of the hole when the bomb went off. Others held on for dear life and prayed, unsure of what to do. Gloria, who was up on the second row with a few other survivors, grabbed their masks and started to climb up to the opening in the plane in desperation. She just hoped she would be able to see Deacon on the other side.

V

Deacon closed the bathroom door, just in case, before he started his ascent to the top where the opening was. *I just know Gloria's doing the same.* As he peered through a window, he saw the other half of the plane was about eighty feet away and a bit higher, yet still distancing itself from the lower half as it spun. He continued to climb, checking through windows as he went, then stopped to inspect. He could see through the windows of the other half when it spun by and saw people climbing to the top where their hole was, as the people in his half were doing.

Then he looked up and saw the people who had reached the top had already either jumped out or allowed the wind to take them—not a good sign. When he finally reached the top, he found out why: they were over a rocky landmass with no chance for survival and just a few thousand feet from the ground. He had lived the past fourteen years on the edge, but when there was no safety net or gadget to save his ass, a new type of fear surfaced. *Damn, this may actually be it. I'm either going to die, or I'm going to shift. I've got to see Gloria again!*

Just then he heard his name being yelled from a distance. *Gloria!* He looked up as the wingless half of the fuselage spun out of control. On the next full spin, he saw Gloria, primed to jump.

Deacon readied himself for the final skydive of this reality. As the fuselage made another round, suddenly, Gloria was flying at him. She used the centrifugal force of the spinning fuselage to propel herself toward his half of the plane but looked as if she was going to come up a few yards short, so he dove after her.

They both directed themselves away from the falling plane halves and tried to match each other's altitude. Once they did, they met up mere hundreds of feet from the ground. Not much time left before they were part of ground zero, but at least they got to embrace and kiss for what seemed would be the final time ... or was it?

VI

This place again? Deacon was perplexed as to where he was and what it meant. The white expanse was limitless, and he was once again a single point of energy. There was no ground or ceiling, no left or right, no cardinal directions or points of reference that he could define, and no reason to have them when he was essentially a sphere in a limitless vacuum. Yet something was different this time. He felt a presence with him, and as he became accustomed to his new form of sight without eyes, which is a three-hundred-sixty-degree panoramic vision of things surrounding him, even above and below, he noticed another point of energy floating behind him. Well, it was what he had deemed to be behind him, since there was no front or back and no up or down.

Deacon was confused and a little frightened, but he felt at peace. He knew the other energy point meant no harm. The point started to move. *I didn't know I could do that.* He sensed the point calling to him, beckoning him to follow. It wasn't vocal; it wasn't even in words, it was more of a psychic summoning. He felt drawn to the other point, and he tried to follow it, but he didn't know how to move without legs or ground to walk on or even water to swim through. There was no physical conduit to achieve movement, so how was the other point moving?

Hey, slow down! Come back! Just then, the other point stopped and came back. *So, this is how we communicate?*

The other point didn't speak; it communicated through its senses. He felt the point agreeing with him, like he was almost right. *But you can hear me though. How do I move?*

The point backed up a bit, and Deacon felt it beckoning to him again. This time he felt the urge to apply the same sensory technique that the point was using to communicate. It was harder than it seemed, like he was using all his senses at once. Then, just like that, he was beside the other point again, although no movement was involved.

Did I do that?

He felt the point agree, yet it felt like he had to learn how to control it and slow down to a movement.

Okay, so who are you? And what are we?

The point changed from a bright white into neon blue, and Deacon felt love emanating from it.

The point began to move away again. *Wait a minute! I have so many questions!* The point kept moving, and Deacon felt it calling to him once again. To express how serious he was, he attempted to say what he wanted to say in the other point's form of communication, through the senses. Deacon tried to project how it felt to be ignored, since that was what was happening. With a little focus and concentration, he projected his feelings upon the other point. It stopped suddenly and returned sporting a soft shade of yellow, as if to say it was sorry.

Seeing the other point change colors again made Deacon realize he had changed colors too; he had turned dark red. *I didn't know I could do that either.* He felt sorry for getting mad at the other point, so he met it halfway, since he had learned how to move. By then he had turned yellow too. *Sorry for yelling.*

VII

The color white is a result of all colors coming together with equal proportions. So, where black is the absence of color, white is the presence of all colors. The most common producer of the color white is light (sunlight, stars, flashlights, and so on). Before Newton proved that light contained all colors, scientists thought white was just the color of light. As Deacon floated in the vast whiteness, he wondered where the point was taking him.

Deacon still wasn't used to the point's method of communication, so he telepathically spoke to it. *Okay, just answer this the best way you can. Where are you taking me? What is this place? All I see is empty white space. Where were you going?*

The point circled Deacon and spoke telepathically for the first time. *Look closer ...* . The voice was soft and echoed slightly, but the information it provided did little to help Deacon.

Look for what? All I see is ... Just then, things started to come into focus. The "sphere vision" took some getting used to. *It's light! It's an infinite array of light balls!*

While he was in the space between the lights, they all blended together and seemed like a vast, empty space, but the closer he got to one, the more it came into focus, as did the rest of them. Since he had met the other point halfway, it put him in a different position, and he was able to gain a better perspective at that different angle. Deacon was amazed. *What is this place?*

The point started to move toward one of the lights, called for Deacon, and then entered the light. As Deacon got closer to it, he was a little apprehensive, but he felt like he could trust the point, so he entered. The light sucked him in with the force of a Dyson vacuum and whirred him through a bright white energy tunnel, like he was on a light-speed anti-gravity rollercoaster.

He saw himself sitting on an oddly shaped couch with some sort of device on his lap and a suspicious look on his face. *Hey, I'm thirty-five again!* The guy looked like he was up to something, and Deacon wasn't sure he wanted to be a part of it. *Note to self: never trust random points of energy.*

As he approached the surrogate, he had other problems to worry about, like, *Where's the brakes on this thing?* He entered the body at full speed and knocked himself off the couch, device and all. When he got up from the floor, he took a moment to take in his surroundings, and then suddenly, the strangest thing happened.

Chapter 15

I

Phoebe flailed her fingers on the keyboard trying to find an alternate feed for the Federation's power grid. She worked in the communications tower, and her job was to monitor the solar satellite array and all the technical connections within her sector. It was a relatively easy job, but it was enough to keep her busy throughout the day. It was also a dangerous job considering the communications tower was usually the first place to get attacked during a raid. The area wasn't previously known to have a rebel threat, and the defectors there were all peaceful, BUT, that day, the rebels in the area HAD made themselves known in a major way.

During a raid, rebels would take out all communication and power and then invade the area, and that's exactly what was happening to Phoebe. A few minutes earlier, the entire solar satellite array had gone down. There were no explosions, and nothing out of the ordinary happened. One minute they were online and kicking, and then the next minute, they weren't. Phoebe didn't have a clue what was happening, since it had never happened there before.

The tower sat in the middle of a crescent-shaped base and was surrounded by a vast array of satellite dishes. Apart from keeping worldwide computers in sync, the dishes also doubled as solar energy converters, providing power for the entire base and the surrounding residential areas.

The tower had its own set of solar panels, but if the line out was compromised, the entire base would go powerless, including the surrounding areas. One would assume the tower was well protected or heavily guarded, but one would be wrong. The sentinels that guarded the base were all robots with predictable routines, which made it relatively easy to sneak in and out of a base undetected.

Bases were raided for a multitude of reasons: supplies, intelligence, politics, but mainly for food. The Federation controlled food distribution amongst the sectors, and the rebels either grew their own or stole their cut. There weren't many rebels in that sector, so the base had never been attacked before, and Phoebe knew nothing about defensive protocol. *I hate using the hive!*

She knew that if she called for help, they would just send the Militia to attack. Even if they got there in time, they would destroy everything. Militia soldiers were trained to shoot first and ask questions last, a bunch of brainless brutes. If someone was in the wrong place at the wrong time, he or she might lose their life just by being there, whether the person was a threat or not. And if the problem was just a blown fuse or a frayed wire, she would have signaled the Militia for no reason.

So, she continued to click away at her keys in search of a possible line out. The Federation's network was un-hackable and had futuristic firewalls and security measures that were unthought of. The problem with that was if the tower went down, the operator basically had to rewrite code to get a line out and then possibly reroute power to the grid.

Ken was the geek who was capable of that, but he had stepped outside to survey the satellites for sabotage. So, Phoebe was in the tower, alone and terrified. *Why haven't they attacked yet? Comms have been down for at least five minutes. I guess the rebels aren't as swift and effective as the stories say. If Ken was here, he'd have a line out by now. Where is that asshole?*

BOOM!

II

"Colonel Stockholm, our ground troops are in place and ready to go, sir."

The colonel crossed his arms and hit his cigar. "Have we heard back from our guy yet?"

"No sir," the scrawny, little communications officer replied, "but everybody else is ready, and we have confirmation that the satellites, the power grid, and the backup systems are down."

The colonel uncrossed his arms, hit his cigar again, and unintentionally blew the smoke in the kid's face. "Okay, get word to the troops. We will attack all at once in five minutes whether we get word from the mole or not."

Colonel Archibald Stockholm was a rebel legend overseas who was responsible for feeding hundreds of thousands and setting in place a standard procedure for attacking Federation bases. He first heard of the starving rebels in the sector from Deacon when he came to request help from the rebel regime in the colonel's sector. He and Deacon shared similar morals and principals, and they had formed a close kinship. When Deacon returned with a rebel colonel instead of food, the rebels there were infuriated. But once the colonel outlined his plan, they all calmed down and gave the man a chance.

His first plan was to establish a secure communication system with his comrades overseas, so attacking the base was a necessity. They needed equipment, weapons, and, most of all, food. If they attacked the base on all fronts simultaneously, they stood a better chance of attaining the things they needed. So, he sent in a mole to do a quick reconnaissance and take out the tower to knock out digital communications and power. Once the mole reached safety, he was to signal the colonel on his walkie-talkie and make his way back to camp. The problem was, the mole never got in touch with the colonel.

With all the troops in place and proof that the base's satellites and power grids were down, the only thing postponing the attack was the colonel's orders. *Alright, he's got five minutes to get the hell out of there. That's all I can do for him. I hope one of those damn sentinels hasn't stunned his ass in there.*

He hit his cigar a few more times, barked a slew of orders, and checked his watch. He had waited long enough. Archie threw down his cigar and stomped it out. "Throw the switch to the explosives, and send 'em in."

III

The comms tower was gigantic. It was a tower in every sense of the word, 250 feet tall with an 80-foot solar satellite on top. Its base was a massive two-story facility, where all the satellite dishes were controlled. Half the building was dedicated to servers and super computers, the other half was where everything was manipulated through the mainframe. Even the basement was full of servers.

Only two employees worked in the comms tower, one upstairs and one on the main floor. It was a lot of space for just two employees, but it was much needed. The basement was rarely ventured into, probably even forgotten about, since the only thing down there were servers that were controlled from the second floor.

The tower's perimeter wasn't heavily guarded, since it was in the middle of the base, and the other parts of the base were guarded well. Other than the three sentinels that patrolled the satellite dishes, the only protection from attack was a ten-foot electric fence that surrounded them. The rebels had been tunneling under such fences for years to steal food and supplies. As Gloria crawled through one of the tunnels at the southern end of the comms tower, she hoped she would make it to Deacon in time.

Gloria never thought she would be crawling through one of the dirty, smelly, bug-infested tunnels again, primarily because she was a high-ranking officer in the Federation's Defensive Intelligence Unit. The tunnel travel had suddenly become a requirement for the mission when it went off course. The main objective was to get to Deacon undetected and retrieve the anti-lithium from him, but when he was spotted by the employee, the plan had to be altered.

The employee who spotted him was beat to within inches of his death, but he saw where Deacon went. However, he was scared to follow him, so instead he went and got a sentinel to do the dirty work.

All the sentinels in the area were charging, so that meant the sentinel required a reboot. She figured she should have enough time to make it to Deacon before the human could reboot the sentinel and get there, but then she intercepted a walkie-talkie transmission to the rebel troops that told her she had five minutes before the attack. She hurried through the tunnel, sending Deacon a message as she left.

The tunnel led to the tower's basement, which had been sealed off years earlier when it was discovered. It was a good distance away, about twice the distance Gloria had to crawl during a previous mission, so, she figured twice the time, which allowed her about thirty seconds of play before the attack. The message that she sent informed Deacon of the witness and sentinel on their way to him and told him to stay where he was. She would come to him.

Gloria possessed the proper tools to penetrate the closing at the end of the tunnel, but she underestimated the time it took to crawl the required length inside the tunnel. *This tunnel's terrain is much more difficult to maneuver*!

She was only a few yards into it when she heard an explosion that shook the entire tunnel. *That wasn't five fucking minutes!* Fearing the worst, Gloria sped through the tunnel—and then the worst happened. The tunnel collapsed in front of her and behind her. She was trapped in the tunnel with limited air and resources. That's when the claustrophobia started to settle in. Now the rescue mission needed rescuing

Well, at least it didn't collapse on me. That's just a matter of time though. I just fucked up royally, but I had no choice. We had to alter the plan. The thing is, if I survive but the mission is compromised, I could get incarcerated over it! I guess that's better than suffocating—at least I think it is.

IV

In this utopian society, everybody got along and worked together. There was no racism or discrimination; everyone was equal. If people pulled their weight, everybody was happy. The entire world was united. There were no language barriers to cross or opposing political views, nothing to divide humanity. Race, religion, politics, class, currency, all were things of the distant past.

The Renaissance era of the 1300s called for a change in the way people thought as a race. The concept spread as quickly as the plague, and over the next few hundred years, the world was amalgamated. Instead of building walls and borders, they built schools and institutions. They also lived according to population control and environmental standards. The air was clean and pure, and there was much more undeveloped land, meaning more forest and jungle for wild beasts and apex predators to inhabit. The animals thrived in this world, where they would otherwise had been on the endangered species list. The balance of the ecosystem kept the rest of the planet flowing harmoniously. And since everyone was working together, people's combined efforts pushed technology and humanity thousands of years ahead.

The humans were a lot more progressive; they even thought differently. They embraced phenomena that were disregarded in Deacon's original reality. Telepaths and people with unexplainable powers were held in high esteem. In his original reality, people consigned them as hoaxers and tried to debunk them at every turn. In this reality, telepaths were bred over the course of several hundred years, and it resulted in humanity evolving into a telepathically connected mind, yet it could be turned off if needed. Everybody needed a little privacy periodically.

They called the mental connection that they all shared "the hive." They used it to communicate, locate one another, send telepathic messages, read each other's minds, and even share knowledge and information across long distances. Granted, not everybody was telepathic, but the hive compensated by connecting with Federation employees who couldn't connect with them. However, if they defected, they would lose all their telepathic capabilities. Different people had different abilities, depending on their ancestry. Not everyone could read minds, but some people's powers stretched beyond the realm of telepathy and into the realm of telekinesis. Still, everybody was connected to the hive at some point in their lives, and it was a remarkable experience.

Nevertheless, the ability came with some disadvantages. Reading minds could be risky and even fatal if done without consent. Furthermore, one telepath was a dangerous being, but an entire race of them was virtually unstoppable. An enemy to the hive could easily be eliminated through mental manipulation. Depending on the severity of the violation, punishment could range from instantaneous death to painful death to paralysis until the rebel could be apprehended for incarceration. There were even accounts of rebels being permanently paralyzed on the spot.

"The Federation" was the name given to humanity's hive mind. Defectors were those who had left the Federation but lived in small communities together and posed no threat. The rebels were defectors who raided Federation bases in attempts to re-establish humanity's previous way of life. Once someone had defected from the Federation, they lost the psychic bond that they shared through the hive but retained their personal telepathic capabilities, if they had any to begin with.

Defectors were harmless and weren't considered enemies to the Federation, but rebels were enemies, and the life of a rebel meant no telepathy at all, so as to avoid detection. It was possible for a defector to rejoin the Federation through a rehabilitation program that was set in place through incarceration, but it took years. There was no rehab for rebels; they were incarcerated permanently or killed instantly.

The world was divided into a grid of large sectors based on global ley lines in which bases sat on intersecting points. The bases handled Federation duties throughout the sectors and were quite large. The Market was where all the food and supplies were, the Tech section was where all the engineering happened, Sector Square was like a city hall, and the Communication Tower was an array of solar satellite dishes that fed the entire base with power and kept all the computers in communication with one another throughout the world.

The Federation saw no need to defend humanity from humans, but they were aware of the defectors and the rebels who posed a threat to their utopian society. To solve this dilemma, they set up three lines of defense. Robot sentinels performed patrols and simple security measures, Militia soldiers trained at secret facilities in remote places to be the violent force for the planet, and the DIU (Defensive Intelligence Unit), was an elite coalition of spies and assassins whose skillsets surpassed that of the Militia.

DIU officers worked covertly and sometimes went undercover. They were the brains that matched the Militia's brawn. They could also match their brawn with brawn. All their operations were conducted discretely, and their chain of command ended internally. That meant nobody knew who they were, including the Federation. Plausible deniability. They were charged with keeping the utopian society "utopian," and that required a certain level of transparency. They infiltrated rebel camps to determine if they were a real threat to the Federation, and if they were, DIU had the authority to either wipe them out or call in the Militia. They were also charged with extraterrestrial relations, and since they were the best that humanity had to offer in every aspect, the job was also quite fitting.

The DIU was comprised of recruited Militia soldiers. The process involved sector elections amongst agents. The DIU operated independently between sectors, but the entire outfit was conducted by a director, who was also elected. The elections that the DIU held for inductees and directors were meticulous but fast, considering it was all done telepathically, and it was not a numbers game. Candidates were telepathically scrutinized by their voters. This way, each voter knew who they were voting for personally, and that increased the chances of the right person getting elected. The winner took the reins and usually picked up where the former director left off.

Sitting in an employee lounge in the tower's basement, Deacon got used to the hive. It hit him like a surge of knowledge at first and almost knocked him to the ground again, but eventually, he learned how to control it. He realized he had a telepathic bond with the entire world, but once he learned how to block them, he still felt "telepathic."

Since the version of Deacon that he inhabited had inherited this telepathy and had had it since birth, it was one of those subconscious, second-nature acts that he had no choice but to acquire, similar to how he became a killing machine with PTSD. The ability would also follow him through other realities.

Once he accessed the hive and used it properly, he figured he knew everything that was going on, and he was itching to spring into action. Through the hive he was able to locate Phoebe and Gloria simultaneously. He saw their situations in cinematic form. Phoebe was upstairs, banging on a keyboard with both fists, and Gloria was crawling through a tunnel on her way to him. He was dizzy with excitement.

The hive couldn't inform him of the rebel group that was about to attack, but it didn't matter, because they were the underdogs. Deacon was a trained killer and a master at hand-to-hand combat in a world with little to no violence. They'd never know what hit them.

V

The explosion that the rebels set off rattled the tower and sent Phoebe searching for a good hiding place. The call for Militia had gone out from somewhere in the Market, and Phoebe realized she should have signaled for them much earlier. *Well it's too late for the Militia now! That sounded like it was right outside!* She unlatched a service panel under one of the computers she sat at, moved a few wires out of her way, and crawled inside. Once she was in the massive computer, she reached out and rolled the chair back in place, then closed the panel, pulling it tight enough for it to latch on the outside. She wasn't concerned with being locked in; she just didn't want to be noticed. *I'll deal with that later.*

No sooner had she heard the panel latch than she heard someone kick in the door. The fact that it was unlocked didn't matter. *I was trying to wait on Ken to get back, but hell, I guess locking it wouldn't have made a difference.* She tried messaging him telepathically but couldn't connect with him. Phoebe suspected foul play. The pounding of platoon boots patrolling the tower made her panic.

The real fear didn't settle in until she heard the squad leader speak. "Destroy all the machines. That way, even if they fix the power grid, they won't be fully functional for a few weeks. Let's make this fast, so we can go help the other factions."

As Phoebe looked through the dark web of wires in front of her, she saw sparks flying and knew immediately what was happening. *I've gotta get out of here, but they'll kill me! But if I stay here, they'll kill me and not even know about it. Maybe they'll have mercy if I surrender. No, they're gonna kill me. I need to figure something out!*

By then she figured Ken was dead, but it didn't seem like he could do anything about her situation even if he were alive. *Fuck it!* She decided to try to get the door open. Just pushing the panel wasn't going to be enough; she had to break the latch on the outside, although she was in an awkward position and did not have much leverage.

Phoebe didn't work well under pressure. Each second it took for her to muscle the door open felt like it was the last second of her life. The destruction was so close that she felt sparks bouncing off her forehead. Death was definite. Even if she managed to escape the computer's guts, she would have to face a squadron of rebels before she reached the exit. So, to avoid any further frustration or an even worse death, she decided to give up on the door and get what was coming to her. *At least it will be fast and painless.*

Just as she was thinking those words, a huge energy-charged axe carved through the super computer mere inches above her head. Sparks flew all over her face, and she smelled her hair singeing. Judging by the length of the axe strikes and the fact that the monitor was directly above her abdomen, she quickly disregarded the entire "fast and painless" idea. The next blow would most likely cut her in half, and she would have to watch it happen.

VI

"I saw him go in through here, but I wasn't about to follow him. That's your job. I don't know why the Federation only allows us a handful of sentinels. You're not even the smart ones. Where the hell were you? You can't guard the tower in standby mode, dumbass."

The sentinel looked back at Ken, emotionless. "Fuck you," it said in its monotone, robotic voice. "I was charging."

"Whatever," Ken replied. "You're useless. Now go on in there and check it out before I throw you in the recycling bin."

The sentinel opened the basement hatch on the back side of tower and started its descent down the staircase. "Asshole."

"Excuse me?"

When Ken left Phoebe to check the satellite linkage, he saw that it had been tampered with and immediately headed back to the tower to get Phoebe and find safety. He took off in full sprint down the grid of satellite dishes back to the tower when he was flanked by the intruder. They were both running at full speed, and the collision knocked them to the ground. As they regained their senses, they jumped up and started throwing punches.

Ken couldn't seem to land a blow on the assailant and ended up taking a few more than he wanted. The intruder delivered a massive right hook that turned Ken halfway around, and then he jumped on Ken's back and put him in a reverse chokehold. They fell to the ground on their backs, and the intruder maintained the hold all the way through with the grip of a gorilla.

As Ken's consciousness drifted away, he felt ashamed for not messaging Phoebe or calling for the Militia when he had the chance. They had never gone over protocol or rehearsed any kind of procedures in the event of an attack, so his gut instinct was to panic and then run. Nevertheless, sending a telepathic message or signaling for the Militia required a certain level of concentration that simply couldn't be achieved while in a reverse chokehold, even less while unconscious.

The intruder's arms tightened around Ken's neck, and his eyes started to roll, but he still had the presence of mind to notice the intruder had dropped a few things when they collided. One of them was a fuse to the power grid from the solar satellite dishes. *Well, that explains why we lost our satellite linkage, but what the hell is that?*

Amongst the other random things that the intruder had dropped—a walkie-talkie, a half-smoked joint, a monocular, and a screwdriver—he also dropped a device that he had never seen before: a small rectangular box that had weird writing and symbols on it. It was made of dull metal, like pewter, yet the seams didn't quite touch, like the box maintained its shape due to some sort of magnetic force. Ken had started to lose his vision, but whatever was inside the small box had started glowing, the intensity of the light increasing gradually. The symbols on the box started to glow red and blink, and the intruder was forced to loosen his grip and push Ken to the side, just as he was losing consciousness.

At that moment, Phoebe was trying to contact Ken to see what was going on outside, but his semiconscious state wasn't accepting any callers. She got the mental equivalent of a busy signal and thought he was either dead or blocking everybody for some reason. If only she knew the situation he was in out there.

Ken lay in a pool of blood, writhing in pain but still alive. The intruder kicked him in the stomach for good measure and then turned to pick up the box, which was blinking red. The light emanating from the seams was bright enough that Ken couldn't look directly into it. The blinking was getting faster, but the intruder just calmly pressed a button on top of the device. It ejected a mist from the seams, and the light gradually decreased until the device was just a small, seamless metal box that was no longer blinking.

Then the intruder grabbed the walkie-talkie, which was broken. He threw it at Ken's face in anger and kicked him in the stomach again. Then he grabbed the half-smoked joint and found his lighter. Ken thought the intruder was going to kill him, but then he simply lit his joint, grabbed the rest of his belongings, and ran off. By the time Ken was able to roll around, he saw the intruder breaking the lock to the tower basement. He opened the hatch, tossed the joint roach behind him, and dipped into the basement, closing the hatch behind him.

Ken was drained. He had never been in a real fistfight before, so the beating had taken a toll. *That had to have been a spy, but why did he leave me alive?* The more he thought about it, the more he realized he never got a good look at the intruder's face. He had been so busy taking punches in the eyes and trying to dodge them that he never had a chance to look at his assailant. As he rolled over and tried to stand up, something down the aisle beside him caught his swollen eye's attention: another blinking red light. *I hope it isn't another one of those little pewter boxes. At least I know where the button is.*

His vision was still a little blurry from being punched in the eyes so many times, and them nearly bulging out of their sockets when he was being choked, but the blinking red light was undeniable. Ken leaned against a satellite and shimmied his way to his feet. Once he caught his breath, he limped toward the blinking light. As he got closer to it, he noticed the blinking didn't get faster, and no bright white light was associated with it. Once his eyes focused, he was extremely disappointed.

The blinking was coming from a foot. Apparently, the intruder had run right past a charging sentinel. Its eyes were red, and its finger was jammed into one of the satellite dishes, drawing power from it. It was standing between two satellite dishes, so its body was hidden from Ken's angle, but once he got closer to it, the rest of the robot became visible. When the power was cut, the charging status was suspended, and the sentinel went into standby mode. *Goddammit, these things are useless!*

Ken was a geek and knew that standby mode required a reboot that could take some time, but his shrewd character cleverly circumnavigated the security measures. He grabbed it by the breastplate and shook the sentinel to life. The action jarred the robot's internal gyroscope and caused an automatic reboot, which was much faster. Once the sentinel was coherent, Ken gave it a piece of his mind. "Man, you guys pick the worst times to charge! I just got the shit kicked out of me, and none of you were anywhere to be found. Where are the others that are supposed to be patrolling this area?"

He released the sentinel with a slight shove, and the sentinel calmly pulled his finger out of the satellite dish. "They were charging too, I guess they are in standby mode as well." it replied, its voice emotionless. "Do you have any injuries?"

Ken couldn't believe it. *All of them charge at the same damn time? Dumbasses! So, who was guarding the tower? Whatever ... .* "Look at my face! Of course I have injuries! I think he might have broken my ribs too."

"Which ones are broken?"

"All of them, asshole!"

The sentinel did a quick scan for broken bones. "Nothing is broken, pussy."

"Excuse me?"

"You heard me; why are you being so belligerent?"

The sentinel spoke in a monotone robotic voice that mocked Ken's intensity and made him lose his temper. "Fuck you, scrap metal! If I was supposed to be protecting you, and you got your ass kicked by some martial arts master motherfucker while I was fucking off with a satellite dish, you'd be cussing me out too!"

"I'm useless with a dead battery."

"You're useless with a full battery! Now come on. I know where he went."

As the two descended into the basement, the sentinel scanned for traps and heat signatures. "I've located the intruder."

"Does he have any weapons?"

"Only the ones he used to kick your ass with."

"Oh, you're a comedian now, huh? That's funny to you?"

"Ha. Ha."

"We'll see how funny it is when he's kicking your ass in a little while."

"Oh yeah. Gulp."

Ken followed the sentinel through the maze of servers. The robot knew where the intruder was and could see him through his infrared filter, but Ken had no infrared filter and was totally unaware and terrified. They turned a corner and heard a loud thud. "Looks like he fell. Maybe we should rush him."

"We? I've already got my ass kicked once while you were finger-fucking a satellite dish. This one is all on you, buddy. Not so funny now, is it?"

Ken thought about it and located Phoebe. With everything that was going on, he had forgotten to contact her. She was upstairs and looked like she was still trying to find a line out. He considered sending her a message but decided against it, since she was in the safest place she could be at the time. There was no telling how many spies were lurking outside, and he damn sure didn't want her to come down to the basement. He also wasn't dumb enough to signal the Militia over a spy. He would've been either exterminated or incarcerated ... transparency. With a hint of fear in his eyes, he turned back to the sentinel. "Have you signaled for reinforcements?"

"The closest sentinel that isn't charging is all the way in the tech section."

Seriously? "Whatever, just go."

As they reached the door, they paused and peeked in. "So, are you going in or what?"

"I'm coming up with a plan." The intruder looked disoriented, so the sentinel decided to attack. "Get ready to back me up."

"I'm not backing up shit. You go in there and do your job."

The sentinel switched its hands to stun. That way, all it needed to do was touch the intruder. It walked into the room, and the intruder looked up at him. The sentinel put one hand out, like a traffic guard telling you to stop. "Halt. In the name of the Federation, I am officially placing you under arrest for assaulting a Federation employee and tampering with—" Just like that, the sentinel's battery died.

Ken was furious. "I swear these fucking things are absolutely useless!"

BOOM!

The explosion jostled the entire basement and was so close to them, they both dropped to their knees due to the ringing in their ears. When they regained their senses, they knew a fight was inevitable. The difference was, the intruder was far more lethal than before and had a bad history with Ken. By that time, Deacon had entered the intruder's body and had greatly increased his killing skills. The assassin's body was as nimble as a cat and as strong as an elephant. Ken had no clue his life was in danger; he figured he would just take another ass whooping, play dead, and transfer to the tech section in the morning. *I've got to get out of this hostile work environment.*

Ken shoved the inanimate sentinel to the ground and lashed out at Deacon in a mad frenzy, only for Deacon to dodge his attack and counter it with two powerful knees to the ribs. This time, they were broken—all of them. He threw Ken to the ground beside the sentinel and stomped on his knees, breaking them too.

As Ken screamed in agony, Deacon walked calmly over to the wooden table in the corner and ripped a leg from it. The table leg was cylindrical and slightly conical, like a baseball bat but much heavier, and it had a tapered lip on the bottom above a thick footing, perfect for a grip.

He twirled the table leg around like it was the bottom of the ninth inning with the bases loaded, but when he struck Ken, it was more like a Mickelson tee-off at the Masters. Blood, brains, and skull fragments splattered across the wall, and Ken was no longer an issue.

However, Deacon continued to bash his head in, just because he had it coming to him from other realities. The more he thought about how Ken had killed his family right in front of his eyes, the more he saw red. He went into a frenzy, beating Ken's carcass with the table leg until his guts were exposed and then stomping on his entrails until he ran out of breath.

When he was done, Ken was just a bloody smear on the ground with a few bones and muscles thrown into the mix. Deacon refreshed Phoebe and Gloria's situation in his head as he wiped the blood from his face with a look of satisfaction. Before he could catch his breath, he headed out of the basement with a taste for blood and an entire group of rebel soldiers at the top of the stairs to beat on.

VII

Before Archie joined the rebel group, they were not much more than a camp of defectors. They grew their own food and kept to themselves to avoid incarceration, but soon the demand was far greater than the supply. The colonel morphed the group of misfits into a military-minded collective. He came with weapons and gadgets and helped organize everybody into troops and squads with ranks. He even implemented a recruiting process to monitor for spies. They were trained according to skillset, and when the colonel decided they were ready to attack the base, they did.

The colonel sat in the command center (which was just a large tactical tent perched in the forest outside the Federation base) monitoring the helmet cams of the squad leaders, which enabled him to see everything that was happening. The company was raiding the base with no loss of life and minimal use of violence. Communications and power were down, the Market was virtually unprotected, the human employees were submissive, and the sentinels hadn't seen it coming. His formula was working flawlessly.

The squad leaders' helmet cams were small and virtually unnoticeable, but they had a wide-angle lens with high-resolution imaging and different filters. The controller at the command center could also interact with them, making them spin for a full 360-degree view or zoom in for a closer look. They had night vision for dark places and infrared in case they needed to pick up a heat signature. The camera that Archie had singled out rested on the head of the squad leader who was charged with taking down the communications tower.

This squad's situation seemed strange from the start. The first thing the colonel noticed was there were no employees in the building. The tower was deserted; not even a sentinel was close by. *Did anybody show up for work today? The chair is pushed in and everything. If I was leaving in a hurry, I damn sure wouldn't take time to push in a chair. Unless … .*

"Setup! It's a goddamned fucking setup! Get those men out of there now!"

He was wrong about the setup, in a way, but it was too late anyway. The one-man ambush breached the basement and bludgeoned the entire squad with a table leg. He moved in swift, fluid motions so as to not get hit with an energy weapon or a stun stick, and he still managed to land crushing blows to his opponents. He easily handled all the colonel's men and inadvertently kept his face hidden from the camera on the squad leader's helmet. One by one, they dropped to the floor as the assassin flipped, twisted and twirled between them. Some of the soldiers received multiple blows and fatal wounds. When the camera twisted around, fell to the floor, and lay there motionless, the colonel knew it was over.

There's no way DIU knew about our attack, so why is an assassin here? And why would he come by himself? This might be an inside job. Archie was perplexed. The colony had been set in place well before his arrival, and they put newcomers through a rigorous screening process. If there was a spy, he or she would have had to be there prior to his arrival. All the evidence led to it being a setup. The colonel smelled a rat that needed exterminating.

From the angle that the squad leader had landed on his broken neck, the commander could see only the lower half of the assassin. He walked out of the field of view for a moment, and then the colonel saw two sets of legs headed toward the door behind the squad leader, well in front of him.

The first set of legs were sexy and leaped over the squad leader's body—revealing a glimpse up her skirt. The second, more familiar, set of legs straddled the body for a moment. Then the colonel saw a table leg coming at the camera like it was zooming in at super-high speed. Suddenly, they lost the feed.

"Play that entire interaction again; and find an image of his face that we can run through the facial-recognition software. I think there's a spy in our happy little community, and I want to know who that filthy fuck is. Jenkins, notify the other alphas, and round them up. We're going after this maniac."

VIII

The tunnel that Gloria was trapped in was about six feet deep in hard clay, hard enough to where she couldn't dig her own way out without proper tools. It was about four feet in diameter, and it had collapsed right at her feet and a few feet from her head, a perfect grave if she stayed there long enough.

As she lay there, sweltering, more claustrophobia settled in. She needed a good distraction, but all she had were her thoughts, and the worst-case scenario was always in the forefront of her mind. *Just give him some time. He's on his way.*

She knew the chances of Deacon finding her in time were slim. Even slimmer were the chances that he would be able to get to her. *Spies are resourceful. He'll figure something out. Just give him time.*

Staying optimistic was imperative, so, to keep the negative thoughts from flooding her mind, she began to sing to herself in her head. She blocked out everything, thought of a song from the place she was from, and replayed it in her head repeatedly until she fell asleep.

IX

Deacon and Phoebe bounded through the vast satellite dish array toward the southern fence. Phoebe was still confused, but she continued to flee with the rebel, because he had just saved her life. Even though he was a rebel, she felt like at his side was the safest place to be during the raid.

Just moments earlier, she had accepted the inevitability of a slow, painful death by energy axe. But instead of the blade crashing through the computer and slicing her in two, she heard a loud thud, like hardened wood hitting a large rock. Then she heard the same sound over and over again, coupled with groans of agony, bodies hitting the floor, and an occasional splash. She struggled to fight her way out of the computer and make an escape, but the panel wouldn't budge.

After a loud cracking sound, a body hit the floor, and then it was quiet, except for the footsteps that were getting closer. *Who knows I'm in here? Whoever it is would have to know me to be able to look for me.*

People had to know who they were looking for to locate somebody using the hive, so whoever was coming to free her obviously knew her and knew *to* look for her. But she couldn't think of anybody who was skilled enough to take out an entire squad. *Unless Ken came back with help!*

"Ken! I thought you were dead! Thanks for coming back to get me. You saved my life! I swear, when we get to safety, I'm going to suck—"

Just then, the latch popped, and the panel flew open. The stranger on the other side presented a big, bright smile. "You were saying?"

The handsome, slim, yet muscular man offered his hand to her, and she grabbed it and weaseled her way out of the computer. He was dressed like a rebel but carried himself like a member of the Militia. Phoebe was captivated. *I still might suck his dick.*

"Are you okay?" he asked in a remarkably calm manner for a guy who had just battered an entire squad to death.

Phoebe enjoyed the irony for a moment. "Shouldn't I be asking you that? Yeah, I'm okay, but you just pummeled that squad all by yourself with that table leg?"

He gave her a wink and a cocky grin. "And they didn't even touch me. Follow me, and stay close. I'm going to get you out of here."

She hopped over the squad leader, and Deacon busted the camera on his head before they left the building. He looked her in the eye and presented his hand, which she took, and they headed toward the southern fence at full sprint. Once they entered the satellite dish grid, it was like a labyrinth, but Deacon maintained a general heading and picked up the pace. However, it wasn't long before a rebel spotted them. They dove for cover behind a satellite dish. "By the way, I'm Deacon. I know you, Phoebe. How I know you is a story for when we get out of here. For now, just stay close. I can't afford to lose you again."

Phoebe was extremely confused but still attracted to him. *I hope he knows where we're going.* She was positive she had never met the man, but he knew her name, where to find her, and everything. *I mean, it feels like I know him from somewhere, but I don't know him. I would remember such a man ... wouldn't I?*

She still didn't understand why a rebel was helping her, even going as far as killing his comrades to save her. At that point though, it didn't matter. If this was what it took to get her out of there alive, then this was what she would do.

Deacon poked his head around the corner and spotted the rebel, who resembled a juiced-up version of the German crony who had aided in his skewering a few realities ago. He was unconceivably massive and walked with a certain type of confidence. "Stay here," Deacon said. "I don't want him to see you."

Then he rounded the corner, twirling his table leg, ready to fight. The bulky rebel grinned, stretched his arms, and rolled his neck. Then he put up his dukes.

The overgrown rebel was sporting metal gauntlets and shin guards that covered his feet, a leather breastplate, some sort of high-tech goggles, and a shit-eating grin. Deacon sized him up, gripped his club, and rushed him with a flurry of blows. The brute blocked them all, but Deacon noticed a force field generated by the metal gauntlets when they were struck.

The rebel launched a counter assault. Deacon blocked those blows too, but the rebel seemed to be holding something back. The final blow was devastating. The rebel squeezed his fists, and a surge of energy coursed through the gauntlets before he delivered a massive blow.

Deacon used both hands to block with his table leg, but the leg shattered in half, and the punch landed square on Deacon's sternum, knocking him onto his back. The rebel squatted to charge his feet. Deacon recognized the charging-up process and rolled out of the way, barely dodging a super stomp that rattled the ground and left a size-twenty footprint behind.

The attack was accentuated with a type of electrically charged sonic technology that electrocuted the opponent and added the power it took to break the sound barrier. If the table leg hadn't had buffered the blow, Deacon would probably be dead. However, the blow didn't hurt him much. It pissed him off more than anything. He had to gather all his lifetimes of experience in hand-to-hand combat to bring this behemoth down.

The large rebel looked to be twice Deacon's size, but Deacon was almost twice his age with an exponential amount of experience and no chip on his shoulder. He was smarter, faster and deadlier, even without a weapon. The rebel didn't stand a chance.

Deacon leaped to his feet and threw the two halves of table leg to the ground. He looked down at himself and saw that the gauntlet had left a charred spot on his chest in the shape of a fist. That infuriated him to the point where he turned red, a feat rarely attained by black people. Deacon wiped off the charred mark and gave the brute a look that was so intimidating, he charged his gauntlets for another attack.

The rebel lunged at Deacon with both gauntlets extended. In one fluid motion, Deacon sidestepped and grabbed the rebel by his arm beneath the gauntlet, folded the arm behind the rebel's back, jumped on it, and rode the rebel to the ground. The rebel hit face first, shattering his goggles and breaking his nose. Before the rebel knew it, Deacon had unlatched his gauntlet, and it was off his hand.

The rebel lay prone, his dominant arm behind his back and Deacon kneeling on it to keep him in place, immobilized. Deacon donned the gauntlet, charged it, and then swung. To him it was just like punching the ground. The brute's thick skull provided little to no resistance, and the gauntlet punched straight through it. His bald head exploded, much like one of Gallagher's watermelons, sending brains and skull fragments in all directions, like the flesh and seeds of the aforementioned watermelon. "Slug-o-matic!"

Deacon grabbed the other gauntlet and the shin guards, strapped them on, and then went back to the spot where he left Phoebe. When he got there, she was nowhere to be found. He looked all around for her and whispered her name but was hesitant to call out loudly; there was no telling who was looking for them. He scanned the area once more and noticed that the power box for the satellite dish beside him was unlatched, and a slip of clothing was hanging out of the panel. He opened it and smiled. "How do you fit yourself in such tight spaces? And why can't you stay put?"

Phoebe giggled as she wiggled around. "Shut up, and help me out of this thing."

X

Alpha squad was an elite group of rebels who would have otherwise been part of the Militia or DIU. They were the smartest, fastest, most skilled group of men and women that the rebels in that sector had to offer. They were also the colonel's personal squad. They had unique skills and oversaw the training of other squads. They trained with their own customized energy weapons and wore different armor than the rest of the rebels. Alphas even had goggles that could identify and monitor life forms and served as a video and audio link with the command center. The rebels had to compensate for their lack of the hive with superior technology.

Moments earlier, the colonel had watched as his largest and best fighter was taken down by the same guy who had abolished an entire squad in the tower. The difference was, this time he saw his face.

When Archie first put the hit out on the assassin, all they had to go on was what he was wearing and a description of his weapon. But one key piece of information, the fact that he had a female employee from the tower with him, gave him away. Once the bully mammoth spotted them, the jig was up. Facial recognition software immediately identified Deacon as the assassin and pegged the identity of the tower employee. The two shared nothing in common, but Deacon had killed his comrades and risked his life for her.

The command center was buzzing. Deacon wasn't just a member of their community; he was a leader. He and a few others had started with a small camp and an idea. It grew into a small community with a high demand, so Deacon had gone to a highly rebellious sector for help. That's when he met Colonel Archibald Stockholm and formed their friendship.

That was when things got complex. Not only had Deacon compromised his DIU mission and the rebel mission, he had betrayed Archie, who was his good friend, and his entire community. As a founder, he knew everybody by first name and was well respected. Everyone he had just killed, he knew on a personal level. The behemoth, Duke, had been his trainer and sparring partner; they saw each other every day. Deacon's behavior also insinuated that he was a Federation spy, meaning the community concept had been a charade. If so, why would he bring Colonel Stockholm, a well-known rebel leader, all the way to that sector?

While the command center was booming with the drama, Archie was seething with fury. He was piecing things together and ultimately decided Deacon's mission was to take him out. The fact that he had allowed Deacon to get so close to him hurt, but the fact that he would kill his close friends indicated he would kill Archie in a heartbeat. *He could have taken me out at any time, and I wouldn't have seen it coming. Why did he wait so long? Why now? Why like this?* The more questions he asked, the more pissed off he became.

The colonel started packing his field bag and donning his armor. "Sargent Terrence, you're in charge. I've got something up my sleeve."

XI

"Is there a reason why we're headed toward the southern fence? The gate is in the opposite direction." Phoebe's level of confusion increased with each step they took.

Deacon pulled her behind a satellite dish. "My partner is minutes from dying. She could be buried alive if I don't find a sentinel and get it to the southern fence, and I mean now. I've tried to contact her, but I think she's asleep or unconscious or something. The sentinel can run a life force scan and dig much faster than—"

CRACK!

"What the hell was that? Stay here."

Deacon stepped out from behind the satellite dish but saw nothing.

CRACK!

Then he saw what was making the noise lying behind a satellite dish a few yards away. At first it looked like a snake with three heads, but then it retracted and lashed out again.

CRACK!

The energy whip was woven with metal strips that resembled a snake's scales; the three heads were the tassels at the tip. His eyes followed the tip as it slowly retracted behind the satellite dish. Once it got to the corner, it lifted off the ground, and Deacon followed it up a fit set of legs with thick thighs and wound into some sexy, supple hands. He couldn't help but keep going up until he saw some perfectly perky breasts that made nipple impressions in the armor. When he got to the top of her long, slender neck, he knew immediately who she was. *I haven't seen her in over fourteen years! But I never got to see her in a leotard. Wow, she's hot!*

Bianca was one of his concubines in this reality, and she was not the same raving bitch from the last one. Deacon didn't know that though; all he saw was a sexier version of his ex-wife. *What a bitch!*

"Look, Bianca, I want to fight you, but I don't want to fight you, okay? Just go back and tell them I got away or something."

"You know I couldn't do that even if I wanted to," she replied. "As surprising as it may be, you've killed a lot of us today, and you're going to pay for it. They didn't deserve that. Duke didn't deserve that."

"Whatever," he said. "You deserve what's coming to you; trust me. I wanted to bust your ass fourteen years ago."

Bianca frowned in confusion. "What? I didn't even know you fourteen years ago."

"Whatever. Let's do this."

Bianca shrugged and then cracked her whip at him for intimidation. She would have been better off saving her energy. The act simply infuriated Deacon even further than he already was. The way she shrugged in the manner that she had in the previous reality brought back all the anger and sadness associated with it. Deacon's memories crashed like a tidal wave against a cliff, and then she cracked her whip, which was insulting at that point. His entire countenance changed, and he gave her a look that was a mixture of hatred and disgust.

She acknowledged the look and retorted with her own. Then she started whirling the whip in a spiral; it looked like a coiled spring spinning. Deacon stood there with that look on his face. Bianca stepped forward and launched the spiraled whip at him while pressing a button on it. As the whip uncoiled and the spiraling energy was transferred to the tip, it was multiplied and electrified.

Deacon twisted his body, dodging the whip, but was able to catch it and choke it off just before the energy surge. Then he pulled the whip tight and gave it a pop on his end, sending the wave of energy back to Bianca. Deacon did it in one solid motion, and it happened so fast, Bianca didn't have time to react. She wasn't trained for this situation and didn't even know it was possible to redirect the energy like that, so instead of sending the wave back to Deacon, she froze in thought.

The intensified wave rode through the handle, up her arm and shoulder, across her neck, through the other shoulder, back down her other arm, and popped her fingertips. It looked like she was breakdancing, and, ironically, she was, because all the bones that the wave rode through broke—*and* she was electrocuted. All she needed was a good techno beat, and she would've killed it.

Bianca died the instant her neck snapped, but she stood there for a few moments afterwards due to paralysis from the electrocution. Once she dropped to the ground, still convulsing and foaming at the mouth, Deacon grabbed the whip and snatched the goggles off her head. The electricity wave had fried the whip's controls and the goggles; they were rubbish. He threw them down and went to find Phoebe.

Again, she wasn't where he had left her, and this time she wasn't shoved inside a panel. She really was gone. *Why can't she just stay put?*

XII

Phoebe darted down the aisle at full speed, hoping to escape the determined rebel that was in pursuit. *Damn, he's fast! I jog every day, and he's still gaining on me!* She cut corners and constantly checked her back. Each time he was a little closer.

She cut a corner, ran a few yards, and turned her head to check if he was behind her before she took another turn. He wasn't there. Instead of following her, he had kept straight and then turned a few yards ahead. When she made her turn, he was right behind her. She saw him, then cut another corner. After a few yards, she turned back to check as she was rounding the corner. He wasn't there, which made her wonder where he had gone, since, moments earlier, he had been close enough for her to hear his footsteps and heavy breathing. The instant it took for her to get around the corner without looking caused her to run into a charging sentinel at full speed.

They both hit the ground hard, with her landing on top of the sentinel. The collision rolled the sentinel's internal gyroscope, causing it to auto-boot. After a few moments, it sat up and looked at Phoebe. Then it raised its hand and looked at it. It was missing a digit. It cocked its head in curiosity and then looked at the charging port on the satellite dish, which housed the missing digit. With its hand still raised, it looked at Phoebe, looked back at its mangled hand, and then back at Phoebe again. "How may I be of assistance this evening?"

"Listen," she said, "I'm being chased by some insane rebel, and there's a human buried alive somewhere near the southern fence. We need to wake another sentinel and go dig this person up. Shit has hit the fan, and all you guys are in fucking standby mode! Now stop worrying about your finger, and get up off your ass. Let's go!"

"But I can't charge again until this is fixed."

"I said move it! A human life is at stake here!"

"Oh shit!"

XIII

Deacon stood tall to survey the area and soon saw a possible reason why Phoebe had ran off. *Isn't that Leroy Jenkins? I really don't want to kill him. He's a good guy, but if he doesn't listen to reason, I've got to do him up.*

Leroy was standing there, awestruck. He didn't want to believe the assassin was Deacon, but he had just seen him kill Bianca and keep on going like she didn't even matter. Even after witnessing him murdering his mistress in such a manner, he still tried to justify it. *Maybe he's sick or something. Regardless, it looks like it's either him or me.* He picked his nose and wiped it on the inside of his pocket, then stretched his arms in preparation for the ensuing fight.

"Listen, Leroy," Deacon said. "I reeeeally don't want to kill you, dude. I didn't want to kill her either, but you guys are attacking me and, well, she had it coming, but you're cool. Just walk away."

"What about Duke?" Leroy asked. "Did he have it coming to him too? Besides, you know I can't just walk away like that. Why don't you just come with me peacefully?"

They looked at one another and then exploded in laughter. The mood was light, but the tension was thick in the air as Leroy continued. "You know, my nephew was assigned to the squad that you massacred in the tower, but I'm not sweating it. You can apologize to him in the afterlife." They laughed again.

"You know what, Leroy?" Deacon said, still giggling. "You've got a pretty good sense of humor for a dead man. I hate that I never got to know you. When I thunderclap your head with these gauntlets, you can tell your cousin that I said 'Fuck him' in person. Well, ghost form or whatever."

They laughed again, and then Leroy gave it a second thought. "Hey, wait a minute," he said. "You were being an asshole, but it was still funny."

XIV

Phoebe, along with two sentinels, arrived at the southern fence in a panic. "Now hurry up and do your little scans. This person is dying!" The sentinels' eyes changed color, and they walked off in opposite directions, scanning the ground for signs of life.

Phoebe paced back and forth between the two sentinels as they ran their scans. The farther away they got, the more unprotected she became. Back and forth she paced, not even realizing her vulnerability. After a few more laps, she stopped. *Wasn't one of them supposed to stay with me?* Then she turned around and ran into a stone wall, at least it felt like one.

"Hey, you guys, I've found the ... hey, where'd she go?"

XV

Leroy unsheathed two long-handled blades that resembled glorified machetes and started twirling them and dancing around until he reached his fighting stance. They weren't laughing anymore. Deacon detected his weak spot from all the dancing, so he just stood there and waited for the attack. Leroy charged, and Deacon charged his feet in anticipation. Leroy's blades crossed right above Deacon's face as he leaned back, dodging Leroy's attack and countering with a super-charged sweep kick that flipped Leroy over, landing him on the crown of his head. Deacon recharged his feet for the super stomp, but Leroy recovered and flipped off his back to his feet. He executed a few more back flips and somersaults before twirling the two machetes in front of himself and binding them at the handle, making a double-bladed spear. He twirled the spear around like he was in *The Matrix* until he assumed a Matrix-esque stance. Then, like Neo or Morpheus, he motioned for Deacon to make a move.

"Hey, that was pretty badass there, Leroy. You've got some moves on you. Perhaps next time we meet I can train you properly, and you won't have a problem with your footwork."

Leroy bristled. "First of all, *we* trained *you*, asshole. Second, I don't have a footwork problem; I can flip over you from a dead stand. Third, the next time we meet is going to be when I die of old age, because you're not walking away from this alive."

Deacon shrugged. "I didn't say you couldn't jump. I said you had footwork problems. That's why it was so easy to sweep you."

Leroy growled and switched his stance in preparation for an attack as Deacon continued. "And after I kill you here, I won't even have to die to see you again."

Leroy charged, screaming with the spear spinning.

"So, in the words of the champ," Deacon continued, unfazed, "'don't take this ass-whooping personally.'"

Leroy swung the spear with all his might, and Deacon dodged it, diving to his side and rolling. All the dancing Leroy had done allowed Deacon to peg his style, and he knew Leroy's next move. After rolling to a stop, he charged his fist in preparation. When Leroy swung the spear, it was cradled behind his left arm, with Deacon crouched behind him and to his right. Leroy spun to his left while thrusting the spear behind him, directly at Deacon's face. Deacon stood and spun toward Leroy, dodging the stab and clocking him with a charged backhand that broke his jaw and spun him back around on his pivot foot. Deacon continued his spin and met Leroy with a devastating knee that crashed through the spear and landed square in the sternum, dropping Leroy to his knees and separating the machetes.

Leroy dropped his weapons and curled up on the ground in the fetal position, unable to breathe. Deacon was trying to be careful not to damage any of the equipment this time, which was why he had kneed him instead of delivering a charged blow. However, the backhand had knocked the goggles clean off Leroy's face. The weapons were still operable though, so Deacon kicked them out of Leroy's reach as he charged his gauntlets. "Don't forget to relay my message to your nephew."

XVI

The sentinels worked diligently to free the buried human. The scans showed the human's heart rate had slowed drastically, and the math proved there was little to no fresh air left in the makeshift grave. They magnetically connected their fingers on each hand and then connected their hands together at the thumbs, making a small shovel that pointed downward. Then they each picked a spot and started to dig. With their hands connected, they angled their wrists and rotated at the elbows, making a motorized shovel.

Once they reached the hard clay, they separated their hands and used them as scoops to take out large chunks. They were making good time; it only had taken about three minutes to get a little over four feet down. That's when the person's heart rate started to pick back up. "I'll take it from here. Go find the lady who fucked up your charging finger."

Down in the tunnel, Gloria was awakened by the sound of scraping above her. The air in the tunnel was thin, but it didn't matter, because she was saved. *Sounds like someone found me!* Earlier, she had fallen asleep, knowing it would slow her breathing and extend her time in the collapsed tunnel. It only gave her a few more minutes, but if she hadn't, she would've suffocated before they even started digging. *I was certain I was going to die!*

Just as she started choking, the clay started to break above her face, and a hole opened up. She pressed her lips to it and took a deep breath of fresh air, then looked out the hole to see a sentinel digging her out.

"Just stay calm. I'll get you out of there."

Seeing the sentinel was a huge relief, but Gloria was happier to finally get some fresh air.

The sentinel pulled another huge chunk away from the hole and then paused and looked at Gloria. "Oh shit, sorry." Then it died with the chunk of clay in its hand.

Gloria started pushing clay away from the hole and digging herself out. *Well, at least he got me started.* Once the hole was large enough, she pulled herself out of the tunnel and looked at the poor dead sentinel. "Guess I could return the favor. I mean, he did save my life and everything."

She disconnected the sentinel's charging hand, which had a fifty-foot wire lead on it, then tossed it out of the hole. Then she climbed onto the sentinel's back and climbed out of the hole. She grabbed the sentinel's hand and plugged it into the closest satellite dish. The dish's panel lit up, and a digital image of the sentinel came up on the display. "Thank you."

"No," she said, kissing the screen, "thank you. Hey, you think you could clear today's events out of the sentinel's databases for me? I'm on official DIU business and, well, you know how it goes."

The sentinel's image on the screen lit up with excitement. "So, you're a spy? A spy kissed me—well, my image? I am honored to have been of service to you! I'll do even better than that. I'll wipe the whole system of your presence and will give you enough time to exit the premises before I do!"

"Marvelous," she replied. "Thanks for your cooperation—and for saving my skin."

"And what lovely skin it is. Calculated at one hundred percent worth saving."

XVII

Deacon stood over Leroy with charged gauntlets and the intention to kill. "I wouldn't do that if I were you." The voice came from behind Deacon. He reared back to swing anyway, and the voice spoke again. "You kill him, I kill her, you kill me, and then my crew kills you. I've got two units on their way here, and trust me, when they see who the spy who murdered their family and friends is, they won't let you out of here alive."

He's got Phoebe! That was the only part Deacon heard. He dropped his fists, backed away from Leroy, and turned around to see Archie standing behind Phoebe with an arm around her neck and an energy-charged short sword across her belly. "All I have to do is apply some pressure, and I can cut this bitch in half. Do as I say, and she lives. Hell, I don't even know who she is, but I'll slaughter this bitch like a farm-raised cow! Now take those gauntlets off, and give them to Leroy, now!"

Earlier, when Deacon was fighting Duke, Archie had tapped in and saw where they were through his goggles. Then he knew where to look for the girl. He intercepted Leroy on his way and told him to keep Deacon occupied. "And *don't die*! I'm going to get the girl and maybe gain some leverage on this asshole." As Leroy watched Deacon outwit Bianca, Archie was chasing Phoebe through the satellite dish array. Once he had taken Phoebe, he returned just in time to save Leroy's life.

Deacon hesitated to listen to Archie but saw the look of terror in Phoebe's eyes, so he did what he said. Leroy, who was beginning to catch his breath, picked himself off the ground, sheathed his blades, and went to retrieve the gauntlets. He would have loved to talk some shit, but his jaw was severely broken, so, he just gave Deacon a swift punch to the belly and snatched the gauntlets out of his hands.

Deacon dropped to his knee and tried to catch his breath as Leroy donned one of the gauntlets. As he gasped for air, he noticed something that the others didn't: an opportunity to get out of the situation.

XVIII

"Squads four and seven, I need you to converge on the western end of the communications tower and wait for further instructions." Archie had previously radioed on the open line for them to head to the southern fence, but back at the command center, Chuck secured a private line with the two squad leaders, and they followed his orders, just like the colonel had sent them himself.

Being one of the four surviving founding members of the community, and Deacon's best friend, Chuck wasn't about to let the colonel kill Deacon like that. He, Deacon, and six other DIU spies from all over the world had started a camp in the middle of nowhere. The purpose of the camp was for the DIU to have an undercover home base. Deacon, the DUI's newly elected director, ran the entire outfit, which put a lot of responsibilities on his shoulders.

He decided that a modest camp in the middle of nowhere was best. The only problem with that was the forest they chose was right on the border between two sectors. Soon, drifting defectors from both sides of the border started to drop in, and with nowhere else to go, they became permanent fixtures at the camp. The defectors didn't have any access to the hive, and there was a negative social stigma against reading each other's minds; it was considered rude outside of the Federation. That allowed the spies to move in silence and carry out missions undetected. Their theory was: the best place to hide something was right under the seeker's nose. That being the case, they didn't see any harm in helping a few people and getting a hand with chores around the camp.

Nevertheless, the community grew to be quite sizeable, meaning more people were defecting. It seemed like their little community experiment was far more successful than expected. So, Deacon devised a plan that involved the community and would cut the head off the snake as well. In his office was a hit list of rebel leaders and ex-DIU agents that is passed down between directors upon death. The struggling community was the bait, and Colonel Archibald Stockholm took it, hook, line, and sinker.

Yet, in that situation, Deacon had no idea what was *really* going on. He only knew parts of what was happening, so saving Phoebe and Gloria was his main objective. Everyone he had killed or maimed thus far he had done so to save Phoebe or Gloria. If he had known the full situation, he probably would've taken a more civil approach. (The fact that he was carrying the fate of the world in his pocket is a different mission for another story.)

His spy colleagues didn't know what was going on with him either, but they backed him fully and weren't going to let the colonel best him. Chuck knew if Archie made it back alive, the jig was up. *But there's only one more alpha out there. If I can keep these two squads out of the picture, we might be alright.*

He left the communications board and went back to the command post, where he had been monitoring the cameras earlier. That's where he had been when the colonel left him in charge, and he had left his drink beside the keyboard when he got up to send the message to squads four and seven. The temperature in the tent had risen nearly ten degrees since he had murdered all the officers in there, and he had worked up a decent sweat during the massacre. He needed his drink. So far, the soldiers in the tent, the colonel, and the alphas were the only ones who knew of Deacon's subversion, and he was trying to keep it that way. He stepped over the putrid bodies of his former comrades and gulped down the entire cup. *All our bases are covered. Just kill the colonel and the alpha, and we'll be alright.*

XIX

About twenty yards behind Archie was a sentinel that looked like it was tracking footprints until just then, it found their owner. The sentinel was missing a finger and was muddy, but it was clear it had just found who he was looking for. Deacon judged the distance from where he was to the whip and the distance from the whip to where Archie was and then smiled.

"Halt, rebel intruder!"

Archie hesitantly turned around, and the slight distraction was all Deacon needed. His uppercut struck Leroy in his already-broken jaw so hard it was like he was wearing a charged gauntlet. Leroy flew back, dropping the other gauntlet as Deacon dove for it, caught it, and rolled for the whip.

"In the name of the Federation, I am officially ... ." The sentinel died mid-sentence, but the distraction had served its purpose. By the time Archie turned back to Deacon, he had the gauntlet on and charged and the whip in hand. Archie raised his arm to take Phoebe's head off as Deacon used the gauntlet to super-charge the whip.

He cracked Archie right in his armpit as his arm descended upon Phoebe, but the short sword never touched her. The whip struck his shoulder, and Archie's arm simply fell to the ground.

Phoebe fought loose from Archie's other arm and ran to Deacon. Even though he was a stranger, she embraced him like he was Jesus. Then they looked in each other's eyes and kissed passionately. It was the first time he had kissed his wife in over fourteen years.

The moment was short-lived though. Leroy had regained consciousness and was gathering his wits. His jaw was shattered, and he was plumb whooped, but he was also seething with vengeance.

The electrical current that struck Archie cauterized the wound when it hit, so he wasn't bleeding out. That, coupled with years of hard-nosed training, allowed him to redirect his focus from pain to anger. Of course, it still hurt and threw him off balance, but he was able to continue the fight.

Leroy scrambled to his feet and gained his bearings. He saw the situation Archie had gotten himself into while he had been semiconscious and felt guilty.

"All is forgiven if we take him out," Archie said.

Leroy already had a gauntlet on his left hand, so he unsheathed a blade for his right hand and assumed his stance. Archie, who was ambidextrous, reached to his back with his remaining arm, drew out a long sword, and then took his place beside Leroy. They looked like a pair of matching vagabonds. Deacon was unimpressed, but Phoebe was terrified. Leroy did no dancing this time. He and the colonel stood there, stone-faced, with their charged energy weapons, and eyeballed an attack.

XX

Gloria's dash down the satellite dish alley came to a sliding stop, and she dove behind a dish for cover. Three rebel soldiers were coming from the opposite direction, and she got out of their path right before they saw her. She knew Archie would call for more than just three men. It had to be an entire squad scattered about, probably two or three of them converging on his location.

Shit, I'm too late! She looked down the alleyway adjacent to Deacon and shuddered at the sight of the soldiers creeping through the array. Deacon was about to take on an alpha and the colonel, and in a few moments, he would have a squad or two to handle too! *I've got to do something quickly, but I can't blow my cover. What do I do? Fuck it ... .*

At first, she thought she could use her status—being a founding member had its perks. In most cases, a founding member's word superseded the colonel's, but it could be two or three units spread out, all converging upon one point. Her other option, the one she approved of, was to attack. If she and Deacon could kill all the witnesses, they could maintain their cover. *I probably would end up fighting anyway, since they're all spread out. So yeah, fuck it.*

She got into position and turned to look back down the alleyway. Deacon's adversaries seemed poised for attack, so she grabbed her knives, turned from behind the satellite dish, and lunged forward—toward the rebels' backs. She rolled back behind another satellite dish and watched as the rebels headed west. *What? Okay, whatever. I guess I can go help Deacon.*

XXI

Things back at the command center were dreary. All the buzz and hype from earlier had died with the rebels, and Chuck was getting tired of sitting there watching the screen. The only relevant screen he had was the colonel's, since Deacon had smashed Leroy's goggles with a well-placed backhand. Deacon looked confident, but from the colonel's perspective, he was outnumbered, and Chuck didn't want to just sit there and watch as his best friend got murdered. So, he set the colonel's location into his goggles, put on his armor, grabbed his weapon, and destroyed all the computers on his way out.

The command center was just outside of the breach in the southern fence, where they had set off the bomb. It wouldn't take him long to get there, but his weapon of choice didn't necessarily require him to be there, and setting the colonel's location in his goggles didn't have anything to do with finding out where the colonel was.

XXII

Leroy had learned that lunging at Deacon wouldn't work. He either had to take him by surprise or land a lucky counter. Since he and the colonel were standing in front of Deacon, the element of surprise was exhausted. The only other way was to counter, but luckily for him, Archie would be attacking too, so the chances of landing a blow had just doubled. Also, Archie was more than proficient in martial arts. He could still handle himself, even with just one limb. *I don't understand how he's still fighting and not on the ground, writhing in agony! Glad this guy is on my side.*

Phoebe took off behind a satellite dish, and they launched their attack on Deacon. Archie swung his sword in a large downward motion, which Deacon blocked with a gauntlet, but Leroy attacked him low, charging his gauntlet and going for the belly. Anticipating this, Deacon grabbed the gauntlet from the inside and used Leroy's momentum against him, thrusting him to the ground. Little did Leroy know, while doing that, Deacon managed to unlatch one of the gauntlet's restraints.

Then Deacon had to block another one of Archie's massive swings with the energy sword. This one came in sideways, on Deacon's right, and nearly knocked him down. It gave Leroy enough time to come to his feet and Archie to reset for the next blow. Archie swung sideways, to the other side, and Leroy attacked with his blade from the right side. Deacon backflipped, and Leroy ended up blocking Archie's swing and being knocked down.

Once Deacon landed, he dropped the whip, charged it, and lashed out at Archie. Archie stuck his sword out to block, the whip wrapped around the sword, and Archie snatched the whip out of Deacon's hand. Deacon was down to only one gauntlet and the shin guards, but he could take them with no weapon at all, and he knew it. He wasn't playing with them anymore.

Leroy, who was so angry that someone could have cooked an egg on his forehead, decided to be proactive and take things into his own hands. *He seems to be doing this to protect that chick, but if she's dead, it might demoralize him. I'm not going to hesitate like the colonel did. I'm killing that bitch and taking the upper hand!* He remembered where she ran off to and looked over there but couldn't see her. *She's around here somewhere ... .*

Deacon saw what Leroy was up to and decided that Leroy had lived long enough. *Man, I gave that guy multiple opportunities to get out of this situation. He has abused my kindness, and now, I've got to take him out.* He saw Archie charging him with the sword again, but Deacon wasn't worried about him. He casually stepped to the side with the missing arm, knowing Archie couldn't hit him on that side, kneed him in the gut, and elbowed him in the back of the neck.

Leroy knew he had to help the colonel, or they would both die, so he charged his blade and hurled it at Deacon while charging him with the other one in hand. Deacon elbowed the colonel again and then swung the colonel around in front of him by the neck. Archie took the charged blade to the chest and died quite painfully. Leroy was still in pursuit with the other charged blade, so Deacon grabbed

Archie by the wrist and used the sword that his dead hand was still gripping to block and counter Leroy's attacks.

Then Deacon took the sword out of Archie's dead hand and attacked Leroy. Leroy flipped over Deacon's sword as he swung, rolled, and grabbed his other blade out of Archie's chest. Deacon was slightly impressed. Leroy was fighting for his life and understood his chances were slim to none, so he was pulling out all his tricks.

The latch that connected the two blades was broken, but two blades were better than one. Leroy attacked Deacon once more, but this time he swung the blades with force and swiftness. The long sword proved to be too heavy to counter both blades, but it had perfect balance for blocking, so Deacon blocked every attack that he couldn't dodge, timing his moves perfectly.

Leroy thought he was doing a good job. He had Deacon backing up, and all he could do was block or dodge. *If I can just land one blow ...* . He displayed his moxie by delivering a massive chop, but that was a deadly mistake.

The hand that Leroy was chopping with had the gauntlet on it. Deacon grabbed the gauntlet, stopping his chop, and unlatched the other restraint. Leroy didn't feel it, so he still had no clue what was transpiring.

Leroy tried to swing his other blade, but Deacon had position on him. He brought Leroy's arm down while he was turning and twisting the gauntlet and then braced it under the armpit that he caught the gauntlet with, which made Leroy twist his entire body around and drop the blade. Then Deacon snatched the gauntlet and threw Leroy to the ground.

Leroy sprang back up and slashed at Deacon's legs, making him take a few steps back and allowing him to get his other blade back. Deacon donned the other gauntlet. Now he had possession of both the gauntlets, the leg guards, and a long sword. Leroy stood up while Deacon latched up the gauntlet, and then he noticed something: a slip of cloth hanging out of the panel on the satellite dish behind Deacon.

XXIII

Gloria showed up at the fight scene and was mesmerized. Deacon was using moves that she had never thought possible. It was poetry in motion. *The way he spun the colonel around and made him take the blade in the chest ... then used the colonel's dead body to defend himself with his sword! Hell, he might have taken out those squads by himself too!*

She stepped back behind a satellite dish and watched as Deacon made taking out elites look as easy as sparring. *The last of the witnesses; we're home free. The only one left is Phoebe. She might keep quiet, but if not, it looks like Leroy is gunning for her anyway. If I just hang out, Leroy can kill two birds with one stone—with him being one of the birds!* She climbed up into the satellite dish to gain a bird's-eye view of the fight. *This should be interesting.*

Two hundred yards away, at the southern fence, Chuck climbed into another satellite dish and opened the bag in which he was carrying his weapon. Back at the command center, his choice of weapon had been up for debate the entire time he was preparing to leave. He didn't decide until he was on his way out, but he had made the proper choice.

He knew he needed range, but he also needed silence. That's why he decided to go with the longbow. It was fully digitized with multiple types of arrows for different situations. It could synchronize with the user's goggles, allowing him to see directly down the sights. Sensors were located inside the bow that detected wind speed and helped the user to adjust for it. It even had an arc projector. Once the target was set, the bow calculated the wind speed and distance and then projected the proper arc and draw back through the user's goggles. The digital longbow was virtually foolproof, but Chuck could peg his target from this distance without all the fancy do-dads and whatnots.

Once he drew his bow, he got into position and looked through the sights. His target was a little over two hundred yards away, and he didn't look like he was doing so well. Chuck decided to take him out anyway. *I didn't come all the way out here for nothing.*

XXIV

Leroy knew what he had to do to get to the other side of Deacon without Deacon realizing what was going on. Whenever his assailant lunged at him, Deacon used their momentum against them, so, Leroy took off at full speed toward Deacon, expecting to either land a blow or get diverted into the satellite dish in question.

He dove at Deacon, who was oblivious to his plan, and Deacon rolled under him, blocking the blow from underneath Leroy, which was totally unexpected but still did the trick. They both came to their feet simultaneously, yet Leroy was wearing a large, mangled grin. He raised his arm and charged his blade. Just then, Deacon saw the slip of clothing hanging out of the panel and knew his intentions.

Deacon's heart dropped. Not only would Phoebe die again, he would see it happen—again. He figured she would have been safe with him, but he was enjoying himself so much that he got caught up in the moment and took his eyes off her. He knew she was in the area, but he was so focused on staying alive that when she hid in the panel, he didn't know exactly where she was.

He also didn't know that Gloria was there watching him. In his mind, she could already be dead. *Man, I lost them both! How did I fuck this up? Well at least I got to kill Ken this time. That felt good.*

Leroy expelled a sinister snicker and slurred a small, indiscernible sentence together with his shattered jaw. Then he cocked his wrist and swung his blade. Everything went into slow motion again as Deacon charged Leroy with the fury of a million Spartans. As Leroy's arm extended, an arrow flew in out of nowhere and lodged itself right in the hinge of his elbow, inhibiting it from fully extending. Deacon slid to a stop, and Leroy groped his injured elbow. A moment later, the arrow exploded, obliterating Leroy's forearm and the hand with which he was clasping his elbow.

Leroy dropped to his knees in pain, and Deacon walked over with two charged gauntlets. "Remember our little conversation?" Then Deacon brought his hands together with a thunderous clap on both sides of Leroy's head. No blood splattered. The force of the thunderclap pulverized his head, and the electrical charge from the gauntlets burned everything that was solid and boiled everything that was liquid. Leroy's head simply dissipated in front of Deacon, and his torso fell to the ground face first—minus the face.

Deacon snatched Phoebe out of the panel and embraced her. "Man, I thought I had lost you again." They kissed again, a lengthy one, then Gloria approached.

"Ahem, you're a little too early for a celebration. We still have to make it back to the base—and figure out what we're going to say. Let's get going. Apparently, Chuck is around here somewhere. Judging from the arrow's trajectory, he should be somewhere near the southern fence where this entire thing started. We can start with finding him and getting back to the command center to figure out what to do next."

Deacon was so happy to see Gloria that he almost ran Phoebe over trying to get to her. They embraced, and Deacon almost kissed her too, but then he realized how awkward that might be for Phoebe, as if her entire encounter with him wasn't awkward enough. "I thought you were dead!"

Gloria dug in his pocket and pulled out the canister of anti-lithium, which was now blinking beyond belief. Just as it started to beep, she pressed the button on the top and relieved the pressure, just in the nick of time. She casually put the canister in her pocket. "Well, I'm not dead yet, and I'm happy to see you too, but we have to get the hell out of here. It's rebels lurking all around the place."

Deacon agreed and dropped the energy weapons without asking about the canister. *It's obviously got something to do with whatever they had going on before I got here.*

They headed to the southern fence, where they met up with Chuck, and then they all fled the scene.

Chapter 16

I

The command center was trashed, and the vile stench of death and feces permeated the air with such ferociousness, it forced the quartet to relocate the tent immediately. They found a nice secluded location a few miles south of the Federation base and pitched camp for the night. Deacon and Phoebe reassembled the camouflaged tent while Gloria got a fire going and Chuck gathered firewood.

They had not exchanged many words since they left the base, but once everything was settled, they convened around the fire to eat their rations and discuss the day's events.

Deacon still didn't fully understand their situation. He thought they were mad at him for killing other community members, but really, he had almost blown their cover in the middle of a covert mission, for a girl that he didn't even know. *And* Gloria almost died because of it. AND he was gingerly carrying a canister of anti-lithium that could have annihilated the planet!

"Okay, Deacon," Chuck said, "what the hell was that all about?"

"Look, man," Deacon replied, "a friend of mine was in danger, and I had to save her, okay?"

Chuck looked at Phoebe and asked her how she knew Deacon. She swallowed her last bite of food before answering. "In all honesty, we just met tonight, but it feels like I know him from somewhere, like maybe we were childhood friends or something. I know it's impossible. I guess he just has one of those faces."

Chuck thought about it for a moment. "Well, I've known him all my life, and I've never heard him mention you. Furthermore, I've never seen Deacon jeopardize a mission in such a manner either. Logic would conclude that you are significant to him, but facts are facts." He looked back at Deacon. "You're the leader of this outfit, but you're my friend first. You know I have your back with anything, but you have to let me know what's going on. Is there some sort of mission that I don't know about or something like that?"

Deacon took a moment to respond. It looked like he was holding back, but really, he was trying to process all the information he had just received from Chuck and apply it to the information he had acquired earlier. Archie had alluded to him being a prominent member of a community, and apparently, he was also the leader of some sort of spy program. *Well, that explains a lot! I guess the community doesn't know about the spy thing. Shit! I think I've fucked up!* This completely changed his perception of the situation, and he couldn't think of a proper response.

Gloria, who had finished eating, rolled a blunt with a fig leaf and lit it before she finally decided to chime in on the conversation. *Maybe I should help him out a little bit ... .* "Well, you see, Chuck, that's the beauty of being a DIU spy: plausible deniability. Hell, the rebels can't access the hive anyway." She passed the blunt to Phoebe and then continued. "They'll only know what we want them to know. I understand your point, but everything turned out okay—that is, if she can keep her mouth closed." They all stopped what they were doing and looked at Phoebe, who in that awkward moment was inhaling a sizeable draw. Then she started choking and coughing.

Deacon saw where the conversation was headed. Chuck and Gloria were looking at Phoebe like she was a pig up for slaughtering, so he decided to intervene before Phoebe could catch her breath. "Look, I brought her into this shit. Her head shouldn't be on the chopping block. Like you said, I'm the leader. I saw something that needed to be done, and I did it. Now everybody just ... just calm down, and let's think this through."

Chuck cocked his head. "Deacon, one thing you've taught me is to close all the gaps. Take no prisoners, and leave no witnesses. What's so important about her? Why is she the exception?"

"It doesn't matter," Gloria said. "She's a witness. So, unless she plans on going through the election process and becoming an official DIU spy, she must die. I don't make the rules; I just follow them."

II

Back at camp, the rebel soldiers started returning from the raid feeling tired, hungry, and confused. Most of the squads came home on their own accord, as there was no leadership in place to give the word. Only two squads knew what really happened: squads four and seven. The ones who had been sent away from the action decided to return to the southern fence area and found the murder scene, where the bodies of all the alphas and the colonel were lying.

They had a saying, "You won't encounter a DIU spy and live to tell about it." So, when all the rebels started to return, and nobody had heard from the other three founding members, Cassandra started to get concerned. She finally came across a member of squad four who had seen the scene inside the communication tower, the massacre in the satellite dish array, and the attack at the command center. He assured her that no founding members were amongst the dead, but upon further inquisition, she discovered their cover could have been blown.

Talk of conspiracy was looming before the other founding members were even there to defend themselves. Cassandra did all she could to keep things calm until they returned—if they returned. However, she had to walk on eggshells while talking, because there was no telling what had happened, and she didn't want to say anything that could make matters worse. She had no way of contacting them while they were in the field, because it was protocol for spies to block everyone who wasn't concerned with the mission. Furthermore, the Federation, as a hive mind, blocked the spies' actions as a security measure. Basically, it hid information from itself. The spies could still utilize the hive and access others, but others couldn't access or locate them. Deacon, being the director, was the one who sanctioned the missions, and if they were on one, Cassandra was in the dark until one of the spies telepathically contacted her.

The system wasn't designed for a spy who lived with a community of defectors though. It was a good cover for the director but a major inconvenience to the spy. Cassandra didn't know what happened to the missing spies or what to do about it. And not being able to contact her team was a major problem. The community was lost without its leader, and she was next in the chain of command.

So, wait a minute, I'm the temporary leader? Okay, so I guess I need to get with squads four and seven and gather all the information I can about the situation, then hold a community meeting to reassure them about the founding members' survival, whether they've survived or not.

III

"This woman isn't dying tonight, especially at our hand. I mean, wasn't this organization made to protect the innocent and defend our Federation?" Deacon tried to rationalize with his partners but seemed to be getting nowhere.

"You've got a point," Chuck admitted. "We do protect the innocent. But to do that effectively, we must remain hidden. This is a witness right here who can peg either one of us in a lineup—primarily you. She's a liability and has to die. You know that; it's *your* policy for all of *your* missions!"

Deacon thought about it for a moment. *My policy, huh? My missions.* "Okay then," he replied, "there's a new mission: ensuring this woman's safety. I'll vouch for her; she's trustworthy."

Chuck scowled. "How can you be sure? How do you know she's not going to squeal? I swear, if you just tell me what's going on, I'll have your back one hundred percent. I just can't endorse this without an explanation, not even from the director."

Deacon turned and took a few steps away to think, like he was in a soap opera and about to reveal some heavy information. *Maybe I should tell them. I mean, what have I got to lose? They seem to be open-minded in other realities, and in this one, there's actually a way to prove this phenomenon is possible.*

Gloria sat back and kept an eye on Phoebe, who was probably ready to run as Deacon and Chuck argued over her fate. They locked eyes for a moment. Phoebe appeared to be terrified. Gloria looked entertained by her fear. However, the conversation seemed to be taking an unexpected turn, and Phoebe's immediate survival became imperative. "Okay, guys, how about this," Gloria said. "In the morning, we can just take her back with us and tell them she's the spy until we can figure out what to do with her." Chuck and Deacon eyeballed each other, but they continued listening. "Hell, Deacon has already made it a mission to ensure her safety, and as long as she's with us, she's safe. If we go back home with her, all of them will wonder who she is anyway. Why not tell them she's a spy? All they know is the information that we give them, right?" She paused to let her idea sink in. "You're the leader, Deacon. Lock her up until we can we figure something out. Once she's gone, the mission will be complete without a failure. Killing her would definitely be considered a failure at this point, Chuck."

Chuck sighed and bowed his head in defeat. "I just wanted to know what was really going on, but I guess you're right, Gloria. It doesn't matter now. Deacon, you know I have your back regardless, right?"

Deacon, who was still a little upset with Chuck, nodded in agreement and relit the fig blunt. "Well, it looks like we have a plan. Let's get our shit together and get some sleep. I'll take the first watch. Chuck can take the second and then Gloria. We'll work on our story on the way home."

Deacon rolled himself another joint and took his post while the others gathered in the tent and made themselves comfortable.

IV

"Okay, I know you guys aren't too excited about me being in charge. I'm not the commander or the most physical person at the camp. Fate just dropped this hot potato in my pretty little lap just as suddenly as it did yours. Now, I might not be in charge for long, but I could be in charge indefinitely. Either way, it all starts right here with you guys."

Cassandra was sweating profusely from anxiety as she delivered her first address to the rebel soldiers. To relate with them, she decided to wear the customary camouflage uniform instead of the flimsy, two-piece, barely covering, or see-through garments that she usually donned. She even pulled her hair back into a ponytail and holstered her sidearm. She was nervous while delivering her speech but felt greatly relieved to be back in a uniform.

She never went on missions with the other spies and was so used to playing the girl next door that she had become acquainted with the lifestyle. They decided to leave her behind as a security measure, just in case something crazy happened. If they all died on a mission, a capable leader was left to take over. She had the fastest wit out of all of them, and the concept of using a defector community as a front had been her idea.

"If the army won't follow me, neither will the people. We have a chain of command for a reason, and if it isn't adhered to now, then everything that we, as founding members, have set in place was for nothing. All we have worked hard for and achieved throughout all these years will have been for nothing, and that tarnishes our legacy as founding members.

"I can't do this alone, so I will be appointing officers tomorrow to fill the positions that today's raid left open. But first, I need to know everything you guys know about the raid. I know it's late, but I need to speak with squads four and seven immediately. I need everyone from these squads to meet me in the mess hall for coffee and inquiry. Everybody else is dismissed until tomorrow's community meeting, unless you have unique information as to what happened."

As her eyes scanned the crowd of tired, sweaty soldiers, she noticed two of them were fresh from the infirmary. Their bandages were already soaked with blood. One of them had a cast on his arm and was wearing a neck brace.

The other had a cast on one leg and one arm, and his chest was bandaged. Both of their heads were wrapped in blood-soaked bandages.

What the hell happened to them? Cassandra wondered. As everyone left, the two crippled soldiers headed toward the mess hall. *They must have some critical information. I should save them for last—just in case.*

V

Deacon sat outside the tent smoking his blunt and tending to the fire. *Okay, let me get this straight. I'm the leader of some sort of spy organization and the leader of a rebel group. Most of the world is psychically connected, and the spy program that I lead is supposed to protect against groups such as the one I live in. I think that's about right. How did I get into this mess? Furthermore, how did I get shit done?*

The more Deacon understood about his situation, the more confused he became. *And what game is Gloria playing? I've spent the last fourteen years with her, and I know when she's full of shit. Why is she playing Chuck and me against each other?* She used to do the same thing to the kids when she had an ulterior motive, and Deacon had noticed the same method of approach that night. *Maybe that's it! But what could she possibly gain from Phoebe's death? Unless … .*

"Hey, Deacon." Gloria climbed out of the tent as if she had not lied down. "I can't sleep. Pass me that weed." She sat close beside him, and he nervously passed it to her. "I should've requested first watch," she said as she took a hit.

"Maybe I would be sleepy by the time this shift is over. With my luck, it'll be time for my watch before I get sleepy."

They shared a laugh, and Deacon looked at her, about to speak, but she beat him to it. "I love nights like this. A clear sky full of stars, cool air with a warm fire, and a thick blunt rolled with natural fig leaf. It just puts me in a ... mood, you know?"

Deacon was already nervous, and Gloria's advances only worsened the situation. *All the time I spent with her, and I clam up now? Come on, pull yourself together.* Deacon was having trouble controlling his emotions in the awkward situation. She gave him the chills—not the type one got when terrified, but the type someone got in grade school trying to figure out how to talk to their crush.

She passed the blunt back, and Deacon took a few tokes before speaking. "Yeah, it's a beautiful night. I used to take my kids out in the backyard on nights like this and lie there in the grass with them. I would point out the planets, stars, galaxies, and constellations. I even taught them how to navigate using the sky. We would joke around for hours until they eventually went to sleep. Then we would carry them to bed. Those were the good old days."

Not only had Deacon just mentioned his children from another life, he had referenced a life he had shared with Gloria, but he did it on purpose. He even threw in the statement "*we* would carry them to bed." Deacon would carry Baylor while Gloria and Randy carried the twins. He knew the chances that she was the same Gloria from the previous lifetime were slim. Just like Phoebe, he would have to start all over again. But it was still worth a try, given her awkward behavior. Even if she didn't know what he was talking about, he felt comfortable enough with her to have that conversation ... yet again.

Gloria seemed to be open-minded about the entire thing, but Phoebe had been too when he spoke to her in the counseling center during his first reality shift. The thing was, this was a different reality with different upbringings for both parties, and Phoebe didn't even know him in this one. *But they're still the same people at the core, right? Well, maybe not. I'm an asshole in most of them. Maybe I'm an asshole now and don't realize it. This is confusing!*

Gloria took a moment to respond. She closed her eyes like she could envision what Deacon was describing in her head. Then she opened her eyes to gaze at the stars and cracked a slight smile. She looked at Deacon, whose eyes were still fixated on the stars. "You don't have any kids, Deacon." Deacon winced but hit the blunt and continued his stargazing. Then Gloria took his hand, and they made eye contact. "But we can practice making one."

VI

Cassandra took a big gulp of coffee from her thermos to begin the long, arduous process of interviewing squads four and seven. The only reason she was interviewing them rather than reading their minds was that they would know she was reading them. It was a two-way street: if she read someone else's mind, it opened her mind to them, and that would certainly blow their cover. The interviews were a must.

"Okay, there are a few things I need you to do to make this process as quick as possible. First, I need you to line up with your squad by rank. The interviews will be conducted in the prep room. I'll be taking squad four first, so line up accordingly." She decided to interview them individually to gain perspective from all viewpoints and not just a collective story. "Also, I need you to be thinking about a few things while waiting to be interviewed. I need to know your position in relation to your fellow comrades, I need to know everything you saw, and I need to know everything you smelled or heard. I need to know every little detail that you can remember. Some may have seen something that nobody else saw."

She also made a point to save the two cripples for last, because they weren't from either squad, and they appeared to know something quite troubling. Going last would also give them time to remember more of what happened. Their battered faces looked confused and frightened, and she knew they had witnessed something big.

The tech team had analyzed the squad leaders' footage and had accounted for all the soldiers. Now all they needed was corroboration and details. The soldiers were able to place themselves well, and each story was unique yet coincided with the others.

The only inconsistency was a small, one-second instant on the helmet cam of squad seven's leader. The techie who caught it couldn't clear it up well enough to decipher what he was seeing, so he wasn't too concerned. He didn't know what was really going on, so he didn't understand the full ramifications of his find. The squad leader didn't even see it, and he was right there, but his helmet cam caught it.

According to the squad leader, the colonel ordered them to converge on his location at the south-facing side of the tower. As they rounded the corner and made their way to the location, they received another transmission from the command center ordering them to head west and await orders, so they did. Once they arrived, one of the soldiers went inside the tower to try to get a visual on the colonel, but instead found a massacre.

The helmet cam showed the squad leader climbing the stairs to the tower and finding the murder scene. Then it showed him throwing up all over his combat boots and walking back outside to get some air. As he stood at the top of the stairs gagging and trying to keep from puking again, his camera caught a glimpse of Deacon and Gloria fleeing with a Federation employee. It also showed someone perched on a satellite dish a few yards away. *Is that Chuck?* The techie who found the clip thought they were three of the soldiers who may have gotten misoriented or maybe were over there fucking off. He had no idea that it was the missing founding members.

Cassandra was able to relax a little knowing her team was safe. *But why hasn't anybody contacted me yet? That's usually the first thing that Deacon does!*

She took solace in seeing that they were safe, but she still had a slew of stymies. *And who was that employee with them? So many questions! Maybe these two are the missing pieces to the puzzle.*

She had saved the two battered soldiers for last and intended on interviewing them privately. *I don't need anything incriminating getting out to the community. If they know too much, well, I know what to do.*

VII

Phoebe couldn't believe she was in the presence of three DIU spies. The entire spy program was a myth to those who weren't a part of it, much like the Men in Black. Everything was done so covertly that few people even believed it existed. However, that allowed them to operate undercover much easily.

The fact that people didn't think they were real was a hard task to achieve, and it didn't come without sacrifice. If someone met a spy, he or she didn't live to tell about it. That's how they maintained their cover. A few witnesses had slipped through the cracks, but those ones were considered loony. The DIU's story paralleled lots of conspiracy stories in many ways. However, Phoebe was now a part of this story, and if the team of spies followed protocol, it wouldn't have a happy ending. Once she realized they were spies, she knew she was going to die unless she could get away from them. That's why when she and Deacon were assembling the tent she had left out one of the spikes in the back of the tent—just enough for a person her size to slip through.

She waited patiently until the perfect time to escape, which happened to be sooner than expected. Gloria had left the tent to frolic with Deacon, and Chuck was sound asleep—more like loudly asleep; his snore was violent enough to wake a hibernating bear. It was so loud, it provided enough cover for her to grab a few rations and a machete from his bag and make her getaway undetected.

She shimmied under the back side of the tent and gained her bearings. Her plan was to make it back to the Federation base, but she wasn't sure which direction it was. As she snuck away from the tent, she heard the sweet sounds of sexual ecstasy coming from the front of it. *Lucky girl ... .*

She didn't use the machete until she was far enough away from the tent not to be heard, and she got back on the path that they had taken to get where they were. *Homeward bound! Just stay quiet and keep moving. As soon as I get far enough away from them to make a silent escape, I'll signal for help, and this thing will be all over with.*

VIII

Cassandra strutted into the prep room with her newly filled thermos of coffee, eyeballing the crippled soldier. The guy looked like he had some juicy information, and Cassandra could hardly wait to get the interview underway. *This looks like the work of Deacon for sure.*

She sat down adjacent to him at the small, sanitized, stainless-steel prep table and took a swig of coffee. "So, start from the beginning. What squad are you from, and where were you guys positioned?"

The soldier, who was still nearly catatonic, took a sip of coffee with his only operable arm and then started to tell his story while staring into nothingness. "Squad nine. We were the ones who got attacked in the tower. Everything was cool. We were raiding the base successfully and all. Our squad came in behind the explosion at the tower and were told to destroy everything and make it quick, so we could join the other squads."

The soldier cocked his head and made a disgusted face, like the memory was more vivid than he liked. "I had the energy axe, so I started to bust up the computers on the main floor. That's when it happened."

He grimaced, like the memory physically hurt him. "He came from out of the basement, and I was the first one he struck. He hit me in the head with a table leg. I dropped my energy axe and fell to the ground. When I regained myself, he had made a round of attacks around the room and was working his way back to me. He was killing people with just one blow. I was scared, so all I wanted to do then was get away from him."

The soldier paused and rubbed his head at the memory. "But he was so fast and fluid with that damn table leg that he cracked me in my knee before I could turn to run. I fell, of course, but not before he hit me in the elbow and across my head again, then kicked me in my chest on my way down. Once I was on the ground, he hit someone else and then stomped me out. I thought I was dead."

Cassandra was intrigued. She knew it was Deacon by the way he had circled the room. He must have been on some sort of drug to have the balls to jump an entire squad with confidence. Her next question was the million-dollar one though. "Did you see who did this to you?"

The soldier thought about it for a bit while rubbing his head. "I mean, everything is such a blur. I've been thinking about that since Junebug woke me up. He was all fucked up too, but we were grateful to get out of there with our lives. But as far as who did this, I don't think I saw his face, or maybe I just can't remember. I took a few blows to the head, ya know."

Cassandra was annoyed. She wanted to read his mind so badly, but that would mean blowing her cover. But if he was lying, or even if he is telling the truth and his memory came back later, eventually, he would say something. *Fuck it. He'll just have to die.*

Cassandra read his mind. She witnessed the entire fight as vividly as a memory can make it. The soldier was lying. She saw Deacon as clearly as he must have. She also saw the other crippled guy, who was waiting for his interview. He actually attacked Deacon, which turned out to be a good idea, because he got countered instead of attacked. That was probably why he was still alive. Either way, they both knew who had attacked them, and they needed to be exterminated.

The mind reading only took a second, but the soldier knew he had just been memory jacked. His confusion lasted for only a moment. Cassandra dove over the table and put him in a headlock. He could barely breathe, but he managed to squeak out, "We were right," just before he passed out. Cassandra dropped his unconscious body to the ground and walked over to the knife block to pick out a sufficient blade to slice his throat.

She grabbed the cleaver. *I've always wanted to use one of these on somebody.* Then she walked over and grabbed the beaten soldier's hair. Using the razor-sharp blade, she sliced his throat from ear-to-ear, literally. Unsatisfied, she hacked at the poor guy's neck until his head was completely off.

After wiping off the cleaver, she scanned the prep room for a good spot to hide the body, then realized she would be moving the body twice tonight when she could just go out there and kill the other guy and dispose of both bodies together.

So, with a devilish grin and a heart full of dark intent, she opened the door to the prep room and spotted the other cripple, who seemed to know his time was up. He stood up and outstretched his operable arm, welcoming his fate, and Cassandra complied. She launched the cleaver at him side-armed, it sliced through his neck and lodged into his spinal cord, nearly chopping his head off too. The cripple fell to the ground, dead, and Cassandra sighed. "Time clean this mess up."

Chapter 17

I

Chuck was snoring so loudly that he woke himself up. (Those who snore know all about the struggle.) His mouth was dry, and he had to urinate. It was still dark inside the tent, so he figured it was still night time. *I guess Gloria took my shift.* He rolled out of his cot and headed out of the tent.

Once he got outside, the first thing he noticed was Deacon and Gloria cuddling by the smoldering fire, naked. *That's one lucky guy there. I don't know how he was able to kill Bianca. She's almost as hot as Gloria!*

He rounded the corner to do his business in privacy. As he was urinating, he was waking up little by little until he was conscious enough to realize what had happened.

It was still dark outside, but it was dawn. The sun had started to poke over the hill as he finished his business. The problem was, he hadn't seen Phoebe when he got out of his cot. *She escaped while they were out here fucking around—literally!*

Chuck was enraged. He ran back in the tent to confirm his fears and found it empty. The back of the tent was hanging loosely, like it hadn't been pinned down properly, and then he knew where she had gotten out. "Goddammit, wake up! That bitch is fucking gone!"

Chuck stormed out of the tent, cussing and throwing things and making his anger apparent. Deacon and Gloria woke up instantly. "What?" Deacon asked, half asleep as he covered himself. "What bitch is gone?"

Chuck looked at him in disbelief. "The bitch that was so important to you that you wouldn't tell me who she was. *That* bitch is gone."

Deacon and Gloria jumped to their feet and got dressed. "When? How? I mean, she was in there with you, right? How did she get out?" Deacon was confused. He had risked his life to save her, and she had left without even saying goodbye. He probably would've let her leave if she had asked. He wasn't going to let the community lock her up in their prison, just because he saved her life. He also wasn't going to let Gloria or Chuck kill her. The only thing he could come up with was to let her go with good hopes, because he believed she could keep her mouth closed about the situation. But the fact that she had planned an escape made him question her motives. *She's gonna fuckin squeal! Imma kill her!*

"So, what are we gonna do now? You're the leader. You got us into this shit. What are we gonna do?" Chuck hadn't calmed down one bit. His "I told you so" attitude made it clear that he would never let Deacon live this down, even if they make it out of the situation without being incarcerated. "What did Cassandra say? I bet she told you to kill the bitch too, huh?"

Deacon didn't know how to respond. He had an idea about how to handle Phoebe, but he had no clue where Cassandra fit into the story. It was the first time anybody had mentioned her. He didn't know he was supposed to be in contact with her. *Shit! Why didn't anybody say something about her last night?* "Uh, I never got in contact with her."

Chuck's disbelief shifted to disappointment. "Well, at least you're still honest." Then he looked down and shook his head. "You know that's the first thing you do, right? What's wrong with you? I mean, you're you, but you're not being, yourself."

Gloria, who felt somewhat guilty for the escape, interjected. *No way am I going to let Deacon take all the blame for this.* "Well, she was in there with you. She left the tent while you were in there with her. You're just as guilty as we are. So, before you go pointing fingers, I suggest you think about the situation in its entirety."

"She slipped out of the back," Chuck said. "How was I supposed to know?"

"Well, how were we supposed to know?" Gloria replied. "Even if we weren't fucking, we wouldn't have known. It's all of our faults, and it's nobody's fault. Let's just work this problem."

Once again, Gloria was right. Instead of arguing about it, they should've been working together as a team to solve their dilemma. Chuck cut his eyes and sat down. "Sorry for the outburst, guys. You know me; sometimes I take things too far. So, what do you suggest? I think we need to see if we can catch up with her. It's the most logical thing I can come up with."

"That all depends on how long she's been gone and how well she bides in the forest," Deacon said. "She's blocking her telepathy, so there's no way of knowing when she left or how far she's gotten. I've had some experience in the forest before. I'll go after her. You guys just head for—"

"No, that won't work," Gloria said. "We aren't going to let you take the fall. We're a team! Splitting up is the last thing we should do. It never works out well. We should stick together no matter what. If you go for her, we *all* go for her, but we kill her when we find her, and that's not up for debate."

Deacon nodded slowly. "Yeah, she dies this time, no question. But sometimes as a team, you've got to know when to split up. Every now and then somebody has to take one for the team, you know? I'm the one who got us into this, so I'll go after her."

Gloria bowed her head, knowing he was right.

"But are you going to have enough balls to kill her when the time comes?" Chuck asked. "I believe you know her well. When I was at the command center, I saw how you found her inside the computer. Nobody would have thought to look there, yet you went straight there like you knew where she was. So, how did you psychically locate her if you didn't know her? It took some thought, but now I believe you. How you know her is still a mystery though. That said, I can't let you risk this entire mission just for you to get there and not be able to complete the mission."

Chuck was right. Deacon still loved her. And there was a slight chance that he wouldn't be able to kill her when the time came. Deacon knew this, and he realized they had a good reason to question his decision making up to that point. "Okay, I understand your point," he said. "But there's no reason for all of us to go down for this. Get in touch with Cassandra, and let her know what's going on. Then I want you two to head back to the base. Let me deal with Phoebe."

II

Phoebe hiked all night on what she thought was the path back to the Federation base. *Damn, it feels like I've hiked twice as far as we did to get there. I should have seen all those bodies from their little command center by now. I'm on the trail, right? Like, who else hikes through here?*

She was lost in the forest, unknowingly following a circular game trail and running out of energy. She sat down next to a tree to eat a ration and gain her bearings. *Okay, the sun rises in the east, and we were headed south when we left, so, should the sun be on my left or my right?* The more she thought about it, the more confused she became. If she signaled for help, it would alert the spies to her whereabouts, but if she didn't, she could die in the forest. She had no friends, and the only person she could contact privately was Ken, who was now dead.

Following that game trail all night and not being attacked was a feat of luck. However, something seemed to be following her. She had heard rustles in the bushes behind her all night, and the one she had just heard was much closer. She decided it was time to get back to the hike. *Can't come all this way to let nature take me out.*

After passing what seemed to be the same tree for the third time, she finally decided to put the machete to use and break away from the trail. She worked out her position in relation to the rising sun and, after much deliberation, figured out which way was north. She didn't have a clue where she was, but she saw some hills in the distance that she could probably use to gain a better vantage point. *North it is. Better than staying on this path and possibly getting mauled by some woodland creature that would otherwise be cute.*

III

Cassandra sat in her room, exhausted. After working all night to dispose of the bodies, she hadn't gotten much sleep. She was trying to summon up enough energy to make a speech. She could sleep the rest of the day if needed. The disposal of two soldiers proved to be a daunting task. Just maneuvering them around the mess hall was taxing. She wasn't about to dig any graves and muscle them out of that building without being seen or without having enough time to clean up the bloody mess involved. Let's just say, Cassie wasn't going to be eating any of the ground beef for a while. *Fuck it, I'm in the prep room.* After cleaning herself and taking a naked nap, she still felt like she had never gone to sleep at all.

She took a gander out her window on the second floor and saw the citizens starting to congregate around the flagpole in the center of the community. *Man, that's way more people than I remember! What am I going to say?* Having prided herself with being the witty member of the group, she was suddenly at a loss of words. She had just murdered for the first time in years, her best friends were missing, and she only had roughly an hour of sleep. She actually had a valid excuse for being off her game, but it was one hell of a time to choke.

She stretched and cleared her mind. *Wait a minute ... Chuck?* Just then, Cassie received a telepathic message from Chuck. He told her that they were safe, but Deacon had gone off on a solo mission and instructed them to return to the base. He didn't go into detail about what was going on, because he didn't want her to panic. Once she told him of her situation and the previous night's events, he felt like it was imperative that she know about Phoebe and the condition Deacon was in. *Why the hell did you let him go by himself? I know he's the boss, but damn! One of you should follow him—just in case.*

After hearing that her friends were okay, a great weight was lifted off Cassandra. She felt much better, even a little energized. She knew exactly what to say now, so she jumped into her uniform and galloped downstairs.

IV

Another one of the second-nature things that Deacon had acquired from the first shift was the ability to track. He picked up on Phoebe's tracks from the back of the tent and followed them to a game trail. He had been following the game trail for a few minutes when he found evidence of her being in the same spot multiple times. He also saw another set of tracks that concerned him.

Eventually, he found a path that had recently been cut out. *So, she left the camp, came across a game trail that obviously runs in a big circle. Looks like she sat here and ate a ration. There are footprints over there, obviously from a different revolution than the one from the snack. There's also another set of tracks here, some sort of big cat. The cat's tracks are covered by her tracks. Either the cat was in front of her or had been following her for a long time. And here's a path that heads north. It really took her that long to figure out which way north is? Anyway, with her being so far off trajectory, she'll end up a few miles west of the Federation facility. She'll figure that out when she reaches those hills over there though. If she isn't too far ahead of me, I can cut her off.*

Deacon climbed a tree and scanned the area for the best route and figured he would follow her path for a mile or two and then cut off to the east. His plan was to cut time by going down her precut trail rather than cutting one of his own. The path disappeared only a few miles up, so she might not be too far ahead of him. He might even be able to catch up with her before she reached the hills. The only problem with that was the large cat that had decided to follow her too.

When Deacon first saw the massive cougar, he was terrified. Not for his own well-being but for Phoebe's. The cat might get to complete the mission before Deacon got a chance, and death by puma mauling is a horrible way to die. *Not today, kitty. I need to have a word with that woman. You better go find another meal, or I'm going to have myself a nice, new puma coat for the winter!*

Deacon hopped out of the tree, grabbed his machete, and headed down the path, on his way to save Phoebe's life again, only to be forced to take her life afterwards. The situation was dumbfounding.

V

Chuck hiked through the forest, seemingly in a daze. He didn't know whether to be angry or concerned. He knew something was troubling Deacon, and he had been close to getting him to talk several times, but Gloria always came up with a solution to whatever they were dealing with, and they ended up losing the moment. Chuck had known Deacon all his life, and even though it would be disrespectful to do it, he didn't need the hive to read his mind.

He knew her for real. Maybe she's an undisclosed mission. Then they wouldn't be able to talk about it. That's got to be the case. If not, there is no other explanation that I can come up with, and he'll just have to talk.

He had realized a long time ago that he had to keep an eye on Gloria as well. *She's been acting a little off too. I don't know; maybe it's got something to do with the exposure to anti-lithium?* The way she had been throwing Deacon off and inadvertently aiding in his secrecy threw up red flags in Chuck's head. *What does she have to gain from all of this?* The entire situation seemed fishy. The fact that they had sex wasn't out of the ordinary, but the fact that they had gone to sleep and didn't even wake him up for his shift was. This wasn't their first time out in the field. They usually waited until it was Chuck's shift to start any hanky-panky, and they usually did it in the tent, so the way the entire escapade had played out was suspicious.

Chuck was also feeling somewhat betrayed by Deacon's secrecy. They had shared everything since they were little boys: clothes, toys, cars, apartments, even women. The fact that Deacon was holding back really bothered Chuck. Deacon usually talked about missions with him, so he didn't understand why he wouldn't divulge the information. Something serious had to be going on, maybe a cause for concern. *He should still tell me though. I shouldn't have to read his mind … .*

VI

After carving out roughly three miles of forest and hiking up a steep hill, Phoebe was beat. She'd never had to work that hard in her life, and she had done it all in the dark without any guidance or sleep. On her journey, she had encountered colorful snakes, spiders the size of her hand, a lizard that got up on two feet and ran at her with its neck flared out, and all sorts of strange insects, rodents, and other creatures. She had become in tune with nature, and she hated every bit of it.

She was lucky enough to come across a freshwater creek that morning where she was able to get a cool drink and wash up. She wanted to take a break and call the Militia, but a rustling in the bushes behind her scared her off. Climbing that massive hill with its steep pitch took a lot out of her, but she finally got to sit down beside a tree and enjoy her last ration.

The beef-flavored ration was enough to bring her to tears. It was delicious, and it filled the pit of her stomach, but the fact that it was her last one made her think it could be her last meal—a vacuum-sealed ration. That thought was what brought her to tears. The last real meal that she ate before she was placed in her situation was a home-cooked dinner that she had prepared for a male companion the night before—a male companion who had ultimately stood her up. She cried over that meal too.

After she was done, she decided to gain her bearings. She knew she couldn't be too far from the base, and it should be visible by now, especially from the top of this hill. If she was close enough to it, she might be able to reach it before nightfall or shortly after. She climbed a tree and wiggled out onto a branch to stand up. Once her eyes caught a glimpse of the base, she felt reinvigorated. *The sun is coming up in that direction, behind the base, so that's east. All I have to do is follow the creek. It looks like it goes right into the base. Hell, it might even be our water source there. It looks like the Militia is still at the base too. I can signal for them now and meet them at the bottom of the hill! I should be far enough ahead of the spies. They'll kill me for sure if they catch up with me, but the Militia will get here first.*

She signaled the Militia, hopped out of the tree with a newfound sense of urgency, and headed back down the steep hill as fast as she could go. All the excitement refueled her body and gave her the proper motivation to keep on moving. *And I'm going straight to the fridge when I get home!*

VII

There were no butterflies in Cassie's stomach as she stepped up to the podium to deliver her message to the rebel community. The jitters and shakes she had throughout her body were due to the amount of coffee she had drank, not nervousness. She knew exactly what to say and was ready to speak.

As she gazed over the crowd, a hush came over it. Everybody was silent and receptive, even more than when Deacon spoke. It seemed like the new leader of the community had their full support and undivided attention.

"Good morning, rebels! Rebels ... has a nice ring to it, doesn't it? Yesterday, we crossed that boundary from defector to rebel. We crossed it for a reason though. A purpose that is greater than us. Yes, we brought back enough food to keep us fed for another year. Yes, we brought back enough supplies and equipment to arm all our soldiers, and yes, we brought back enough tech gear to keep my team busy for months. But yesterday, we crossed that boundary to send them a message. It's not about the food or the equipment; it's about freedom! It's about being able to do what you please, when you please, and with whomever you please! It's about not having to worry about incarceration or waking up to go to work for them just to feed yourself and your family. We want liberty! Yesterday, we sent that message. We let them know that we will not just sit here and bide our time while we slowly die off. No! We will continue to grow! We will continue to fend for ourselves and fight for our freedom! Not just for us but for our future, for our children, and for theirs. Sadly enough, we lost a few people yesterday, but we gained something too: brotherhood, teamwork, something real to fight for. Yesterday was about freedom. We are rebels, and we won't go quietly! Now let's continue the fight, so our brothers and sisters won't have died in vain. Let's give them something to be proud of. Let's fight for something to be proud of, so we can build something to be proud of!"

The community erupted. If nobody knew where they were, they did after that speech. Cassandra electrified the crowd with her powerful delivery. She was able to use the success of the raid and the deaths of the fallen to motivate the community. She also effectively cast doubt on any thoughts of the founders being spies.

As she backed away from the podium to a round of applause, one set of claps was louder than the others. They were going about half the pace of the rest of the claps, like someone was genuinely proud. The crowd hushed again and looked around, thinking the claps were coming from behind them, but they weren't. When they realized the claps were coming through the speakers behind them, from the microphone on the podium, they all looked up to see Chuck emerging from behind Cassandra with a huge smile. "Nice speech, Cassie."

VIII

I think I just might have to decapitate this asshole. Deacon lay prone on a tree branch waiting for the puma to get close enough to strike. After following it down Phoebe's path for a mile or so, it branched off, so, Deacon decided to follow the cat instead of staying on the path. He didn't want the cougar getting the drop on him, so he stayed behind it and hoped it would slip up.

He stayed on the cougar's trail for two more miles until he finally got within range of it. He saw it stop and lie down beside a creek. It wasn't sleeping or getting a drink; it appeared to be waiting for something. So, instead of attacking it and getting mauled before he got a chance to complete his mission, Deacon decided to climb a tree and wait for the perfect moment to attack. He found a decently thick branch that was in perfect position near the cat and silently wiggled out onto it. There were no branches under him, so all he had to do was wait until the cat got close enough for him to drop down onto it.

Deacon had his machete and his field knife unsheathed, and his senses were overloading. He closed his eyes and took it all in. He felt the westward wind wafting the hair on his forearm. His mouth was dry, but he could still taste the pork ration he had eaten before he got on the game trail. His fingertips and toes tingled with anticipation, and he could hear every single bug making its signature noise within a sixty-yard radius.

But wait, what's that? Footsteps?

Deacon opened his eyes and looked at the cougar, which was still lying there but had apparently heard the same thing, judging from its attentiveness toward the footsteps. Deacon looked in that direction and was happy the large cat wasn't perched in the tree with him, because he could see over the foliage that was blocking the cougar's view. He looked back at the puma, and it saw it was looking behind Deacon, like it had heard something else. *What is it now?* He looked in that direction, and his jaw dropped. *Yep, gonna have to cut its head off.*

IX

Deacon didn't leave a clear path for Gloria to follow. If it wasn't for the two ration wrappers (one from him and the other from Phoebe), she wouldn't even believe she was headed in the right direction. She was better at tracking than Chuck, so they decided she should go after Deacon while Chuck headed to the camp. But they had underestimated how well Deacon fared in the wilderness. He was virtually untraceable; there were no footprints, snagged clothing, or odd depressions for her to go by. She never tried to locate him or contact him, because she didn't want him to know she was following. So, she decided to follow Phoebe's trail, assuming Deacon did the same. When she saw the poorly cut path off the circular game trail, she knew she was getting hot.

Gloria followed the path for a mile or so until she noticed a break in the path. *Was it Deacon or Phoebe? If Phoebe cut the path, and the cut path continued, Deacon was the one who had deviated, but why? He may have been trying to cut her off, but if that was the case, he would've gone the other way, right? Besides, the base is that way. Maybe I should just stay on the path. At least I know it'll lead me to Phoebe.*

She continued down the path until she found another one of Phoebe's ration wrappers. When she reached down to grab it, she inadvertently grazed her hand across one of the largest, most colorful spiders she had ever seen. Its colors matched the foliage that had fallen on the forest floor, so she didn't see it until she brushed its fur. It was bright orange, like a mango, the size of a cantaloupe, and fuzzy as a coconut. Its teeth looked like viper fangs, and it didn't look too pleased about being disturbed.

The menacing spider raised its front four legs and hissed at Gloria—at which point she stomped on it quite vigorously. The last stomp was so hard it squirted guts out, and the spider's legs shot off the body from under her boot. *Damn, I didn't even see that thing! It was fuckin' camouflaged. I wonder how many of them suckers I've stepped on so far without knowing it.*

Once she calmed down, she heard water in the distance. *Is that a creek?* She took a few steps closer and then stopped to survey the area. The first thing she noticed was an unbeaten path that came around a bend and stopped at a tree. The second thing she noticed was another path that went out of the jungle toward the creek. The third thing was the rustling of leaves from footsteps that seemed to be coming down the hill in the distance. *So, is that Deacon, Phoebe, or some other woodland creature that I should be worried about?* She didn't know whether to run to it, run from it, or grab a weapon. Being a logical person, she chose the logical decision: she ducked behind a thicket of tall grass and grabbed her field knife.

X

Phoebe hustled down the hill, stumbling, falling, and rolling. She didn't quite understand the danger she was in; all she could think about was getting to the bottom of the hill to meet up with the Militia. She tripped and fell, rolled downhill, then jumped to her feet, ran a few more yards, tripped, and started the entire process again. *At this rate, I'll be at the bottom of the hill in no time!*

Once she reached the bottom of the hill, she gained her bearings and made her way to the creek. The water was so clean and clear, she could see all the way to the bottom. She could even see fish and the tadpoles swimming below. She decided to kneel and take another drink, so she lay prone and closed her eyes, then put her lips to the water to drink, like a gazelle. The water was cool and refreshing, like ice water without the ice. No particles or mineral taste, just cool, crisp, fresh water. *Mmmm!*

When she opened her eyes, her shadow provided enough background for the creek to act like a mirror. Her eyes finally focused on the image that the creek was reflecting, which was that of a large, intimidating, angry mountain lion. It was right in front of her on the other side of the creek, just within pouncing distance.

The puma had snuck up on her so silently that if she had not opened her eyes, she would have passed on without even knowing how she died. It had been hunting her all night and had finally caught up to her.

Okay, so it knows that I see it. No sudden moves. She slowly looked up at the large cat, and it dipped its head low. She hadn't had to use the machete since she headed up the hill, so it was sheathed on her side. She had to come off her belly to reach it. She slowly rose off the ground, and the cougar growled. She froze, petrified. After a few moments, she decided to try again. She leaned a little more off the ground, and the cougar dipped even lower, preparing to pounce. She froze again, unsure of herself. She didn't know how much longer she could hold herself off the ground in that position, but she knew the puma wasn't going to stand there and play the inching-up game with her much longer. It was do or die time.

The best plan she could muster was to twist her body as she dropped to the ground in the hope that she could reach the machete in time. She had to be fast and flawless, because the puma had already calculated its pounce and was ready to jump at the perfect moment. She was fully aware that she wasn't going to make it out of the battle unscathed, but if she made it out alive, she was good with that. *And it will make for one hell of a story*! She took a moment to mentally prepare herself for the attack. She was scared, but it was going to happen whether she wanted it to or not, so she got set. *Ready ... steady ... GO!*

She was moving so fast that everything else seemed to be moving slowly. She dropped her body and spun simultaneously, landing on her shoulder and rolling the rest of the way over. She saw the cougar leap in her upper peripheral as she reached for her machete. *Oh shit!* Her reaction wasn't the shock of having a two-hundred-pound cat pouncing after her; it was the fact that the machete wasn't in its sheath. She must have lost it while tumbling down the hill.

As she lay there, ready to accept her fate, the most unexpected thing happened: another machete seemingly materialized out of thin air, sliced cleanly through the puma's neck, and then stuck in the ground next to her. The cougar's head landed in her lap, and its headless body landed in the creek.

All the horror from the situation struck Phoebe at once, and she sprang to her feet while releasing a scream so vicious that all the wildlife in the vicinity fell silent—even the insects. Once she had regained her wits, she assessed her status. *Okay, so I'm alive, and without a scratch! Now, where the hell did that machete come from?*

XI

Chuck and Cassandra sat in the mess hall and sorted things out over some fresh coffee and a fig leaf blunt. Cassie still had questions, and even though she knew Chuck was tired from his hike, she needed to know what he knew. *Hell, at least he's had some sleep.*

She sat across from him at a small table with her coffee, took a sip from it, set it down, and folded her hands in front of her. "First of all, it's good to see you alive and to know the rest of the crew is alive. I thought I was alone for a minute there. That's why I need to know everything. What happened out there?"

Chuck took a sip of his coffee and a pull off the blunt. "I really can't tell you; I don't know. Deacon has something going on with the little employee he saved. He knows her from somewhere, but he's not telling us. I guess we'll find out when all this is over. Before he left, Gloria and I convinced him to make her death a mission, because we didn't trust that he would do it. When you had us split up to follow him, there was hardly any debate. Gloria *wanted* to do it."

He hit the weed again and passed it to Cassie. "By the way, Gloria has been acting strangely too," he continued. "I don't know what's going on with those two, but something is up. Maybe I'm just being overly analytical again—or paranoid, as you guys would say. I just tried my best to act like I wasn't suspicious until I got another opinion."

Cassandra hit the blunt and took a moment to put things together. *So, sometime during the middle of the mission, Deacon went rogue and started killing his own people for a female that he has no past with? Then he risked our freedom by bringing her with them? Chuck is right; that is uncharacteristic of him. Gloria should've never went along with that either. Something is up.* She hit the weed again, passed it, sipped her coffee, and folded her hands. "Man, you two could've killed her at the base, and we wouldn't be going through this right now. Why didn't you take her out when he brought her back?"

Chuck looked at her like he smelled something sour. "You weren't there. I saw how serious he was about her survival. He did acrobatic shit I had never seen him or anybody else do before. I wasn't going to deal with that over her."

He paused to smoke. "If you had asked me a few days ago who would win in a fight between Deacon and me, I would've said it would be close, but I could take him. Ask me that now, and I can tell you in all honesty that I won't stand a chance, not even with you and Gloria helping me. He is on an entirely different level now, and I don't know where he acquired these new moves and skills. He's, like, twice as fast and stronger than anyone I can think of, and I didn't want any part of it. That's why I didn't kill her. I didn't even touch her. Gloria didn't, and you wouldn't have either."

After retrieving the blunt from him and taking a large pull, she grinned, then tested his testosterone. "So, you didn't kill her, because ... you were scared of Deacon?"

Chuck gave her the sour smell look again and then realized she was just busting his balls. "Very funny. But seriously, he was so adamant about her that I couldn't make him choose between the two of us. If I would've tried to kill her, that's the situation we would've been in. And that would've been like asking a man to choose between his best friend and his wife. A real friend wouldn't put a man in such a situation."

She nodded in agreement and passed the weed back. "Okay, I understand. There's just one more question: does he have the fortitude to kill her? I guess we'll just have to wait and see. By the way, don't eat the beef for a few weeks."

XII

Deacon hopped out of the tree with a sense of satisfaction. Even though he had lost track of Gloria, he had still managed to save Phoebe, and that was all that mattered to him.

When Phoebe reach the bottom of the hill, she had attracted the cat's attention, and Gloria was able to slip away so slyly, she was totally undetected by the cat or Deacon. Once the cougar crept up on Phoebe, he wasn't as concerned with Gloria anymore, since the cougar had clearly made its choice.

The cat was too far away to drop down on, so Deacon had to throw his machete. Timing was key. He had to wait until the puma pounced, because it had its head dipped into its shoulders and could possibly pounce after the machete was thrown. The kill had to be done in mid-flight, and Deacon only had one shot at it—that is, if he wanted Phoebe to survive without a scratch (he had his field knife as a close-range plan B).

The cat pounced, and Deacon threw the machete with perfect aim. The cat was decapitated, and its body lay in the creek with blood squirting out of its neck and flowing downstream. Phoebe was safe.

I told you I was going to cut its fucking head off! No need for plan B!

When Phoebe saw him hop out of the tree, she was so full of emotion that she couldn't control it. If it wasn't for him, she would've died that day—and a couple of times the day before. She ran to him and embraced him the same way she had in his original reality, and Deacon couldn't contain his emotions anymore either. They both cried.

She pulled back, and they made eye contact. Something in Deacon's eyes comforted Phoebe, and she knew she was safe in his arms. Deacon saw the love emanating from her, like the point of energy in the white place. In the short moment that their eyes locked, it felt like he had gone back to his original reality, and nothing had changed.

They both closed their eyes and leaned in for a kiss that had the passion of a prime-time soap opera. Deacon's brain flooded with memories of his original reality. The only thing that was flooding Phoebe's brain was cold steel. Her body went limp in Deacon's arms during the long passionate kiss. He didn't understand why at first. As her head fell away from his lips, he saw a field knife handle sticking out of one side of her head and the tip of the blade sticking out of the other side through her hair. He knew the knife had came from Gloria, but that wasn't the pressing issue. Phoebe had just died again. She wasn't as safe in his arms as she thought.

Deacon fell to his knees with Phoebe's dead body in his arms and screamed. He couldn't believe this had happened, in this way, no less. Once again, he had to watch his wife die right in front of him, reliving the ordeal that Ken had put him through in his first shift. The agony, the physical pain, the mental anguish of losing her again in such a manner took its toll on him, and he became weak.

He gently placed her body down beside him in the cold creek water and then vomited. Once he was able to catch his breath, he heard helicopters in the distance. *Wait a min ... what's that? A helicopter? Could it be the infamous*

Militia? Fuck 'em, and fuck this reality. I just want my Phoebe back! He wiped the sweat from his brow and the puke from his chin, washed his hands off in the creek, and placed his face in his clean hands to cry.

XIII

Helicopters? That bitch signaled for the Militia? Gloria was surprised they had been able to catch up to her anyway. Phoebe obviously had no experience in the forest. *She should've made it to the base by now, but I guess she went up the hill to see where she was at. At least she got north right. But now we have to deal with the Militia too!*

The way Phoebe came down the hill had attracted the puma's attention and allowed Gloria to slip away. She found a good hiding spot under a thicket on the other side of a tree. Nobody could see her there, yet she could see everything that was going on—except for Deacon, who was in the same tree above her.

She had her field knife out just in case she had to deal with the cat, but at the moment, the puma was preoccupied with a nice piece of easy prey. So, her idea was to permit the puma to pounce on Phoebe and then sneak up on it while it snacked. Phoebe didn't even have the machete that she had so maliciously stolen, so she was unarmed. When the puma pounced, Gloria grinned. Then the machete dropped, and she gasped. *There he is! Goddammit!*

It happened so fast that she didn't have time to react. She had no clue where Deacon was up until then, so she didn't factor his intervention into her plan. She calmed down and thought her situation through again. *Okay, assuming he doesn't know that I'm here … .*

She figured she would wait to see if he would finish the job or fail. If he killed her, everything would be okay, and they could go home. If not, she would have to kill Phoebe herself—and maybe even Deacon.

So, she watched and waited, hoping Deacon would make the right move. Moments later, the soap opera kiss forced her to make the toughest decision she had ever made. Logically, killing Phoebe was the right thing to do, but once she saw Deacon's reaction, she felt like she had just made an epic mistake.

Gloria thought she was going to have to fight Deacon after killing Phoebe, but quite the opposite happened—she had to run out to stop him from killing himself.

"Why can't I be with her? If I can't have her, I don't want to live anymore! Why couldn't I have just died in my car? Why do I have to endure this torture over and over again? What did I do to deserve this?"

He had taken the knife out of Phoebe's head, licked the blood off it, raised his head, and closed his eyes. He raised the knife up high over his head. That's when Gloria grabbed him by his wrist and disarmed him. She had already pulled the machete out of the ground and sheathed it, just in case Deacon got slick.

They made eye contact, and all she saw was sadness and despair. "I'm sorry for your loss," she said. Deacon's countenance turned from sadness and despair to sadness with a hint of curiosity. "That's the Militia," she continued. "We have to get out of here."

Though Deacon was curious about why she had said what she said and how she had said it, the fact that Phoebe had just died in his arms was overpowering. He also wasn't going anywhere with her murderer. "I'm staying. I can't just leave her here like this. They'll have to kill me."

Gloria was offended. "No, they're going to zap your ass, beat the shit out of you, and then incarcerate you for her murder! Now get up, and come on. You don't even have to come with me; just leave here."

As the choppers became visible in the distance, Deacon stood up and looked at Phoebe's body. "Somebody has to be held accountable. I put her here. It's my own fault." He stopped crying and stiffened his chin. "And I don't blame you; you were just doing your job. Now get out of here while you still can."

Gloria's jaw dropped, but she did what he said and took off up the hill to find a good hiding spot. Once she was settled, she turned to watch as the Militia tried to take Deacon. He put up a good fight. *They better be happy they came with more than one chopper full of goons!*

Deacon was knocking people out and throwing people into people, breaking off limbs and using them as weapons. For a minute, it looked as if he might defend himself against three helicopters full of Militia soldiers—until one of them touched Deacon on the leg with a stun stick on his way to the ground. *Game over.*

The soldiers who were still able to fight swarmed him and stomped his lights out. Then they helped the others who were still alive back onto the choppers. One chopper was dedicated to the dead. That's where they put Deacon, amongst all his victims—including Phoebe. Gloria watched as his feet dangled out the side of the chopper, twitching. He was still alive, but just barely.

When the helicopters took off, two of them went in one direction, and the one with Deacon went in another. They were headed toward the mines. *Incarceration.* The other choppers were headed toward the hospital.

Chapter 18

I

Deacon fought the swelling of his two black eyes to crack them open for the first time in a week. When he arrived at the mine's infirmary, he was suffering from fatigue, dehydration, broken bones, busted lips, black eyes, torn ligaments, and a severely whooped ass. His survival was a testament to the human's natural instinct to survive, even when he or she didn't want to anymore. As his eyes adjusted to the light, the first thing that he thought about was the unexpected murder of Phoebe in his arms. *Why?*

Other than the memory of Phoebe, he didn't remember most of that night a week earlier. He didn't even know it had been a week. The last thing he remembered was the sting of the stun stick on the side of his leg, and then everything went black. So, he worked his way backwards from there. Then he remembered the hive.

He tried to access it but was denied. It wasn't as if he no longer possessed telepathy; he was just blocked from using the hive. *Well that's a devastating blow.*

After scanning the dirty, moldy recovery room, he looked down at himself to assess the damage, and it was brutal. *Geez, I'll never recover from this!* One arm was broken in two places, the other one had a wrist sprain, a few broken fingers, and a dislocated shoulder. One of his legs was broken, and the other had a boot on it and a wrapped-up knee. He could feel his broken ribs with every breath he took, and the neck brace he was wearing inhibited him from looking anywhere but straight. The bandages on his head were for the gashes on his forehead but added a nice, soft support for the back of his head on the pillow, which was good, because he was probably going to be there for a while. *But wait a minute, how am I supposed to take a shit?*

He laid there in pain for a few moments when a scantily clad nurse walked in and noticed he was awake. Her hair was in pigtails, and her nurse's uniform looked like she had acquired it from a children's playset. "Oh, you're finally awake. The warden wanted me to fetch her as soon as you were conscious. I'll be right back."

He tried to get her attention before she left but then realized that not only was he practically immobile, he could barely talk. She didn't even hear him and walked swiftly out of the room. *What the fuck?*

A few minutes later, the young, sexy nurse returned with a large grin on her face. She took a few steps into the room and then did an abrupt about-face. Deacon could see her nice, shapely ass hanging out of the bottom of the dress and heard her giggling as she stopped. She looked over her shoulder at him and winked, then faced the door to introduce the warden.

"It is my pleasure to introduce the warden of this facility. She is the judge, jury, and executioner of the mines. No inmate leaves here without her personal approval, and no inmate ever meets her approval. She's the alpha, the omega, the big wig, the finishing line, the—"

"Get on with it already!" a familiar voice shouted from outside the room.

The cute nurse giggled. "Okay, sorry. Introducing, Warden Joeckel! Yay!"

She clapped as the warden sauntered in. Deacon knew who it was instantly. *Janice! If this bitch doesn't let me the fuck out of here immediately, I swear, I'm actually going to get my hands on her this time.*

Shut the fuck up, inmate! Janice interrupted his angry rant mid-thought with a telepathic message. *You're going to be here indefinitely!*

It was a much healthier version of Janice due to the eating habits of this reality, but it was no doubt his mother-in-law from his original reality. Joeckel was her German maiden name (which is a totally different story). She wasn't married in this reality.

When Deacon realized what was going on, he seized the opportunity to clear his name and claim his freedom. *Okay, so you can read my mind. Check this out Janice: I didn't kill your daughter!*

Janice furrowed her eyebrows and peered down her glasses at him. *How did you know my name, and how did you know that was my daughter? And what are you showing me? I don't see anything.*

Deacon was getting frustrated. *I'm showing you my memories, see? I didn't kill Phoebe, I loved her!*

Janice cracked a slight smile. *Whatever, spy. I've heard of you guys' brain games, swapping memories and creating false ones to throw off inquisitors. Besides, all the evidence points to you. You were the only person found in the vicinity. Your field knife matches the wound perfectly, and her blood was all over you. It was even in your system, indicating you licked the knife clean after the murder. You licked the knife clean! You maniac! I'm going to make sure you serve an eternity in here!*

She had Deacon in a bind. He didn't want to snitch on Gloria, but he wanted to be cleared of his wife's murder. Even though he was innocent, he wasn't going to snitch, so, he just lay there and thought of the last time he held Phoebe in his arms. Then he blocked Janice from his thoughts to piss her off.

"It doesn't matter. Hell, telepathy is blocked in here anyway. I don't need to read your mind anymore. Besides, I wanted to tell you this verbally. For what you did, you will be here for the rest of your life. And believe me, you will die in here—way before I do." She cut her eyes at the nurse, who backed up in fear and allowed Janice to walk closer as she continued. "I'm not going to kill you, but I'm going to make damn sure the workload does. As soon as you can walk, you will be exiled to the mines for a lifetime of servitude. By the way, I've come to visit you since you arrived and have wrung your neck until you turned purple every day for a week—and I will continue to do so until your ass is out of recovery and in my mines!"

Janice jumped up on top of Deacon, removed the neck brace, and proceeded to choke the consciousness out of him. At first, the way she jumped on top and straddled him was extremely sexy. She was wearing a business-like skirt and he could feel her clitoris through the thin hospital-like robe they had him in. She stroked his penis as she wiggled into position and reached for his neck. The sultry moment was ruined the instant she got her hands around it. The fact that Janice was actually getting off to strangling him was slightly disturbing to Deacon.

Her move was totally unexpected to him, but the nurse knew what was coming. She exited the room as Janice began to violently expel her anger. She had the grip of a table vice and the pugnacity of the Hillside Strangler. Deacon felt the blood vessels bursting in his face and eyes as he slowly fell into unconsciousness from the Janiconda's choke hold.

II

"We can't break Deacon out of incarceration! We'll all get caught and join him in there." Cassie had been trying to talk her fellow spies out of the risky maneuver for the past week. After Deacon was abducted by the Militia, she became the new director of the DIU via a worldwide telepathic vote amongst the spies. The next candidate wasn't even close. She was beautiful, smart, and deadly—three of her most vital qualities, but not all of them by far. She was also a weapons expert, an electrical engineer, a master at hand-to-hand combat, a technology guru, and a long list of other things. She was a well-qualified leader, not the dimwitted secretary from the last reality. The fact that she hadn't been on a mission in a long time didn't matter. She was the perfect candidate, and a personal friend of the previous director.

"You know we could get in and out of there without detection. They won't even know he's gone." Gloria pleaded with Cassie for her executive help in the matter. Chuck backed Gloria's plan, but he was a little less adamant about it. However, Gloria felt extremely guilty for Deacon's incarceration. She had killed Phoebe, not him. If anything, she should be the one who was incarcerated. "I'll go by myself if need be. Just give me the mission, and I'll be gone today!" She didn't want to go without it being an official mission, because that would be considered going rogue. Deacon going rogue was what got them into this whole mess.

Cassie shook her head. "If anything goes wrong, you'll get caught. I can't lose you, Gloria; you know that. That would be a large blow to the agency to lose Deacon and you within a week of one another. I can't be responsible for that. Besides, what if you get there and he doesn't want to leave? I mean, you guys said he had been acting weird. Hell, what if he attacks you in there? You never know. That's why I can't authorize it."

"I'll go with her," Chuck said. "She doesn't have to do this by herself. I'm his best friend, and you know me. Fuck it, I'll defect for him. That's my brother. I'm in."

Cassandra couldn't believe it. "I'm damn sure not sending both of you guys to get caught and me be stuck here by myself with a community full of idiots depending on me! Fuck that!"

Gloria looked at her with all sincerity. "Come with us then. We could certainly use your skills in there, and I know you care as much about him as we do, if not more. Now, I know this isn't an easy decision to make, and if I was in your shoes I would be having a lot of difficulty with it too. But please don't let politics cloud your judgement on this. We're his friends, his *real* friends. He's innocent, and we're the only ones who know it. We have to do this ... for him. Don't make us go rogue."

Cassie leaned back in her seat and crossed her arms. She knew Gloria was right, but she still had a problem going along with it. She gave Gloria a questioning look, which was matched by an equally serious look from Gloria. Then Gloria raised an eyebrow, "If it was you in there, Deacon would've already sanctioned the mission, and we would be inside the mines by now."

"Okay, Gloria, you're very persuasive. I'll do it as long as we do it together—the right way. This is treading on unknown territory. We'd be breaking a *lot* of DIU codes. I mean, we put people in there, not the other way around. None of us have even been to the mines, so this is going to take some recon and surveillance. But yeah, I'm in."

Gloria and Chuck both cracked huge smiles on the victory.

"I can't make it a mission, because it goes against so many codes," Cassie continued. "And we can't do it anytime soon, because that'll draw too much attention to us. We'll just have to take our time planning this thing out and go rogue when the time comes."

III

Deacon woke up to a familiar feeling. He looked down to see that the sexy little nurse had mounted him and was enjoying his morning erection as much as he was. Her back was turned, so she didn't know he had woken up. Deacon watched as her nicely shaped ass clapped as it bounced up and down on his solid manhood. Apparently, he was one of those lucky guys to whom such stuff happened.

She got off, and then she got off, but when she turned to look at him, she noticed he was awake. So, she proceeded to give him a blowjob—lucky guy indeed. He did his business in her mouth, and she gratefully swallowed. Then she winked at him and exited the room. Not a word was exchanged between them.

Not long after he caught his breath, he noticed his legs weren't in casts and bandages anymore. They were in some sort of mechanical braces. So were his arms. At first, he thought the sex had numbed his pain, but in actuality, he just wasn't hurting anymore. He rolled over and sat up on the edge of his bed. Everything seemed to be functioning properly, and he felt no pain at all.

He stood up and moved around a little bit in the mechanical suit. *Not too agile, but at least I can move again.* He twisted and turned a few more times, and then a voice spoke to him over the intercom system. "So, I see you enjoy being able to move around again, huh? Working in my mines will make sure that feeling is short-lived. I figured I'd had enough fun with nearly killing you every day for a week. It's time to put you to work. I had Julia inject you with a numbing agent before installing the equipment on your legs and arms. It has certain side effects that she was able to take advantage of, but trust me, when it wears off, you will be in a world of hurt like you've never felt before.

Now meet me in my office, so I can issue your work area and living quarters. There's a guard outside your room who'll escort you here."

Deacon walked out of his room. When he saw the guard, he got excited. "Hey I know you! You're, uh ... my chauffeur!"

The guard looked at Deacon, slightly puzzled, and then responded with a thick Jersey accent. "Uh, the word is 'escort.' I am to *escort* you to her office. The word 'chauffeur' implies that there is some sort of vehicle involved. *Escort.*"

Deacon giggled. "I know, I'm talking about ... uh, never mind. Phil isn't it?"

The guard looked at him with an even more puzzled expression. "Yes, but how did you know that?"

Deacon smiled and patted him on the back. "Don't sweat the small stuff, Phil. I have this feeling we're going to be close friends."

Phil sighed. "Good, because most of the people in here are dicks. The inmates, the workers, the warden, even the other guards, they take their jobs way too seriously around here."

"Well, you won't have any problems out of me buddy," Deacon replied. "So, who won the game last night?"

Phil gave him another puzzled look, and Deacon responded with a look of surprise. "Football?" Phil's expression didn't change a bit. "You guys don't watch sports in here?"

Phil frowned. "What kind of numbing agent did she give you?"

Deacon laughed. "So, you guys don't have any competitive sports in this one, huh? Guess we're just going to have to do this ourselves, right, Phil?"

"Once again, I have no idea what you're talking about, but hell yeah, I'm with you," Phil said.

Deacon smiled. "Yeah, we're going to get along just fine, Phil."

"Now you say football, I guess that involves kicking a ball around, huh?"

Deacon shook his head. "No, that's soccer. Football is ... ."

IV

"What the hell is this?" Cassandra, being the new director of the DIU, was tasked with handling all the previous director's belongings. It didn't matter what the director had going on; the next person to touch his belongings would be the new director. Federation spies weren't allowed to have families or people who depended on them. That was a liability that the DIU couldn't afford. If they died on a mission, that would leave a broken family wondering what happened to their loved one and asking questions. It also made their family a target for any rebel spies or assassins who found out about them. That's why they made being without family a prerequisite for DIU operatives. They weren't as strict in the Militia.

Only a director had the authority to handle another director's belongings, so, as Cassie sat at Deacon's desk, rummaging through it, she found a list of names that all sounded vaguely familiar. The name at the top of the list was the one that stuck out to her. "Colonel Archibald Stockholm? Is this a hit list?" She continued to read the list and saw other familiar names. *Some of these are DIU agents. What is this indicating? Double agents? But how is that possible?*

Defection from the DIU was punishable by death or incarceration, depending upon the circumstances. The agents on the list had defected but had strong genetic telepathic abilities and were still on the run. That made them the most dangerous people on the planet. Once Cassie realized the gravity of the situation, she was angry that someone would turn on the prestigious agency. But then she became afraid—for her life and the lives of her friends. "These rogue spies are a disgrace to our agency, and now they could come after us, probably gunning for me! I've got to warn the others!"

With the hit list in her hands, she stood up with a sense of urgency. The implications were mind numbing and sent a chill up her spine—until she tried to turn around. That's when she realized the cold chill wasn't from the shock of her realization, but from a knife that had been shoved into her back. She turned slowly to face her murderer. "Why? What did I ever do to you?"

V

Phil led Deacon down a long corridor that had a window running almost the full length of it. Deacon tried to keep pace with Phil and still admire the glorious scene outside. *This place is built inside the mountain? This is an amazing view!*

Phil paused to allow Deacon to take it in. "Beautiful, isn't it?" he said with an equally inspired look.

"It's magnificent," Deacon replied.

"Enjoy it while you can. It's probably the last time you'll ever see sunlight."

They reached the end of the corridor and rode the elevator all the way to the top. Then they walked down another shorter corridor that had a large door at the end of it. It was solid steel with an eye scanner and a palm scanner for clearance. Phil consented to the scanners, and the large steel door slid out of the way. Then he stepped to the side and motioned for Deacon to proceed.

Once Deacon was inside the large office, the door slid closed. Janice's office was more like a small apartment. If she was constantly supplied with food, she could have lived in there indefinitely. He scrutinized the office from right to left. *Kitchen, bathroom, bedroom, living room, office, desk, Janice ... Janice!* "Good morning, ma'am."

Janice cut her eyes and sucked her teeth. "What's good about it? I've got a staff full of idiots, watery diarrhea, a pulsating migraine, and my only child's murderer standing in front of me. It's a horrible morning."

"Well, at least the view is immaculate," Deacon said.

She sucked her teeth again as she pulled a remote from her desk. "Hologram. Here, want to go to the beach?" She pressed a button, and the scenery changed. "Boom. Beach."

Deacon realized he wasn't going to get anywhere with her and decided to get down to business. "So, seeing how nice your spot is, where's my living space?"

She laughed. "Your space is a joke in comparison! You'll see." Then she stood up and walked around her desk. "You'll see lots of things. Most of them will shock and even terrify you, but you will grow accustomed to some of it. Dead bodies in the corner, the rancid stench of rotting carcasses and rat shit in the morning, the aches and pains of sixteen hours of hard labor every day, and the hunger of being fed just enough to work the next shift. I'm going to break you down for the rest of your life, and you will die a miserable, lonely, pathetic, inmate's death."

By the end of her tirade, she and Deacon were face to face. She had a menacing look about her, just waiting for a plea for mercy, but Deacon said nothing in response. He just stared into empty space like she wasn't even there. Even though he was innocent, there was no way of proving it, and Janice was so hellbent on his demise that it wouldn't have mattered anyway. She was going to make sure he rotted in there.

Janice backed out of Deacon's face and started pacing behind him. "I usually don't have people come up here for this, but I wanted to issue your duties personally. You, sir, are assigned to the catacombs. That's the hardest labor on this planet. It's where death goes to die. You understand?"

Deacon continued his blank stare as she continued. "Your living space is in the hole, a seven-mile trek from the catacombs, and the pit of disgust, as far as living is concerned."

Deacon lowered his head—not because he had just been sentenced to death but because he had begun to think of how he had gotten into this situation: Phoebe's death in his arms.

"I wanted to issue your sentence personally. Not just for the sheer pleasure of dealing the death card to my daughter's murderer, but also so I can see you before your decline. Five years from now, you will be a twig, a mere shadow of your former self. Ten years on that line is enough to kill anybody, but most give up and kill themselves within five."

She returned to her desk and giggled. "The workers and guards often bet rations on how long an inmate will last. I've got a year's worth on your death by seven years. Spies are resilient; you're not the first one to end up here, and I'm sure you won't be the last. Hell, we've got spies in there now who have been here for twenty years. That's the only reason why I give you so long. Otherwise, you wouldn't last a week. Now get out of my office. Phil is waiting outside to take you to your living space."

Deacon wasn't even paying any attention. He had been daydreaming about his life before the reality shifting began. His wonderful kids, his two jobs, his beautiful wife, his best friend; memories of his original reality consumed his thoughts to the point where anything else was irrelevant.

After a few seconds of him staring off into nothingness, Janice scoffed. "I said get out of my office, inmate!" Deacon snapped out of his trance and exited with haste.

Outside the office, Phil was waiting patiently for Deacon. The door slid open, and Deacon strode out of there with the look of a man on a mission. Phil noticed Deacon's countenance. "Normally, people come out of there shook up, but you seem to have come out of there with a newly found sense of self-worth. What's up?"

Deacon paused for a moment before responding. “I’m getting out of here, Phil. I know you must hear this all the time, but I am truly innocent. I’m not about to be stuck in here with her on my ass when I didn’t even do it.”

“Okay,” Phil replied, “but do you realize you just told a guard that you’re going to attempt to break out of his facility?”

VI

“What? Did you guys think you could just do whatever you wanted to do? Fuck that! He killed my cousin, and you killed my brother, and somebody’s got to pay!”

Drew Drake (Junebug) loomed over Cassandra’s bleeding body, wishing he had brought another weapon. The distraught leader of squad four felt like he had seen enough to convince him of the founding member’s betrayal and sought vengeance for the deaths in his family.

“I’m not the villain here,” he said. “I’m a victim! So, I’m not going to stand here and waste my time with a speech. I’m going straight to my squad and expose you all as frauds!”

After he received the transmission from Chuck that basically instructed he and his squad to abandon Archie, it set off alarms in his head. But, being an obedient officer, he stood down and followed orders. When they found the massacre in the tower, he saw that his cousin was amongst the dead, and his brother was in bad condition. He helped his brother and another ailing rebel back home. On the way back to camp, they confessed as to who had attacked them, and Drew was even further confused.

When they got back, and Cassandra called the meeting, the plot thickened. He was the first to be interviewed, so when he was done, he went across the street, sat under a tree, and waited for his brother to give his account of the story. One by one, they exited the mess hall by rank until both squads were accounted for. Apparently, she had saved them for last. That's when he started to fear for his life, but he waited diligently for his brother.

Eventually, he fell asleep under the tree—he was tired, and it was late. When he woke up, he saw Cassie exiting the mess hall alone. So, he went home, expecting to see his brother there, but he wasn't. *James! What did she do?* After a week of him not showing up with nothing being said, and people getting sick from the meat, Drew started to piece the puzzle together. When he heard that the other injured soldier never returned home from his meeting either, that's all he needed to connect the dots and figure out that the founding members weren't who the rebels thought they were.

"I'm actually impressed at how long you guys have put up this little front, but the jig is up. Your legacy ends here, today!" Then he headed out the door just as quietly as he had entered it, leaving Cassie to die with the knife still stuck in her back.

VII

After going back down a different, biometrically secured elevator and another long corridor, Phil and Deacon reached an expanse that had been cut out of the middle of the mountain. *You could probably fit three football fields in here easily!*

Phil looked back at Deacon. "This is called the fork. All tunnels start and end here, so if you ever get lost, just get back to the main tunnel, keep straight, and you'll end up here. The tunnels are all labeled with signs, so getting back here is a cinch. The large tunnel over there heads downhill to the living quarters. Unfortunately, yours is all the way in the back—in the hole."

As they headed toward the tunnel, Phil continued. "It's fucking foul down there. The good thing is, you won't have many neighbors. Most people who get sentenced to that place usually die within a year or so."

Deacon cut his eyes at Phil. "Thanks for the encouragement."

"No, don't take that the wrong way or anything. I'm pulling for you," Phil said. "Who do you think everybody is betting? I run the house, buddy. If you last even a day longer than seven years, I'll have enough rations for a lifetime."

Deacon raised his eyebrows in surprise. "Oh, really now? What are my odds?"

Phil shrugged. "I don't know; nobody has ever lasted that long."

Deacon shook his head in disappointment. *Good thing there's no Vegas here.* "Well, I'll tell you what: I'll stay alive, no problem, but I'm pretty sure I'll find a way out of here by then."

Phil giggled. "That's not the first time I've heard that. Dude, there is no way out of here. You are literally inside a mountain. The only way out is the way you came in. It's biometric too. You'll need a guard or Janice to escort you out. *Escort*, there's that word again."

They laughed and continued down the long tunnel. Once they got a good distance, it got dark, the only illumination came from motion-sensing lights that came on while there was motion in their field of view. If Deacon and Phil stood still for more than a few seconds, they were in complete darkness.

"This tunnel actually has a slight curve to it and spirals downward; it's just so miniscule that you can't really see it," Phil said. "That's why light from the fork doesn't reach that far down here. By the time we get to where you're going, the fork will be a little over a quarter mile above your head."

Deacon nodded in comprehension. *Interesting bit of information there.*

"There are two community showers down here and four community toilets. The closest to you is a mile away."

Deacon sighed. "So, by the time I get back home from taking a shower, I'll need another one. Great."

Phil laughed. "Well, if you need to use the toilet, we're about to come up on one now."

Deacon looked ahead and spotted a faint glow in the distance.

"Looks like one of the janitors is making it nice and fresh for you right now," Phil said.

Deacon walked into the bathroom and saw the gray-haired janitor with his back turned, diligently cleaning the sinks. "Don't stink it up too bad in here," the old man said. "I still got a ways to go."

Deacon paused on his way into the stall. *Don't I know that voice?* After urinating, he flushed the toilet and walked up to the sinks to wash his hands. He tried to steal a glimpse of the janitor's face, but he was turned just slightly out of Deacon's view, until he turned to say, "Come down here. I've already cleaned that one."

"Chalmers!" Deacon exclaimed. "You're the last person I thought I would see down here!"

Chalmers Marr looked youthful and spry compared to the Chalmers from Deacon's original reality. Health care was free here, so people were able to live full and healthy lives, and people like Chalmers could get the medical attention they needed without any hassle.

The peppy old man stepped back and scratched his gray head. "Forgive me, but I don't remember you. I'm getting old, and I haven't been telepathic for so long that now my brain itches."

Deacon cackled. "My name is Deacon Russell, sir. I wouldn't expect you to know who I am, but I'll put it like this: you have my utmost respect and won't have a problem from me. You should come by my place sometime and chew the fat."

Chalmers took another step back. "I haven't heard that expression in ages. I might just take you up on your offer sometime. Where are you sentenced to?"

Deacon bowed his head. "The hole."

Chalmers giggled. “The old bitch up there must not like you very much, huh? What did you do to get put down there?”

This was where the conversation got tricky for Deacon. So, apparently, Janice had slept with Chalmers at some point and had a child: Phoebe. For some reason, they never got married, seeing that Janice had maintained her maiden name. Even so, Chalmers had to watch his daughter being raised by that monster while he was stuck down there cleaning bathrooms. It appeared Chalmers had endured a great injustice for many years, and even though he seemed chipper, the fact remained, he was Phoebe’s father, and Deacon had been incarcerated for her murder, innocent or not. Chalmers might not even have known his daughter was dead, so Deacon had to be careful with what he said. “Uh, I’m in here for murder, but I’m innocent ... seriously.”

Chalmers grinned. “Yeah, I am too—seriously. But hell, you can ask any inmate in here, and they’ll tell you the same thing. I’ve dealt with a lot of people in here throughout the years, and without telepathy, you learn how to discern people’s character with natural wit. You, my friend, are sincere, and I believe you’re innocent. All I can say is stay tough and stick it through. I’m not going to sugarcoat it though; you’re never getting out of here.”

Just then, Phil burst in the bathroom. “Hey, when I said use the bathroom, I didn’t mean jerk off. Oh, what’s up, Chalmers? I see you’ve met Deacon.”

Chalmers smiled. “Yeah, he seems like a straightforward guy. Don’t think we’ll be having any problems out of this one.”

VIII

Cassie had bled out so much that it had formed a red pool around her. She didn't realize it until it tickled her cheek. Death was inevitable, and she was disappointed, yet death wasn't the cause of her disappointment. She was dying and couldn't signal for anybody. Even if she could, they wouldn't have enough time to make it to her before she died. A telepathic message was too risky. It also took a lot of energy to send a telepathic message, energy that she didn't have. Yet she felt obligated to message someone, giving her new prominent role within the DIU's ranks.

As she lay there dying and debating about she should signal for somebody, Chuck strolled into the room and saw her on the floor. He had been on his way to Deacon's room to gather some memorabilia. He had just lost his best friend to the system, and he wanted to make sure a few pictures and sentimental items didn't get lost with him. The dying body of another friend was the last thing he thought he would see.

"Cassie! Fuck, man, can't I get a break?" He knelt beside her and checked for a pulse. *She's still alive!* "Cassie! Wake up, baby. Who did this? Just give me an image."

Cassie opened her eyes, gurgled, and coughed up a puddle of blood that oozed down her cheek. "Listen, there's not much time," she said as Chuck cradled her in his arms. "You two have to get out of here. Our cover is blown. They know who we are and are gathering together right now to come and kill you two." Chuck could no longer hold back the tears as she continued. "Read my mind, Chuck. There's important information in there."

Everything came to Chuck in flashes. First was a third-person view of her watching a video off a squad leader's helmet cam and seeing him fleeing with Deacon, Gloria, and Phoebe. Then the scene shifted to her murdering the two soldiers in the mess hall and grinding up their bodies.

Then she was looking at a list of names in the first-person point of view. Some of them were well-known DIU operatives who had come up missing over the past few years. The others were infamous rebel leaders who had become a thorn in the Federation's side. Then, still in the first-person, she spun around to look her killer in his eyes. Then everything went black. Cassie died in Chuck's arms as he was reading her mind.

He pulled the knife out of her spine, picked up her body, and laid it on the bed. Then he covered her with a blanket. The list was soaked in blood on the floor, and the killer was long gone and probably ratting them out, but Chuck had extracted enough information from Cassie's memories to grasp the gravity of the situation. They were in immediate danger and had to flee. The rebels had found them out, and there was a hit list full of DIU agents and rebel leaders who were probably hunting them down right now. *Shit, I've got to get Gloria and dip the fuck out—but not before we pay Mr. Squad Leader a little visit.* He rushed out of the room on his way to get Gloria and avenge Cassie's death.

IX

The fork of the mountain was spacious with numerous tunnels ranging anywhere from fifty to eighty feet in diameter. Some had tracks for carts, and others didn't, but all were the product of labor provided by inmates and workers for over seventy years. Workers could come and go as they pleased. They checked in at the gate and were escorted by a guard down the elevator. Not many people chose to work there, so the guard could usually get them all down the freight elevator in one trip.

Incarceration wasn't like jail or prison—well, in a way it was, considering inmates couldn't go anywhere else. However, incarceration was more like indefinite servitude to the Federation. Workers chose to be there; inmates had no choice. Workers lived in a house away from the mountain and had to travel for miles every day to get there, which took a level of dedication that few could comprehend. Inmates lived inside the mountain but had to walk miles to reach their living and working spaces, which also took a certain level of dedication to keep from committing suicide.

The fork also served as a social hub where everybody ran into everybody on their way to and from work or home. Not much mingling went on in the mountain, but if any happened, it happened there. Deacon and Phil crouched in the middle of it trying to recover from their long hike.

After walking all the way down to Deacon's living space (which was simply a cot with a locker enclosed in a ten-foot cube) and all the way back up the long, spiral hill, they were exhausted. All living spaces were grouped together down skinny tunnels that branched off the large corridor. Deacon's was the last space, on the last branch, at the end of the corridor. He had no neighbors for almost a mile, and it was so quiet he could hear the rats scurrying around in the dark. Phil would only have to endure the extensive hike once. Deacon had to walk it daily, indefinitely. By then, the numbing agents and pain meds had started to wear off, and every inch of his body was in pain. The metal contraption he was fixed inside of was supposed to aid his movement, but it seemed to be weighing him down.

Once they caught their breath, it was another four-mile hike uphill to Deacon's work area. "Let's get going," Phil said. "We aren't getting any younger sitting here. It's through that tunnel; follow me."

As they began their ascent, the first thing Deacon noticed was the lighting. The tunnel was illuminated continuously by floodlights; no motion sensors involved. Phil explained that there was always a shift of laborers in the tunnels, so the lights were always on.

He also explained how the cart system worked. The automated carts exited the tunnel and headed to the smelting area, which was in a different section of the mountain. Once the cart left the tunnel, another one was sent back in to the miner. It was an intricate dance that the carts played with one another, allowing the miners to continue working instead of pushing carts all over the place and wasting time.

They were winded again about a mile up the hill, and they still had three miles to go. They stopped to take another breather and sat down on the side of the tunnel. "Man, I'm sure glad I don't have to make this trip anymore," Phil said. "I'm starting to feel really sympathetic for you right now."

Deacon took a deep breath and looked up, about to respond, until he saw another familiar face. *Junior?*

X

Chuck rushed into his home, grabbed his field bag and a few provisions, and then ran back out the door. He and Gloria resided in the same building, so that made bugging out that much easier. He ran into her place, packing her things as he explained the situation. "Cassie is dead, murdered by a disgruntled soldier, and our cover is blown. The word is out, and we have only precious moments to leave before the entire community is on our heels."

Gloria was sold with the first statement and helped him pack.

"I got there just in time to read her mind," Chuck continued, "and there's a lot I have to tell you. But not now; we don't have time. I'll tell you once we leave. But first, there's someone that we have to see on our way out."

Gloria looked up. "Man, I hope it's that disgruntled soldier motherfucker."

As they went out the door, they heard a ruckus forming outside the front of the building, so they went out the back. They snuck around behind a few more buildings until they reached the last one on the row. Then they turned the corner, so they were able to witness the uprising undetected. It seemed like the entire community had been notified and was out to take part in their torture. At the front of the crowd was the face that Chuck had seen in Cassie's memory of her murder.

"There he is. You might want to get your binoculars for this one." Chuck took out his longbow and a yellow arrow as Gloria grabbed the binoculars from her bag. The yellow arrow was designed for speed and power; Chuck handled the accuracy part. He drew the arrow, took aim, then let it fly. As Drew stood on their front porch, preaching to the crowd, the arrow speared him right between the eyes and stuck into the building's front door. The arrow was so deep into the wood that it hung Drew's dead body upright with his feet dangling off the ground. All the chanting and rioting ceased, transforming into screams of horror.

"Okay, let's go." Chuck said as he and Gloria grabbed their bags and weapons and headed out. "What did you bring to eat?"

"A couple of rations and some leftover burgers," Gloria said. "Why, you hungry already?"

"Nah, not yet. Toss the burgers though. I'll explain that on the way."

XI

Phil and Deacon finally made it up the long hill, and Deacon got introduced to his mechanical chisel. The entire time Phil had been explaining how to use it, Deacon was only partially listening. He couldn't believe the mess he had gotten himself into this time. He had gone from being the wealthiest man on the planet to a lowly inmate. He knew he could kill everybody in there if he had to, but that would do him no good if he was still trapped in the mine.

Another thing was bothering him: he had just seen Junior. When he approached him, of course, Junior didn't recognize Deacon, and his name wasn't Junior, but Deacon knew it was his son when he saw him. It was *his* son!

The boy went by the name Chandler and was eighteen years old, so, apparently, Phoebe did know the Deacon from this reality, but somehow the memory was gone. She didn't remember him, and his immediate assumption was Janice had something to do with it. *She had to! Phoebe wouldn't knowingly banish her child or give up a chance of having a family; that's all she ever wanted out of life.* He knew that, because the same mentality had rubbed off on him before he found himself in this reality shifting situation. Now, he just wanted his family back, but in every reality that he visited, it was impossible. *Why can't I ever go to one that's normal?*

"Hey, have you been listening?" Phil snapped his fingers in front of Deacon's eyes. "Wake up. Fuck it. You'll be doing this the rest of your life. You'll get the hang of it eventually. Once your sixteen hours are done, your machine will automatically shut down for recharging, and you can go home, but you have to be here tomorrow to pull another sixteen. If you don't have them done within the twenty-four-hour timeframe, she'll send a few guards to physically persuade you to make it to your station. Hopefully, I won't have to be one of those guards."

Deacon grinned. *Yeah, for your sake I hope you're not one of those poor bastards either.*

Phil yawned. "Well you know what you've got to do. Get to work. I think I'll take one of these carts back downhill. See you around ... uh, Deacon, right?"

"Yep. See you around, Phil."

Chapter 19

I

"So, you know if we do this, it means we will be going up against a former DIU director, inside a fortified mountain, that's filled with guards, and it's only two of us, right?"

After nearly seven years of being on the run, nothing could intimidate Gloria anymore. She and Chuck had been hunted and chased by DIU agents for the past few years and have had to forage and fend for themselves like defectors out of fear of being found. They'd had shootouts where innocent bystanders were killed, been captured and had to fight their way out, and they were being chased at that very moment. The DIU were chasing them because they held vital information about their organization, and the rebels were chasing them for taking out a leader. They seemed to be on everyone's hit list, and seven years of being chased by agents and rebels was enough for Gloria. She was ready to get Deacon out of there. For her, it was now or never. She cocked her eyebrow and looked at Chuck. "It'll only be two of us until we reach him ... then it'll be three."

They stood on the top of a mountain, between two large solar satellite dishes, observing their target through Gloria's binoculars. The mountain they were standing on ran parallel to the mountain that the Federation was mining. It used to be the mountain that was mined until all its resources had been exhausted. The mountain still stood strong; even though it had been virtually hollowed out, most of its tunnels and shafts were still intact and traversable.

Inside the mine was a large tunnel that was used to transport tools and equipment from the old mine to the new one. It followed a large mineral vein that led under the valley. Seventy years later, they had carved out an intricate system of tunnels in the other mountain, and the annex tunnel had been blocked off and forgotten. The new mountain now housed an entirely new generation of inmates and guards who were oblivious to the annex tunnel. The warden didn't even know about it.

The plan was for Gloria and Chuck to find the lost tunnel and make it to the other mountain undetected. From there, they could blend in with the regular workers until they found Deacon and could utilize the annex tunnel for their escape. Infiltrating the mountain would be a cinch, but finding Deacon would prove to be a task, since his telepathy was blocked. There are tens of thousands of inmates and employees, it could take a few days or a few months; that is if he is still alive to begin with. They could be there for a while.

Regardless of the circumstances, Gloria was going to get Deacon out of there no matter what. *He has been in there long enough.* She put her binoculars back into her field bag and tied it up. "You ready to get dirty?"

Chuck shrugged. "Hell, at least in there I'll be able to take a shower."

II

After working diligently on his escape plan for nearly seven years, Deacon was ready to get the hell out of there. He had met a lot of interesting people, formed new bonds with new friends and close relationships with some females. The thing that he was most proud of though was being able to indirectly raise his son, whether the boy knew he was Deacon's son or not. Deacon had watched Chandler grow into a respectable young adult and was proud of him. The only thing he was disappointed about was the fact that he was leaving before Phil would be able to cash in on his seven-year anniversary. *I told him I wasn't going to be here that long.*

Deacon had devised a scheme to escape as soon as he arrived. He learned the guards' rotation and had chosen the perfect candidate for his plan. The way he figured it, if he was to take the regular way out, they would see him coming from far enough away to alert other personnel, and they would be authorized to kill. Plus, it was a three-mile hike uphill.

But since the fork was about a quarter mile above head, all he had to do was dig upward at a slight pitch, and he would have his escape passage. It only took a few years to excavate with his personal miner's tools, but it took a few more years to master the climb. His plan for the biometric scanners was simple: one of these unlucky guards was going to have to sacrifice a hand and an eye for his escape. Most of the guards were cool except for one asshole who enjoyed abusing her power: the perfect candidate for Deacon's plan.

He knew he wouldn't be able to waltz out of there without a fight, but fighting was right up his alley. He had been beating on the guards the entire time he had been in there, and those guards were no match for him. If he didn't feel like working, Janice would send a pack of guards to try to "motivate" him. It always backfired though. She would end up sending half of her squad to get beat up before having to allow Deacon the day off. She couldn't afford to lose too many guards on him. It could lead to an uprising that she wouldn't be able to handle with just a fraction of her security. She also couldn't authorize a kill for such a minor infraction without ending up incarcerated herself, so he would beat the hell out of the guards, take a day off, and then return to work the next day like nothing had happened. Fighting the guards during his escape was the least of his worries.

His only problem was the fact that he was unfamiliar with the territory outside the mines. If he escaped, he wouldn't have a clue where to go. A few years earlier, Chandler had given Deacon directions to his home, but they were joking around during that conversation. There was no way to know if he was telling the truth or just going along with it. *Only one way to find out ... .*

Being stuck inside a mountain for any length of time without a day to night reference had certain effects on people. Most inmates trained their body to a certain time and went about their lives pulling third-shift hours and not even knowing it. Deacon's case was a little different. If he was going to escape, he wanted to do it during the night, under the cover of darkness, so he would be difficult to spot.

To remedy this, Deacon judged the hour by when Chandler came in. Chandler said he worked on the first shift, so he could get home and have the rest of the day to himself. That being the case, Deacon trained his body for a third-shift routine, spending time with his son and working on the escape tunnel in the morning, sleeping during the second shift, and working on the third shift. He wanted to be wide awake and alert when it came time to escape.

Every year that Deacon remained alive, Phil got a huge payout of rations from betting on his life, which he gladly split with Deacon for not killing himself or getting himself killed. Those extra rations provided the extra fuel that Deacon needed to fight with the guards, pull sixteen hours of hard labor, and dig a quarter-mile vertical shaft. With all the climbing practice, fighting guards, and heavy machinery operation, Deacon was fitter and more powerful than he was at the beginning of the reality shift. His seven-year anniversary was coming up in a few days, and he was fully prepared to break camp.

III

The layout of the mines inside the two parallel mountains mimicked one another in terms of where the offices and elevators were, but the shafts were different, considering they followed the mineral veins.

Chuck and Gloria entered the mountain through an air vent that led to the warden's office. The place was dark and smelled like centuries of sweat and piss. They took out their flashlights and then followed the long corridor down to the freight elevator, which was inoperable. Unfortunately, they had to climb down the long elevator shaft, hoping the two-ton freight elevator didn't decide to fall during their descent.

Once they reached the bottom, they were stuck at a crossroads. They stood at the center of what would be the equivalent of the fork in the other mountain. They were flummoxed; the layout was so vast and complex that they couldn't decide which way to go.

After much debate, they decided to go down the least decrepit tunnel in the hope that it was the newest. That would indicate that it was the last one dug and the one that headed to the other mountain, but they were wrong. All the tunnel did was lead out of an older-looking one, and they realized they had just walked in a large arc. However, Gloria noticed something upon exiting: a small sign that was covered with so much dust that it had been camouflaged with the surrounding rock.

She walked over to it as Chuck cussed about the time wasted on their hike. "What are you doing?" he asked as she wiped off the sign.

"Figuring out which way to go."

Chuck leaned in closer and read the sign. "MT6-I? What do you figure that means?"

Gloria took a step back and thought about it. They had seen only one other sign. It was above the large freight elevator and read "FE2." *Okay, so if that meant freight elevator two, then this must be some sort of acronym also. I wonder if… .*

She rushed back over to the tunnel they had started in, three tunnels down. Chuck followed her like a lost puppy. She found another sign, cleaned it, and confirmed her theory. "These were mining tunnels, and that one is the sixth entry." Chuck finally caught up to her as she continued her explanation. "That sign read MT6-I, mining tunnel six, in. This one here reads MT6-O—"

"Mining tunnel six, out," Chuck said, finishing her sentence. "So, I guess now we've got to find one that doesn't have 'MT' in front of it."

"Precisely," Gloria said. "Let's split up. I'll go this way, and we'll meet in the middle. Yell if you find something."

They went their opposite ways, splitting the task of finding the proper tunnel. One by one, they wiped off signs, only to feel the sting of disappointment before they continued their search. The problem was, the tunnels weren't placed in succession; they were numbered in the order they were dug, which meant the second tunnel was *across* from the first, not beside it. And the tunnels twisted and curved in all directions following the veins, so, the end of the tunnel wasn't next to the beginning of it either. There was no way of telling which tunnel was right unless they checked each individual sign, and there were twenty-two mining tunnels in total, meaning forty-four including the exit tunnels. However, three tunnels weren't included in those forty-four: the inmate's tunnel, the tunnel that led to the smelting area, and the annex tunnel, which happened to be the one that they were looking for.

"Hey, I found something!" Chuck yelled to Gloria, and she came running. The sign he found was on the wall of a large tunnel and read "IT." "I guess this is *it* ... get it?"

He giggled as she shook her head and responded. "Yeah, I get it. But it's the inmate's tunnel, clown. Still, the size of this tunnel just gave me an idea. Wouldn't you think that an annex tunnel would be larger than the rest?" Chuck scratched his head as she continued. "I mean, they would have to transport all their equipment through this tunnel, and I'm pretty sure they've got some big shit. The tunnel over there is the biggest one in here. Let's go check it real quick; it may save us some time."

The duo ran to check the large tunnel, and to their luck, the sign read "Annex Tunnel."

"Sweet!" Chuck exclaimed

Gloria and Chuck started down the long, dark, smelly tunnel with a reinvigorated hope of retrieving their lost comrade. Every few yards, a motion light came on to light their way. Apparently, the solar receivers were still working. They tucked their flashlights away and headed down the long tunnel.

About halfway down the tunnel, Gloria dropped to her knees with a searing pain coursing through her brain. Her body folded to the ground as it started to spasm, and she screamed at the top of her lungs

Chuck reached in his bag for a bottle of painkillers. "What's the matter?" he asked.

"I don't know. I think it's ... Deacon!"

IV

Deacon lay in his living space, crying his heart out, basically, having an anxiety attack. He was planning to leave in a few days, but he didn't want to be on the run for the rest of his life. *What if I can't shift anymore? I don't want to be a fugitive, but I also don't want to live a life of servitude for a crime that I didn't commit. I want my life back! I miss my wife and kids!* Deacon rolled around on his cot in pain, unable to get comfortable and trying to deal with his emotions. He still loved Phoebe and his children from his original reality, but they weren't the wife and kids he was referring to. *Gloria! If you can hear me, say something, please!*

Deacon had a massive headache, and his body was seizing so much it was causing cramps all over. He could feel something going on, like his brain had a conflict of interest with itself. Something was happening to him; he was changing, and he could feel it. It was like when he would catch the flu. He could feel when it was coming and could tell he was getting sick. Right now, he knew something was going on and could feel his connection with Gloria getting stronger. *I know you can hear me. Say something. Please, say something!*

Deacon! How? Gloria finally replied. She was happy to hear from him yet confounded as to how he had managed to send her a telepathic message.

I don't know, he said. *Where are you? I can sense you're somewhere near me.*

Yes, I am—I mean, we are. Chuck is with me. We're in a secret tunnel that leads to the mountain that you're being held captive in. Sorry it took so long, but we're coming to get you, Deacon.

Deacon sat up in his cot, filled with joy. The pain and convulsions stopped, and suddenly, he felt as strong as a rhino. To hear her voice, even telepathically, was rejuvenating, and he was ready for anything. For him to know they were coming to get him and were practically close enough to knock on his door gave him a boost in confidence and worked wonders for his morale. He stood up and danced a jig in celebration, jumping, stomping, and laughing. Then there was a rumble.

At first Deacon thought the rumble was him, until the light in his room went out. He looked around in the dark for a moment, and then his light turned back on. *What the fuck was that?* Then it happened again, this time longer and louder. The mountain was experiencing a major cave-in, and multiple tunnels were collapsing.

Oh shit! Gloria, are you still there?

After a few moments of silence, panic settled in.

V

Chuck opened his eyes and removed the few rocks that had fallen onto him during the cave in. When Gloria told him that she was speaking to Deacon telepathically, he was staggered. He tried to locate Deacon and send him a message but failed. For some reason, Deacon was only able to link telepathically with her. She told Deacon that they were on their way to get him, and Deacon had given her the schematics of the entire mountain, including a tunnel that he had dug himself and the layout for a foolproof escape plan. They were impressed with his plan but were sure he would abandon it once he learned of the annex tunnel.

Once her pain subsided and she was able to stand up, Gloria embraced Chuck in jubilation. She was so ecstatic about Deacon contacting her that she could barely stand it. As they hugged, Chuck noticed a popping noise. As they continued talking to Deacon, Chuck realized an electrical transformer seemed to be malfunctioning.

He wasn't an electrician; that was Cassandra's forte, so, he tinkered with it for a few minutes as Gloria and Deacon conversed, trying to find the kill switch. None of the switches seemed to change the faulty transformer's condition, so he decided to keep moving. That was all they could do anyway.

Gloria was unaware of the situation but followed Chuck as he backed away from the transformer, then continued down the annex into the next motion light's field of view. When the light came on, it set off the transformer, and it exploded behind them, blowing a huge hole in the wall.

Gloria's link with Deacon was severed due to her concentrating on the matter at hand. She and Chuck ran for their lives as the tunnel collapsed behind them. They looked like two Olympic gold medalists competing in the hurdles, but instead of hurdles, they were leaping over stones. No matter how fast they went, they couldn't outrun the destruction, and soon they were overwhelmed by the boulders that were following close behind them.

Chuck cleaned himself off, put on his flashlight (which could also strap to his head), and looked for Gloria. When he finally found her, she was covered with big stones. The only way he spotted her was a small patch of her hair sticking out from between the rocks that covered her head. He limped over to the pile of rocks and observed her situation. Much to his surprise, the stones had landed in such a way that not many of them landed on her; they had landed on themselves, forming a pyramidal structure, so she was trapped in a makeshift tomb but largely uninjured.

So, there she was, buried alive again, and having to be excavated again. Chuck rolled away the big stones and hurled the small ones, slowly uncovering his partner in espionage. Once she was clear of rocks and debris, he noticed she was still breathing. *Okay, so no need to check her pulse. How long is she going to be out though? I might have to carry her the rest of the way ... .*

He stood up and inspected his situation. The transformer had caused a massive cave-in, and their exit passage was now barricaded by boulders. *Now I'm wondering what HIS escape plan is!* There was still a good bit to hike, with a hurt leg, and while carrying his partner. *Well, this tunnel isn't going to hike itself.* So, he stretched and got ready for the long, arduous journey ahead.

He looked down at Gloria to see where the best place would be to lift her dead weight. *She's top heavy AND bottom heavy!* He reached down and hooked her under her knees with one arm and underneath her shoulder blades with the other, then lifted her up. As he did, one of Gloria's perfectly round breasts popped playfully out of her shirt. Of course,

Chuck noticed. He had wanted it to happen so badly that when it did, he felt guilty, not because he was getting an unconscious flash, but because it was almost as if he had willed it to happen.

He stared at the voluptuous tit and started to salivate. He had never looked at her in that way or even thought of her like that. He knew she was sexy, but he had never been in such a situation with her. He pondered putting her back down and zipping it up, but that would mean he would have to dead lift her weight again. He had much trouble with this decision while staring at her perfect boob, by which time the coin-sized nipple had hardened.

"My eyes are up here ... ."

"Gloria!" he exclaimed. "You're awake! Are you okay?"

She giggled. "I should ask you the same thing from the way you were drooling all over my tit! But I guess I can't blame you. I personally know you haven't had any for at least seven years."

Chuck, who was still staring at her boob, acknowledged her shot at his inadvertent abstinence. "Very funny. Why don't you pull the other one out and make my decade?"

He put her down, and they laughed as she fixed her breasts, found her flashlight, and strapped it to her head. She looked around as Chuck gave her a status update. "Our escape route is blocked. The only way out is through the other mine, so let's hope Deacon's plan can accommodate three. Oh yeah, why don't you try to contact him?"

Gloria closed her eyes and concentrated.

VI

The mountain that Deacon mined suffered significant damage during the cave-in. Many people died, inmates and guards alike, as multiple tunnels suddenly collapsed due to an explosion that rocked the fault line and caused a small quake. The only thing that Deacon was concerned about was if the freight elevator was still functional. *Hell, if I can get the doors open, I can get out of here, and right now seems like the perfect time to make my escape while the authorities are in disarray. Gloria, where are you?* He had called out to her repeatedly for a while but had been unsuccessful, so he didn't really expect her to answer him this time either, but she did.

We got stuck in a tunnel. Our escape route is compromised. You got room in your escape plan for two more?

Gloria! I see you're not too far from me. Hell, I think you might be ... yeah, you're right on the other side of this wall! The annex tunnel led right up to Deacon's back porch, figuratively speaking. Once the annex tunnel had reached its destination, the first thing they started with was living quarters for the inmates, and then they worked their way upward. Once the base of operations had been relocated, they sealed off the tunnel and built living quarters in front of it. Not many people had even been back there through the years unless sentenced to the area. Nobody wanted to live all the way back there, which meant traveling an extra mile to work and an extra mile to home each day. Deacon didn't mind it though; he liked the quietness and seclusion, plus the extra steps helped keep him fit.

I can't tell how thick this wall is though; besides, how do you guys plan on getting through this rock?

We have a laser and a couple of small charges. Enough to get us to you, but not enough to get us out of here. We have to use your plan.

By that time Deacon was so antsy that he had the jitters. *That's fine. Just hurry and get here. Our window of opportunity is closing.*

VII

Chuck and Gloria reached the barricade, and Gloria sensed Deacon on the other side. "Let's hurry and get this done," she said. "Apparently, our little incident with the transformer caused collapses in more tunnels than this one and, long story short, they're a bit understaffed right now."

Chuck took out a fancy device that scanned the rocks and displayed the depth of the wall and its weak points. Once they found a spot that was strong enough to support a hole, they broke out the laser, set a depth, and started cutting. The laser made short work of the stone. It resembled a plasma cutter blasting through thick sheet metal. Deacon stood on the other side of the wall and watched as the hole formed right beside his cot. He was so excited about seeing Gloria and his best friend that he could barely contain his anticipation. He was also ready to break out of incarceration, so his excitement level had peaked.

As the laser cut through the rock, it vitrified into glass that collected at the bottom of the hole and fell off in large globs. Once the hole was done, they pushed the cut-out rock into Deacon's living space and peered through. "Hey, Deacon, I've missed you so much!"

Deacon couldn't contain his elation. His smile was ear to ear, and he was jumping for joy. "Well, get in here and show me some love. Where's my homie? Chuck, poke your head through the hole."

Chuck looked through with a big smile. "That's what *she* said."

The two crawled through the hole and hugged Deacon. It had been so long since the trio had been together that they had almost forgotten the situation they were in. Yet, to their displeasure, Gloria had to remind them of the journey ahead. "We're only halfway through this thing, fellas. Let's pull it together and get it done. We can celebrate outside."

Deacon detailed his escape plan, and they all seemed confident. "The only thing I'm not sure of is if the freight elevator was damaged in the collapse. If it was, we might have to improvise."

Chuck and Gloria looked at each other. "Dude," Chuck said, "we have enough equipment here to cut our way through the freight elevator and climb up if need be."

Deacon smiled. "Let's get started then! Given our current situation, we could take either route: a three-mile uphill hike or a quarter-mile diagonal climb. The climb is much faster."

Following a unanimous decision, they scaled the tunnel above and made it to the top. Deacon had a large rock set in place that followed the landscape on the other side, undetectable by the naked eye. "Once I push this rock out, there's no turning back. We have to mangle the guard within seconds of breaching the tunnel. She can't be allowed to signal the other guards telepathically. I'll take her out, since I'll be the first one out of the tunnel, but if anything goes wrong, one of you will have to have my back." The others nodded in agreement. "Next is a long corridor to go down before we reach the freight elevator," Deacon continued. "It's usually empty, but I'm pretty sure she has a guard or two in there in light of the current situation. We'll have to take them out, but I can almost guarantee they will be able to call out before we're able to kill them, so we'll have to make it to the elevator before the back-ups do. There aren't many guards up there, so it should be a cinch."

Chuck gave a rundown of the plan, just to make sure he had everything straight. "So, you take out the first guard, then we sneak over to the corridor and take out the other guards in there. Use the elevator to get to the top and take out a few guards up there, and then we're home free. Correct?"

Deacon nodded. "Let's do it!"

He shoved the rock out of the way and ran full speed at Ruth, the guard he had preselected to be his first sacrifice. He wasn't sure there would be other guards in the corridor to use, so he stuck with his original plan. During his seven-year stretch, he had become acquainted with several interesting inmates, one of them being a smelter who he got to construct his weapon for escape. It was a crescent-shaped blade with a handle that protruded about an eighth of the way up its spine. When he gripped it, the blade ran the length of his forearm and had sharp points at the fist and elbow. It was a multifunctional weapon that Deacon had plenty of practice with during his incarceration.

Ruth heard footsteps behind her, but by the time she turned around, it was too late. Deacon sliced her head off with one swift swipe of his forearm. Then, in one fluid motion, he swiveled the weapon around and sliced her hand off on the down stroke. It happened so fast that her body didn't have time enough to start falling before her hand was cut off. He caught her severed hand with his free hand and kicked her head back to Gloria, who was next to come out of the tunnel. She caught the decapitated head as Deacon told her to retrieve the eyes from it.

Gloria dug out the woman's eyes, no questions asked, then helped Chuck out of the tunnel. They gathered at the well-hid corner that Ruth guarded and surveyed the area. The corridor was roughly fifty yards away, but amid the current chaos, it seemed as if they could make it there undetected.

They took off across the fork. Once they got there, they took cover behind the entryway. Deacon poked his head around the corner and saw three guards, two of them close enough to reach before they could signal the others. The last one was guarding the elevator at the end of the hall. Deacon faced Chuck. "I got this."

Deacon and Gloria rushed into the corridor, weapons drawn. The two soldiers didn't know what hit them, and their attackers were so fast and fluid that there wasn't much they could have done anyway. Gloria dove in with her wakizashi and stabbed her target through the neck. It pierced all the way down to his heart, killing him instantly. Deacon simply punched his target in the head with the sharp end of his weapon. The last guard down at the elevator was the one Chuck said he would handle, which he did.

He rolled out from behind the wall with his longbow drawn. He had one yellow arrow saved for a moment like this. The arrow zipped down the corridor with sonic swiftness and found its mark on the guard's forehead, pinning him to the elevator door before he knew what was happening.

"Good job, team," Deacon said. He felt like he was on a mission with his old team again. Once they utilized Ruth's eyes and hand, they threw them down and got onto the elevator, still undetected. He was excited, but there was still more. He had found out how to overcome the mental block, but that wasn't it. He felt ... different, like there was more to it ... like he was missing the bigger picture.

He had felt that way since he had endured the pain of regaining his telepathy. But he felt as if he had gained much more than just telepathy. This was something significant, and yet he couldn't quite put his finger on it.

The elevator stopped and opened to reveal that they were on the corner of two converging corridors. "That one leads to the warden's office, the other one leads to freedom," Deacon said as he led his team out of the large elevator.

They ran down the long corridor and kicked the door open. There, at the bottom of the steps, stood Janice. She was accompanied by what had to be every guard and sentinel that she could muster. The door closed behind Deacon and his companions and locked. They were trapped.

"The only way you're getting out of here is through me—and my bodyguards." Janice snickered as the guards and sentinels fortified their position. Then, just like that, Deacon had an epiphany. *Gloria, I get it! If you can hear me, I love you, and hopefully I will find you in the next reality.*

No, I'll find you. I'm your lucky charm, remember? Then, just as fast as a thought can travel, Deacon was at the white place again.

VIII

So, here I am, in the white place again, yet alone.

Deacon stood there—well, floated there—for a few moments in solitude. It took him a few seconds to readjust to the "sphere vision" again and having to appoint a direction as "front." The other energy point wasn't there, but he had a good idea who it was the first time, and he was on a mission to find that version of her again. *I think I've about figured this thing out. There are still a few questions that I would like to ask, but they can all be answered in the future. It appears I'm immortal or something.*

So, with all the time in the world, he decided to start at the next white light. *This place seems to be some sort of grid that can be maneuvered. The only way I can find out is if I explore.* He headed into the light with the knowledge that if he wasn't pleased with the results, he knew how to leave. Either way, he had a mission: to find his wife and get some answers.

Chapter 20

I

The tropical setting that Deacon found himself in was not far from paradise. Big trees, clear skies, sandy beach, clear water with waves beating against the rocks, everything was perfect. He was sitting on a rock admiring the sunrise when his energy arrived. A cool breeze gusted across his face as a massive wave crashed against the rock he was sitting on, true paradise.

He looked around and spotted a long wooden pier. At the end of it stood a child, a little girl in a bright red dress and a pink satin sash. She looked like she was either waiting for somebody to return from sea or mourning the loss of somebody at sea. Deacon made the trek to the pier and approached her, gently placed his hand on her shoulder, and knelt down to her level. He didn't know what to say, because no other adults were around, and she could have come to the pier with him. He also didn't know what was going on in this reality, and he had learned not to assume anything. Her parents could be dead, for all he knew, so he had to choose his words wisely. "Are you feeling any better?"

The child sadly shook her head then turned to look at him. "Uncle Deacon, do you ever miss Aunt Phoebe?"

With that question, Deacon understood a lot more about his situation. He had no blood siblings, and the only person he would consider that close was Chuck. So, apparently, this was Chuck's child. Another thing that he concluded was that Phoebe wasn't with him again. She was either somewhere else, with somebody else, or dead. Either way, she wasn't there. He sighed. "Every day, kid. Every day."

The child started to cry, then hugged Deacon's neck. All he knew to do was to hug her back and try to console her. There was no telling who she had lost. Besides, one always comforted an ailing child. The little girl wiped her tears and then grabbed Deacon's hand and led him off the pier. He figured she was ready to go home. He needed to talk to Chuck anyway.

He spotted a path ahead that he hadn't seen earlier. It appeared that the little girl was leading him toward it. On their way, Deacon encountered the strangest thing: a waddle of emperor penguins making their way toward the sea to go fishing. *Penguins? Wait a minute, that means we're in the Antarctic!*

II

At the base of the Queen Maude Mountains in Antarctica, near the basin, was a small community of friends and family that had lived there for generations. They could trace their lineage back to pre-disaster times and had elders who recorded their history on the walls of the local caves for the future generations. They lived off the land, hunting the animals that their ancestors brought to that land and fishing the waters that surrounded them.

They had a residential area near the coast, so everybody had a great view, and they had a rural area, where all the agriculture took place. They all ate together and took care of each other. They even had a pub, where everybody gathered to drink away the night. The pub was a community hangout, and the grumpy old man who ran it chose to name it after himself: Chalmers'.

The entire gang was there at one table having a blast. Chuck playfully flicked a fishbone at Archie, who sat across from him. Gloria and Cassie both toasted and drank a shot while Julia passed a joint to Phil. They were all smiling jubilantly and seemed to be thoroughly enjoying themselves.

The conversation was sparked about how the elders had sought out this land of paradise. "Even though this is a massive continent, people from around the world came here when shit went down," Archie said. "I'm pretty sure we'll soon overpopulate this area and put ourselves in an even worse situation." He always had a negative outlook on humanity.

Chuck didn't share his negativity but agreed with him in this aspect. "We, as humans, don't realize how bad we've fucked up until it's too late. Even though we lost a large percentage of our population during the impact and the aftermath, we're still the fastest growing population of mammals on this planet. Overpopulation is a crisis that we have to address as a civilization, or we could doom future generations."

Julia and Gloria were both pro-life, being nurses and all. "Wait a minute," Julia said. "So, you're saying we have to regulate our right to live? So, what do you suggest, we start killing people over a number?"

Cassie laughed. "No, silly. What he's saying is we have to regulate the number of people we bring into this world."

Gloria grimaced. "Killing babies?"

Phil laughed along with Cassie. "Wrong again, sister. We're all responsible adults who know we have limited resources and limited space available on this planet. We need to regulate ourselves."

Archie grinned. "I'm glad to see there are actually people who understand me."

III

The warm beach weather had Deacon fooled. Even though it was at least seventy-five degrees out, he was as far south as he could go. Centuries earlier, an asteroid had struck Earth with an extinction-level impact. The thirty-mile-long devastator hit the Arctic Circle with enough force to hurl glaciers across the northern hemisphere, glaciers that eventually melted and flooded much of the world's land mass—at least what was left of it after the asteroid melted the Arctic Circle. With not much left to reflect the sun's light, Earth's temperature reached historic heights, and Antarctica soon melted away too, exposing the expansive landmass underneath.

Antarctica provided a livable climate, valleys that caught plenty of melted glacier ice for freshwater lakes, and mountainous regions for diverse livestock. What was left of humanity packed its bags and headed south, bringing all sorts of creatures with them. Penguins, however, were indigenous to the Antarctic region, and that's how Deacon deduced where he was.

The little girl stopped in front of the pub and looked up at Deacon. "Daddy is in there if you need to see him. I'm going to bed."

Deacon looked perplexed. "Don't you want me to walk you home? There are all sorts of crazies out here."

The child laughed. "Silly Uncle Deacon. I live right there. I'm sure I can make it a few feet without getting lost. And who's crazy?"

She giggled again, and Deacon was at a loss for words. "Well, I mean, you know ... strangers."

She laughed hysterically. "Who's a stranger?"

Deacon stumbled over his words. "Uh ... goodnight, sweetheart. See you tomorrow."

The girl walked off, still laughing. "Goodnight, Uncle Deacon!"

Deacon smiled at the awkward moment he had just shared with her. *Cool little tike there.* Then he looked up at the pub. *Chalmers'?* He shook his head and walked in with a slight smile.

IV

"Hey, it's Deacon!" a voice called out from the back of the pub, and everybody acknowledged his arrival.

"Hey!" He looked around and spotted everybody he knew as he waved at people on his way to Chuck's table. *Hey, there's Leroy over there, picking his nose, and that's Ken with him ... smiling?* The list grew as Deacon realized everybody in there were close friends and family. *Is that Bianca with Duke? And over there ... that's Janice laughing!* He had never seen Janice laugh without insulting him first. Even then, most weren't jokes. She was serious with her insults, to the point that it wasn't funny to her. To see her laughing like that warmed his heart. *Damn, I feel like I'm on the set of* Cheers*!*

Then he saw his ace-in-the-hole, his main man, his right wing. "Chalmers! Man, it's nice to see you outside!"

Chalmers smiled and gave him a big hug. "Yeah, it's nice to see you too, Deacon—but we're inside."

"Yeah, man, you've gotten me through some tough times, dude," Deacon said, "but I'm glad to see you're out of there in one piece."

Deacon walked away with a large grin and left Chalmers wondering if he should cut him off before he even started drinking.

Deacon finally made his way to the table and spoke to everybody that was there. They all seemed to be waiting for him to arrive. Chuck and Phil both lit a joint as Archie poured shots and Cassie went for a round of beers. Gloria sat across the table from him and blew him a kiss. His heart sank. *Can you hear me?*

She winked. *I sure can.*

Deacon sat down as drinks were passed out. Then Chuck raised a glass. "Let's toast! Good times, good friends ..."

They all responded in unison. "Good friends, good times!"

V

They sat at the table for a few hours, smoking, drinking, and shooting the shit. During that time, Deacon conversed with everybody while telepathically flirting with Gloria. They sent each other images while playing footsie under the table all night.

It was late, and the pub had started to clear out. One by one, Deacon's friends left the table until it was just Gloria, Chuck, and Archie left with him.

Is there somewhere we can go to talk? Deacon had to ask, because Chuck had a cast-iron stomach when it came to alcohol, and he and Archie were in a deep conversation about the universe, one that didn't seem like it was going to end any time soon, seeing that they were both drunk.

Sure, we can go anywhere you want, Gloria replied. "*My place, your place ... hey, let's go to the cove!*

The cove was a tall, secluded cave entry at the basin that not many people had the gall to visit. They could get there by swimming, but it was a dangerously long swim from the beach. Climbing down was more dangerous than climbing up because of the loose rocks. It was possible to feel them going up, but on the way down, one could dislodge right from under the climber's foot and send the person plummeting to his or her death. The locals who had the proper amount of crazy in their system took the shortcut, jumping from the cliff into the sea and swimming back into the opening. The cliffside had large sharp rocks, and the waves below were treacherous and unforgiving, but if a person could get the proper amount of air, he or she could stick it.

Deacon and Gloria tossed some dry firewood, their clothes, and a bag full of other items down into the cave as they prepped themselves for the jump. Jumping at the wrong angle would result in the jumper's body decorating the cliffside. Hitting the water at the wrong angle could break a person's bones and make them a permanent resident of the seafloor. Deacon understood this, yet he had brass balls. This wasn't his first time he had attempted such a death-defying act, and Gloria's experiences with him in previous realities assured her that he was up for the task. She probably had more butterflies in her stomach, even though she was used to making the jump. He had experienced a lot in his lifetime, and it would take a lot more than a jump and a swim to scare him. Maybe if a panther was chasing them or something ... .

Gloria stood there naked and stared at Deacon, who couldn't contain his erection. "You better get that thing under control before you jump," she said. "That's one bone we don't need to break for sure!"

They laughed and counted down for the jump. *Three, two, one, go!* They bolted at full speed and hurled themselves off the cliff. If someone didn't know any better, they would think they had just committed suicide together.

VI

After swimming into the cave and gathering their things, they didn't even bother getting dressed. Gloria rolled a joint while Deacon built a fire. The entire time they didn't say a word, Deacon was trying to figure out where to start while Gloria was waiting for him to start asking questions. Once the fire was lit, they cuddled up beside it and made love; they didn't even smoke first. Deacon had seven years of emotions pent-up for this woman, and as soon as he got his arms around her, he couldn't hold them back anymore. He couldn't stop either. Even after ejaculation, he kept going ... three times total. And she was all over him like a rabid meerkat, scratching, biting, and drawing blood. The fire cast their shadows across the cave wall, dancing together for hours into the night.

After the third time, Deacon was exhausted, and his groin was numb, but he was much more focused and knew exactly what he wanted to say. They got up and rinsed off in the sea, then came back to the fire to dry, feeling refreshed. Gloria lit the joint off the campfire, and Deacon decided to finally speak. "So, what happened to me? Am I dead?"

The question of "what happens when you die" had stumped humanity since we became self-conscious. Philosophers had devoted lifetimes in search of answers to the question, and entire religions were based upon the assumption of an afterlife. Humans feared what they did not understand, and death was one of those issues, since not many people were able to study it and live to tell about it.

There was, however, the rare occasion of a near-death experience where someone would be considered clinically dead for a length of time, but under certain circumstances, was revived. They all came back and told similar stories, yet scientists disregarded them, explaining that what they saw were hallucinations that occurred as the cells in the eyes were dying. They used the fact that they all saw roughly the same thing to support their own argument, since all of them were clinically dead at the time. A scientist would rather believe this far-fetched explanation than take the word of the people who had experienced the phenomena firsthand. Irony.

Gloria hit the joint and then passed it to Deacon while trying to answer his question as straightforwardly as possible. "This is going to be difficult to explain—and trust me, I've been trying to figure out the best way to do it for centuries. No, you're not dead; you're just able to access a higher plane of existence. I could easily say that what you have been experiencing is what happens *when* you die, but your situation is much more complex."

Deacon was enthralled. He hit the joint again and passed it back to her as she continued. "You, my love, are aware of your conscious self. You've reached a level similar to what the Buddhists call enlightenment." She hit the joint once more, then passed it back while she exhaled and continued speaking. "Monks work their entire lives in search of this, starving themselves and devoting lifetimes to meditation and prayer. But, you have the ability to exit this plane of existence and travel between realities as fast as a thought."

Deacon was slightly knowledgeable about Buddhist beliefs and could kind of see where she was going. He passed the joint and took the opportunity to speak. "So, I just woke up with these powers that take monks their entire lives to achieve?"

Gloria took a hit and nodded. "Not all monks achieve enlightenment, and the ones who do may not reach this level of it. There have been reports of them returning as different people on an entirely different timeline and exiting their bodies to witness events that took place on the other side of the world. But you are still much more powerful than that, and it didn't take any prayer or starvation."

Deacon cocked his head in curiosity. "Interesting. Okay, go on."

Gloria passed the joint back to him. "We are able to shift through *realities*. Meaning, we're not simply hovering over our bodies and going around the globe, just to return to the same reality with a hell of a story to tell. We can go to an entirely different existence and be in a totally different situation. It's not like we're taking over someone else's body; it's still you, just in a different reality. There really is no designated term for us, since we've never had to explain it, and I don't want to be the person to coin one either. But I guess we are ... perpetual ... or incessant beings."

Being able to identify what was happening to him was somewhat relieving. Things were starting to come together a little bit, but he still had a plethora of questions in his mind. He took another toke of the pot. "Okay, so, have I always had this power, or did it just suddenly kick in when I *died*?"

Gloria was already reaching into the bag of weed. "That explanation, my love, will require another smoke."

VII

After the joint was rolled, they settled back into their cuddling position in front of the fire. Even though Deacon was having a tough time swallowing her explanation, it was the only one he had heard so far, and it came from the only other person who knew what he was experiencing. The least he could do was hear her out.

Gloria lit the joint before she began. "You've always had this power. It was inside of you; it's inside of every human. You just don't know it's there. It's the same as how you acquired your combat skills and telepathic powers. You didn't know you had it until it was awakened. I just helped to ... awaken it." Deacon nodded in understanding. She took another hit before continuing. "There's also something I need to share with you that you probably have figured out by now, but it hasn't been officially addressed. In another lifetime, we were a couple—we were *the* couple. We were spending time in a reality in which the entity you know as Ken gutted you in a bar, in front of everybody, for no reason at all. I've returned to that reality numerous times trying to witness the events that take place with Ken leading up to that moment, but nothing happened to make him commit such a heinous act. He led a shitty life and was a shitty person. You two didn't even know each other in that reality; it was just a random act of violence."

Deacon nodded. "I think I get it. You were looking for me the same way as I was looking for Phoebe. I totally empathize with you." He turned to face Gloria and cleared his throat. "I had to look you in the face, so you can see how serious I am. I understand your situation, and I'm glad you decided to 'wake me up.' Otherwise, I would be dead. Plus, I would have never gotten the chance to meet the one I was made for. Gloria, I knew we were meant to be together since our first real conversation at the kitchen table. Back then, you had a thick Spanish accent and ... hey, wait a minute, when did you lose that?"

Gloria giggled as she passed the joint as she spoke on the exhale again. "I lost it ages ago! I had to portray that version of myself for the version of Deacon that was there before you, but once I was sure it was you, I gradually lost it, just so nobody would notice. Hell, you lost your southern twang after a few years too."

She giggled again, and Deacon smiled, but he had something else on his mind. He hit the joint and attempted to talk as he exhaled, like Gloria did. "So, I've noticed that time doesn't apply to us like everybody else." He coughed viciously before continuing. "How was I thirty-five every time I shifted? And just how long have you been alive?"

"I can show you better than I can tell you," she said. "To do that, we have to go to Purgatory. The trick is—"

"Purgatory?" Deacon interjected. "What, the white place?" He had heard of Purgatory before, but in association with religious texts.

She nodded. "Yes. It was created by my people eons ago. Purgatory is outside of our spacetime, so to you, it would only be a few years ago, but to me ... come on; I'll show you. The trick is, we must be touching in order to go there together. It's very important, and I'll explain all of that when we get there."

She grabbed Deacon by his hands. "I see you have learned how to shift. Do you understand it at its core?"

"Yeah, it's love. I realized that when I regained my telepathy in prison. It actually helped me to regain it. It wasn't like the telepathy that the hive shared, more like a mutual telepathic bond between *us*. The love I have for you was so great that it physically hurt me to be away from you anymore. Then I thought back to all the times I shifted and what the last thing on my conscious mind was, and that's when it hit me."

Gloria wiped a tear. She hadn't realized that he loved her that much. "Well, since you understand, let's shift." She looked him in the eye with a soft, warm, compassionate look. Deacon didn't see it at first; he had to look beyond her. It was like something nonphysical was encapsulating her. It was her aura. The more Deacon focused on it, the brighter it got. Then he saw his aura too, and it was magnificent. He was engrossed as he gazed back into her eyes, and then love engulfed them and took them to Purgatory, together.

Chapter 21

I

I know you've been here numerous times now, Deacon, but I would like to officially welcome you to Purgatory, the place outside of space and time. Gloria telepathically spoke to Deacon instead of using her native *emotional* language, so he could fully understand her.

It took him no time to adjust to the sphere vision again. He had finally learned how to see past the visible spectrum that he was used to in his physical form. He could see their auras in great detail, and it was spectacular. Gloria's was glorious; she looked like she was wrapped with an aurora borealis. He could see the small orbs of light much more vividly too, but more importantly, he recognized a pattern. "So, is this just a large timeline?"

Gloria was surprised at how fast he was catching on. "Well, in a sense, yes, but much more complex. Think of it as an infinite time grid. I'll explain it like this: there are an infinite number of possibilities that could happen at any moment in time, so every decision you make or action you take puts you in a different location in here. You don't even have to make the decision or take the action. It doesn't even have to affect you. The area that we are in is during a time when this version of you is thirty-five. This place is outside of spacetime, and anything that could possibly happen in history is here—anything."

Deacon was intrigued. "So, how far does this level go?"

"Infinitely."

"And the level above?"

"Infinite also. Get it? Each level represents an instant in time, and each orb represents one of the infinite possibilities that could be happening at that instant."

"Well, why didn't you just go back and get your version of me?"

"Good question," she replied. "It may seem like we have devised a way to cheat death, and in a way, we have, but we are not immortal. If we die, that's it; our energy moves on to our next physical presence on our own timeline. That's why shifting together is so important, because if not, you go to your own timeline. If I was to go back to a different reality where you were alive, or even in the same reality just before the murder, it would be on my timeline, in which you would be a totally different guy—in your case, an asshole."

Deacon was in deep thought, trying to understand. "So, let me make sure I understand this correctly: since each level contains an infinite number of instances, the bottom begins with birth, and the top ends with death, right?"

Gloria tilted her head from side to side. "Good assumption, but wrong. The levels go up and down infinitely too. This is where the concept of reincarnation comes into play—another thing that the Buddhists kind of got right. Like I said, once you die, your energy moves on to your next physical presence. There's no telling what you may look like or how you may be. The only thing I had to go by was your aura."

"Wow, that's deep." Deacon was stunned by the lengths she had gone to find him. "So, you were in a reality with me, and I died. When you returned here alone, you were on your own timeline. There was a different version of me there, because my energy had transitioned to a different version of myself on my own timeline, right?"

"Precisely. Now you see how Purgatory works. See, there are different versions of me down your timeline, but if I'm here with you, then we go there together. So, when you died, I was forced to go there alone. There was no way for me to know where you went, so I thought I had lost you for good."

II

Deacon and Gloria floated down the aisle they were on. Deacon, who had gotten used to looking beyond things and seeing the metaphysical and astral aspect to them, was noticing much more detail in the orbs. He could see the situation that he would be in if he entered it. He assumed that Gloria was seeing something different while looking into the same orb, since it would correspond to her existence. "How many of these things have you entered during your search for me?" Deacon asked, curious about the lengths she had gone to find him.

"I would have to use scientific notation to put a number to it," she said. Then she turned neon blue. "I've seen so many things and been to an abundance of realities. Billions upon billions of different versions of you, none of which were *you*. I've spent more time searching for you than I spent with my version of you to begin with—and we spent eons together! I knew it was you by your aura. It's a strong, loving aura, one good for shifting, and your aura matched his lumen for lumen. You walk like him, smell like him, feel like him, you even make love like him. It's like you're a copy of him that is in a different reality, exactly what I've been looking for."

"Wait a minute: how did you find me throughout all the infinite possibilities?"

Gloria changed to a bright blue color again. "I lived entire lifetimes and searched for eons until I finally found you, dying on a hospital table right in front of me—again. It was totally by chance that our paths crossed again. See, time has no boundaries here. Whenever the shift from the hospital table went awry, I had to go back to my timeline and live entire lives until, by chance, your energy entered that particular reality. If you never showed up, I just had to continue the search until I found you again."

III

Deacon turned yellow when he found out all she had gone through to find him. In his original reality, she was a nurse who worked with Phoebe at the hospital until Phoebe quit her job to take care of her parents. He was unaware of this, but Gloria was one of the nurses who was working on his dying body when she awakened his shifting powers.

In the next reality, she was a stripper in the bar who tried to gain some alone time with him. She saw him sitting by himself looking confused and tried to get him to come to a room with her. She was ready to tell him what was going on right then, and her attempts were very persuasive, almost successful, but he declined her seductions, and that night he was gone.

She spent entire lifetimes just to encounter him once, until he fell into his fourth reality. She knew it was him by the change in his aura and the way he received her fellatio. She wasn't going to lose him again either. The original Deacon in that reality paid her to bathe and have sex with him. She *wanted* to do all that once he had shifted there. She was ready to spend eons more with him. Once they were ready, she was going to teach him how to shift, and they would start all over again in another reality. But the shift had to be done prematurely due to an assassination attempt that didn't even target them. The difference was, they were able to shift together.

She led him to a reality where they could live off the grid, and would also awaken his telepathic abilities. But when they got there, and Deacon was aware of Phoebe, he was focused on her first and foremost. Even though saving Phoebe threw Deacon off his mission, Phoebe was ultimately the reason why Gloria was saved by the sentinels. However, one could argue that if Phoebe wasn't a factor, Deacon would've come and saved Gloria. It appeared that even after spending fourteen magnificent years with Gloria in a reality where Phoebe was dead, Deacon was still in love with her.

When he shifted out of incarceration without Gloria, she knew that she would see him again, and he was just one lifetime away. He walked into Chalmers' pub, and she knew instantly it was him by his aura. He was glowing brilliantly on the metaphysical spectrum, whether he knew it or not. She had a lot of pent-up emotion that she had to expel and couldn't wait for some alone time.

IV

Deacon's thoughts were everywhere. Gloria had explained a good bit, and it was a lot to take in. The labyrinth of orbs began to feel overwhelming for Deacon. If he wasn't paying attention, he could easily get lost in there. As he floated past the orbs, he saw himself in a multitude of situations, many of which he wouldn't want to be in. Getting lost in there is a bad idea, so, as Gloria floated a little farther and took a left, Deacon followed close behind her.

Many of his questions had been answered, but he was still unsure about a few things. As they floated down an aisle of orbs, he asked another question. "So, when you saw me dying on the operating table, how did you awaken my powers?"

"I was helping the doctor operate," she recalled. "Then I saw your aura flickering as you drifted in and out of death. I knew it was *your* aura, so I had to act fast. I attempted to shift with you. The problem was, your love for Phoebe was too strong. The shifting process is based off love, and your love was focused so strongly elsewhere that when we shifted, we drifted."

Gloria turned yellow. "I didn't mean to put you into that situation either, having you shift without anyone to explain things to you. You must have been terrified!"

Deacon hadn't thought about his first shift from that perspective. He remembered being more confused than scared. "I was a little afraid, but I just wanted to know what was going on. Everything felt like a dream—or more like a nightmare."

Gloria stopped for a moment, as if trying to remember where she was, then took a right. "It felt like a dream, because it was—well, sort of. They say sleep is a close relative to death for a reason. When you're dreaming, the subconscious overtakes your thoughts. It's what the 'enlightened' monk accesses during meditation, the subconscious. In there, the gloves are off. You can be in the future, in the past, or in an entirely different reality. It can take you anywhere. That's why dreams seem to predict the future or coincide with events that take place in your life. It's also why life seems like a big dream, because it is. If you were wondering why you don't remember your previous lifetimes, it's the same as not remembering all your dreams. The same concept is why you didn't know that you could shift until I awakened it."

She stopped to allow that to sink in. "Anyway, I wish I had the time to talk to you before throwing you into that situation and ripping you away from your family."

A theory developed in Deacon's mind. "So, when we shifted together during the freefall, it only worked because I didn't love Phoebe as much anymore?"

"No," she answered abruptly. "You still loved her with the same conviction, and proved it in the next reality. The shift worked, because you also loved me. It's possible to love more than one person, as I'm sure you have found out after all you have been through. You still love her now, and yet you love me too."

Deacon turned dark purple. "Did you kill her out of jealousy?"

"Of course not," she replied, then turned green. "Okay, maybe a little bit. But honestly, the bitch had it coming." They laughed as they continued down the infinite aisle of orbs.

V

Deacon had been through a lot. His first few shifts were only a few days long, but the last ones were one hell of a roller-coaster. He had lived as a rich man on top of the world, and he had lived as an inmate working for the Federation for a crime that he didn't commit. He had experienced more ups and downs in the past twenty-one years than he had in the thirty-five that he had spent in his original reality.

When this entire thing started, he just assumed he was having a bad dream, or was maybe in a coma from the accident. However, it only took a few shifts for him to abandon his dream theory. The coma theory was still in play, but he wasn't so confident in it either.

His first encounter with Purgatory didn't come in his first shift, because he wasn't able to perceive it fully. He just fell right back into another reality. The next time, he was able to see it for a split second before he fell into another one. He didn't know how to float or move in there, so he kept falling into different realities, but he began to grab glimpses of Purgatory. To him, it just looked like a vast whiteness.

When he went there with Gloria, she taught him a few things, like how to move and how to see and focus. That was the first time he was able to see the orbs, and they were splendid. He felt like he was standing inside a disco ball.

Gaining telepathy was probably the most entertaining thing. He wasn't so excited about the hive, but the mental connection with other humans was what he felt like people had been missing in life. He was convinced that if we all thought the same and worked together, there wouldn't be any limitations to humanity's capabilities. Interstellar travel, clean energy, and plenty of food. Cooperation would catapult humankind into the future. It was the premise of the speech he delivered at his fundraiser, and he wondered if that had anything to do with why Gloria led him there.

At that point, he still wasn't sure if it was Gloria or Phoebe who was in the white place with him. For all he knew, it could've been Chuck. It took seven years of incarceration for him to realize who it was. He missed her every day, and even though he missed Phoebe too, his love for Gloria was consuming. Each day he spent away from her only made him want her more intensely. Once they regained their telepathic connection, it confirmed his belief that she was the other point of energy. He felt totally different inside, like he wasn't living but just controlling a body. That is how he knew he could shift. Just one more question remained.

VI

Gloria took a right, and Deacon followed. She seemed to be leading Deacon somewhere, but he didn't realize it from all the complex thought she had him doing. They floated through another aisle of interesting situations when Deacon broke the silence with another question. "So, you've lived entire lives in search of me, and you were there when this whole thing started. What happened to my body after I shifted?"

Gloria stopped to reply. "That's another good question! The answer is short, but it isn't quite as simple. An infinite number of possibilities could have happened."

Deacon thought about it for a moment and related it to how Purgatory worked. Then he realized something. "Hold on, so, I can go back to my original reality? There's an orb here that I survive in? I can see my family?"

"Yes," Gloria said. "It's right over there." The entire time, Gloria had been taking him back to his original reality.

"Now we can simply go back to before the explosion, and you can call in sick to work, or we can go to one where you survive the explosion ... whatever you like."

VII

The decision shouldn't have been so easy for Deacon. This entire time he had been searching for his way home. He missed his lovely wife and his sitcom-like family. Sure, his life wasn't perfect, but compared to the other realities, it ranked highly. There was no telling what an inmate would do to have such a wonderful family. He missed holding his cute little daughter and playing video games with James. He missed father-son talks with Junior and cuddling with Phoebe as they fell sleep. He missed getting high with Chuck in the basement and joking around on the grill line at his second job. He even missed his version of Janice ... in a weird sort of way. He missed his old life.

Even though he longed for his original home, he had endured some serious trials on his way to where he was and been forced to look at life from a different perspective. He missed his original friends and family, but along the way, he had made new friends and raised a new family. Now that he grasped the concept of infinity, he realized the possibilities were endless.

It should have been a hard decision, but Deacon responded rapidly. "Okay, so that's my original reality, and this entire area of orbs here is my original timeline, right?

Well, which one of these other orbs is the one where you and I live happily ever after in paradise?"

Gloria turned bright blue, with the brilliance of the sun. "Follow me!"

She led him to a reality where they lived alone on a secluded island, and they simply revisited that reality whenever they wanted. There was an infinite number of possibilities to explore, and they had all the time in the universe to do it.

The End?

Lightning Source UK Ltd.
Milton Keynes UK
UKHW041419090421
381719UK00002B/565

9 781525 530906